Knit the Season

"Arrives just in time for the holidays . . . Readers who anticipate comforting, heartwarming stories from Jacobs's series will not be disappointed: Curling up with a Friday Night Knitting Club novel is like visiting with old friends. . . . This holiday entry is sure to please fans and leave them hungry for the next installment."

—*Booklist*

"More than a few craft-lovers will find this yarn under their tree."

—*BookPage*

"The newest addition to Kate Jacobs's immensely popular Friday Night Knitting Club series . . . [gives readers a] warm, fuzzy feeling."

—*Family Circle*

"[A] holiday special."

—*Library Journal*

"Jacobs's prose is pleasant, and she smoothly juggles all the story lines."

—*Kirkus Reviews*

Knit Two

"Jacobs stitches together another winning tale of the New York City knitting circle. . . . This sequel is as comforting, enveloping, and warm as a well-crafted afghan."

—*Publishers Weekly*

"Fans [will] eagerly snuggle in to see how the friends piece together their knitting projects while finding solace in one another's company."

—*People*

continued . . .

"As [the women who made Walker and Daughter yarn shop their second home] turn out afghans and booties, [they] also knit the pattern of their own lives in a plot that travels as far as Rome before returning, of course, to Seventy-seventh and Broadway."

—*The New York Times*

"Reading Jacobs's second knitting novel is as warming and cheering as visiting old friends."　　　　　　　　　　　—*Booklist*

"Readers are left with a sense of how the craft has calmed these souls as they journey through their individual stories of acceptance and personal growth. Fans of Debbie Macomber's Blossom Street series will find much to enjoy here."　　　　—*Library Journal*

"As the story presents the challenges that each woman faces, it becomes a beautiful celebration of life, friendship, knitting, and the bonds that tie us together. A delight to read." —*Romantic Times*

"[*Knit Two*] reflects the relationships among women in real life—their willingness to help each other, their caring attitudes, their discretion when needed, their openness, and their lack of pretense in an emergency."　　　　　　　　—*Omaha World-Herald*

"For legions of readers awaiting a reunion with their friends from the bestselling novel *The Friday Night Knitting Club*, novelist Kate Jacobs's warmhearted sequel, *Knit Two*, is certain to be a cozy companion on a blustery winter night. . . . Jacobs has embroidered [the novel] with snippets of sage advice applicable to both knitting and life: 'You know enough now that you don't just have to follow someone else's pattern.'"　　　　　　　　—*BookPage*

The Friday Night Knitting Club

"It's all here—dating, love, motherhood, career, estrangement, death and, especially, friendships that span generations. . . . [A] quick, fun, poignant yarn."　　　　　　　　　　*—The Seattle Times*

"The book's great—worth reading *now*."　　　　　　*—Glamour*

"An absolutely beautiful, deeply moving portrait of female friendship. You'll laugh and cry along with these characters, and if you're like me, you'll wish you knew how to knit."

　　　　　　　　　—Kristin Hannah, author of *Winter Garden*

"If you are looking for an inviting group of gals to spend a few winter evenings with, pull up your afghan and snuggle in with *The Friday Night Knitting Club*. . . . [It] makes you yearn for yarn, even if you're not a knitter."　　　　　　　　　　　*—USA Today*

"Knitters will enjoy seeing the healing power of stitching put into words. Its simplicity and soothing repetition leave room for conversation, laughter, revelations, and friendship—just like the beauty shop in *Steel Magnolias*."　　　*—Detroit Free Press*

"[A] winning first novel . . . Impossible to put down."　　*—Booklist*

"If you like to write or read or knit, your first reaction to *The Friday Night Knitting Club* may be pure jealousy. . . . Readers will come to root for nearly everyone in the sweetly diverse cast of characters."

　　　　　　　　　　　　　　　—Concord (NH) Monitor

"What begins as an unlikely hodgepodge of women soon evolves into an unbreakable sisterhood as the characters learn from each other's differences and bond over their love of knitting."

　　　　　　　　　　　　　　　　　—Vogue Knitting

continued . . .

"A *Steel Magnolias* for the twenty-first century."   —*Kirkus Reviews*

"Poignant twists propel the plot and help the pacing find a pleasant rhythm."   —*Publishers Weekly*

"A really great story."   —*Marie Claire*

"Celebrates the power of women's independence and is essentially an urban counterpart to *How to Make an American Quilt*."
—*New Statesman*

Comfort Food

"Fresh, tasty *Comfort Food* goes down mighty easily. . . . A satisfying read that showcases Jacobs's skill in creating endearingly flawed characters . . . The kind of book you rush home to finish."
—*USA Today*

"Gus and the show's cast, with their humor, moods, and romance, are the sparks that bring this warm and irresistible story to life. Highly recommended."   —*Library Journal*

"Lighthearted."   —*Kirkus Reviews*

"Meeting the heroine of Kate Jacobs's new novel, *Comfort Food*, is not unlike breaking bread—or perhaps organic blackberry scones—with an old foodie friend. . . . Jacobs has once again crafted a luxuriant yarn of a story. . . . *Comfort Food* is good for the heart and the soul, serving up a rich pastiche of friendship and motherhood, with a savory side of romance, too."   —*BookPage*

"A delectable table and a truly fun read."   —*Romantic Times*

knit the
season

kate jacobs

berkley books
new york

THE BERKLEY PUBLISHING GROUP
Published by the Penguin Group
Penguin Group (USA) Inc.
375 Hudson Street, New York, New York 10014, USA

Penguin Group (Canada), 90 Eglinton Avenue East, Suite 700, Toronto, Ontario M4P 2Y3, Canada
(a division of Pearson Penguin Canada Inc.)
Penguin Books Ltd., 80 Strand, London WC2R 0RL, England
Penguin Group Ireland, 25 St. Stephen's Green, Dublin 2, Ireland (a division of Penguin Books Ltd.)
Penguin Group (Australia), 250 Camberwell Road, Camberwell, Victoria 3124, Australia
(a division of Pearson Australia Group Pty. Ltd.)
Penguin Books India Pvt. Ltd., 11 Community Centre, Panchsheel Park, New Delhi—110 017, India
Penguin Group (NZ), 67 Apollo Drive, Rosedale, North Shore 0632, New Zealand
(a division of Pearson New Zealand Ltd.)
Penguin Books (South Africa) (Pty.) Ltd., 24 Sturdee Avenue, Rosebank, Johannesburg 2196, South Africa

Penguin Books Ltd., Registered Offices: 80 Strand, London WC2R 0RL, England

This is a work of fiction. Names, characters, places, and incidents either are the product
of the author's imagination or are used fictitiously, and any resemblance to actual persons,
living or dead, business establishments, events, or locales is entirely coincidental.
The publisher does not have any control over and does not assume any responsibility for
author or third-party websites or their content.

The recipes contained in this book are to be followed exactly as written.
The publisher and author are not responsible for your specific health or allergy needs
that may require medical supervision. The publisher and author are not responsible for
any adverse reactions to the recipes contained in this book.

PRINTING HISTORY
G. P. Putnam's Sons hardcover edition / November 2009
Berkley trade paperback edition / November 2010

Berkley trade paperback ISBN: 978-0-425-23676-5

The Library of Congress has cataloged the G. P. Putnam's Sons hardcover edition as follows:

Jacobs, Kate, date.
Knit the season : a Friday Night Knitting Club book / Kate Jacobs.
p.   cm.
ISBN 978-0-399-15638-0
1. Young women—Fiction.   2. Grandmothers—Fiction.   3. Americans—Scotland—Fiction.
4. Knitters (Persons)—Fiction.   5. Knitting—Fiction.   6. New York (N.Y.)—Fiction.
7. Scotland—Fiction.   8. Christmas stories.   I. Title.
PR9199.4.J336K55   2009   2009034108
813'.6—dc22

PRINTED IN THE UNITED STATES OF AMERICA

10   9   8   7   6   5   4   3   2   1

knit the season

thanksgiving

How essential to stop, reflect, be grateful. For food.
For family. For subtle joys, such as the feel of soft
yarn on fingertips, for the sense of ease that comes,
stitch upon stitch, from following the rhythm of the
pattern. Honoring the spirit of the holidays can also
be a celebration of the experience of crafting.

chapter one

New York seemed to be a city made for celebrations, and Dakota Walker loved every moment of the holidays: from the shoulder-to-shoulder crowds breathlessly waiting for the lighting of the gigantic Christmas tree in Rockefeller Center, to the winter-themed department store windows displaying postmodern Santas, to—her favorite—the kickoff to a month of fun with that ruckus of a parade on Thanksgiving morning.

Dakota's grandmotherly friend Anita Lowenstein—who, nearing eighty, could text almost as well as some of her college classmates—had escorted Dakota to the parade when she was small. Last Thanksgiving morning, in a fit of nostalgia, the two of them bundled up in layers, chunky handmade cable-knits over cotton turtlenecks, and staked out a spot near Macy's just after sunrise to watch the river of floating cartoon characters and lip-synching pop stars and freezing-but-giddy high-school marching bands flowing down Broadway. Just as it should be.

But what Dakota most enjoyed about the beginning of winter was the crispness of the air (that practically demanded the wearing of knits) and the way that tough New Yorkers—on the street, in elevators, in subways—were suddenly willing to risk a smile. To make a connection with a stranger. To finally see one another after strenuously avoiding eye contact all year.

The excuse—the expectation—to bake also played a large part in her personal delight. Crumbly, melty shortbread cookies and iced chocolate-orange scones and whipped French vanilla cream cakes and sugary butter tarts: November through December was about whipping and folding and blending and sampling. Though she'd spent only one semester at pastry school so far, Dakota was eager to try out the new techniques she'd learned.

Still, she hadn't stopped to consider how it might feel to roll out crust, to pare fruit, to make a meal, back in what was her childhood home, as she adjusted her bulging backpack, groceries in each hand, and climbed the steep stairs two floors up to Peri's efficient little apartment situated one floor above the yarn shop her mother had started long ago, the tiny shop—the shelves packed to bursting with yarns fuzzy, nubbly, itchy, and angel-soft, its walls a kaleidoscope of cocooning pastels and luxurious jewel shades—that Georgia Walker had willed to her only child and that Dakota had, finally, come to truly appreciate.

The white-painted cupboard door creaked loudly as she opened it, surprising not because of the unpleasant volume but because Dakota realized, in that moment, she had forgotten the quirks of this particular kitchen. At the same time, overflowing bundles of yarn spilled—burgundies and cobalts, wools and acrylics, lightweights and doubleknits—from the shelves, tumbled to the grocery bags she'd just set on the counter, and then bounced to the linoleum tile floor below. Almost as an afterthought, a tidy pile of plush plum cashmere dropped noiselessly through the air, just missing her head, and landed directly into the small stainless sink.

"This isn't a kitchen!" cried Dakota, reaching out her arms as widely as was possible in her heavyweight white winter coat, trying to hug yarn and food and prevent all of it from rolling off the edge. "It's a storage facility!"

She hesitated. What she'd wanted was simply to find a bowl, something in which to pile up the apples she'd purchased, and she'd approached Peri's compact galley kitchen in the apartment above the Walker and Daughter yarn shop as if on automatic pilot. Distractedly running through a to-do list in her mind, Dakota lapsed into an old pattern and went directly to where her mother stored the dishes once upon a memory, back when the two Walkers lived in this same walk-up. And what did she find? Knitting needles of all sizes and woods stacked in the flatware drawer and oodles of yarn where the dishes ought to be, raining down from the cupboards. She wasn't sure she ought to risk a peek in the oven now that Peri lived here.

It had been a long time since she'd cooked in this location, making oatmeal, orange and blueberry muffins for her mother's friends, the founding members of the Friday Night Knitting Club.

"Seven years," marveled Dakota, her voice quiet though no one else was around. Seven years since she'd puttered around this kitchen after homework, smashing soft butter and sugar together as she contemplated what tidbits would go inside the week's cookies.

"Careful now," murmured Georgia, the shop ledger in front of her on the cramped kitchen table. "Maybe don't put in everything that's on the shelf. We went through two bags of coconut last week."

"Uh, those muffins were my best ever, Mom," said Dakota, prancing around in a victory dance on the worn linoleum. "The supreme moistness I've been searching for! You can't stand in the way of a chef."

"As long as this chef remembers that we're on a budget," Georgia said mildly, brushing away some bits of eraser from the page before her. "I think I created a monster the afternoon I taught you how to measure flour."

"Okay, Mom," said Dakota, sliding into a chair at the table. "Should I not make so much?"

Georgia's eyes crinkled as she regarded her lively daughter, whose ponytailed hair was falling loose from the neon-pink scrunchie she'd knitted herself.

"Never stop," she said, gently tugging her daughter's hair. *"Don't give up something you love just because there's an obstacle. Find a way to work around it. Be open to something unexpected. Make changes."*

"Like what?"

"Like if you run out of sugar," she said. *"Use honey."*

"I did that last week!"

"I know," said Georgia. *"I was proud of you. We Walker girls are creative. We knit. You bake. But above all, we never, ever give in."*

Dakota surveyed the room. The kitchen was almost a relic, one of the few places in the apartment undamaged by last year's flooding, the bathroom down the hall being the source of the water that ruined the yarn shop in its previous incarnation but reminded all of them—and especially Dakota—of the importance of a mother's legacy. The store reopened soon after with a clean-and-simple style, with basic shelves for the merchandise, though she and Peri planned a massive remodel to begin in the not-too-distant future. That was all they'd talked about for months. The idea was to devote the shop space to a boutique for Peri's couture knitted and felted Peri Pocketbook handbags, and to adapt the first floor from a deli to a knitting café. Dakota's father, James Foster, was in charge of the new architecture but—due to frequent changes from his, ahem, difficult clients—hadn't finalized the drawings. It was a grand plan, a vision that required Dakota to hurry up and graduate from culinary school. Peri had been keeping everything under control for a long while, and the strain was showing.

"I don't want to miss my moment, Dakota," Peri reminded her, though she admitted she wasn't sure what that moment might be. Indeed, as Dakota grew older and struggled to keep her schedule in check, it had gradually begun to dawn on her how much Anita and Peri and even her father had worked tirelessly to fulfill her mother's dream of passing the store to Dakota. And even though Peri had a small ownership stake, even though Anita had helped out financially eons ago when Georgia bootstrapped her shop into being, even though James was her dad, everyone's sacrifices of time and energy belied self-interest as motivation. Amazing, truly, to know that one woman—her mother, who always seemed just so regular and everyday with her reminders to zip up jackets and sleep tight—had the grace of spirit to inspire such devotion.

Still, changes were coming all over, it seemed. Since leaving the V hotel chain, James's focus had been on his own architectural firm. Unfortunately, business wasn't exactly booming. The knit shop was also facing smaller revenues this quarter. Dakota didn't see the adventure in uncertainty. Too much change, she knew, could come to bad ends.

She eyed the clock, assessing the tidying she still needed to complete in the apartment. Dakota knew Peri was downstairs in the shop, finishing up the day's sales and awaiting the arrival of the club for their regular get-together. Those same women who were now Dakota's very own friends and mentors. The big sisters and, on some days, the surrogate mothers who were around whenever she needed to talk. The group would be gathering in the shop in a few hours to knit a little and talk a lot, catching up on one another's lives and prepping for the upcoming holidays.

To be fair, Peri had warned her, when the two of them struck their deal last week as they went over the bookkeeping for the week, that she had nothing in the kitchen. Absolutely nothing. Dakota was accustomed to that style of New York living, had other friends whose refrigerators held only milk and bottled water, a selection of cereal at the ready for every possible meal or snack. She had shopped for staples today, even salt and pepper, knowing full well to expect very little. The turkey and produce would come Wednesday, when she planned to make all the dishes and leave them for day-of reheating. Tonight her goal was merely to organize the space and stock the shelves.

Although these shelves were already overstocked with surplus inventory from the knit shop. Clearly.

Gingerly, Dakota stepped over the yarn and away from the green canvas totes covering the tiny strip of countertop between fridge and stove, their long handles flopped over every which way, as the onions and spices and celery threatened to spill right out of the bags with just a nudge in any direction. She glared at the groceries, hoping the power of her stare would keep them still, as she figured out where to unload the yarn. She listened for movement, in case the bags began to topple, as she pulled the door to the fridge just enough for the light to come on inside. Mercifully, it was empty—not a yarn ball in sight—and held only a dozen bottles of handcrafted root beer and a door filled with nail polish. Hastily, Dakota shoved most of the groceries into the fridge, even the five-pound bag of organic sugar.

But the relief at crossing something off her mental to-do list passed quickly. The truth was, her mind was bursting. There was just too much swirling around her. The past year had been the busiest of her life. Convincing everyone she was all grown-up led to a hard-won realization: She had to act like an adult. She had to handle new responsibilities. And it was a lot. Life, just the day-to-day, was a lot. She worried. Often.

Her mother had been a worrier as well. Everyone said so. But she'd been a smiler, too, witty and generous and seemingly able to make things fit together.

Right now Dakota spread her worries around, allowing time for concerns large and small. She worried about finding time to make two turkey dinners in the next week, mastering a perfect chocolate truffle cake before Monday's class, reading Catherine's latest installment in her mea-culpa novel about two former best friends who reconnect, and finishing the tidying of her room so her grandparents, Joe and Lillian Foster, would be comfortable staying at her father's apartment during Thanksgiving next week. That had been a task put off for too long, and Dakota spent several weekends earlier in November pulling boxes from her closet and underneath her bed, chuckling over sixth-grade book reports and old report cards and printouts of endless photos from the summer in Italy, waiting for frames or albums. She'd also spent a quiet, lonely day sifting through some of the odds and ends that had belonged to Georgia. Admiring the pencil drawings that accompanied the original pattern designs for the hand-knit suits and tunics and dresses her mother had outlined in a binder, the simpler sweaters destined for the charity pattern book she'd been assembling with Anita. And she read again the notes on knitting that her mother had kept in a small red journal that was passed on to Dakota after her death.

It was soothing to see Georgia's handwriting again, to imagine her mother curled up in a chair and scribbling.

"Get Christmas list from Dakota" was what her mother had scrawled in the margins of one of the pages. That comforted her, somehow. The proof of being on her mother's mind. To confirm what she already knew.

Dakota had taken to carrying that red journal with her, tucked in the bottom of her knitting bag—an original by Peri—along with an oversized unfinished camel-and-pastel-turquoise striped sweater she'd found. She'd kept all of her mother's UFOs, all the fun projects her mother never had a second to complete because she was too busy knitting her commissioned pieces, and just tucked them away for a later time. Every fall, Georgia's habit was to choose one of those on-the-go creations and finish it by the end of the year. A little gift of satisfaction to herself. That particular sweater was Georgia's UFO of choice the fall that she died, Dakota recalled vaguely, and Anita had bundled together all the knitting that hadn't been completed and placed it safely away. Too painful to look at, too precious to throw away: The unfinished objects had simply lain in wait until Dakota was ready. This she knew.

It struck her, as she was sorting and organizing, just how close she was getting to the age her mother was when she had arrived in New York.

During the great cleanup, she uncovered an old Polaroid that was fading and loose at the bottom of a box, of Georgia standing at the top of the Empire State Building, a knitted cap pulled down low on her unruly corkscrew curls and her mittened hands resting on her pink cheeks as she affected a look of surprise. She wondered if her father had been the photographer, if the two of them enjoyed their bird's-eye view of the skyscrapers all around. Dakota liked how the snap captured Georgia's goofy side, and she liked this concrete evidence that she had her mother's wide eyes, proof that the two of them were the same, just with different shades of skin. She tucked the photo into the red journal after scanning it onto her laptop, to the folder that held her story, with its images of Gran and the shop, and a picture of Ginger and Dakota standing in front of the Roman Forum.

She felt guilty that she hadn't spent as much time with Lucie Brennan's daughter, Ginger, since she started culinary school, and that she'd broken four lunch dates with KC Silverman in as many weeks. She had planned to finish a pair of matching fisherman's sweaters for Darwin Chiu's twins, Cady and Stanton, when they turned one; of course, they were already over eighteen months and the sweaters were now too small. She'd have to save them for a decade until someone else she knew had a baby.

Not to mention that she fretted whether Anita and Marty

Popper would finally say "I do" at the wedding they rescheduled for New Year's Day instead of submitting to yet another manufactured delay caused by Anita's son Nathan Lowenstein. (How many almost heart attacks could one very fit fiftysomething man invent, she wondered? And when would Anita stop getting suckered?) And as much as she wanted the wedding to be a go, she felt surprisingly nervous about seeing her friend Roberto Toscano since their summer romance in Italy more than a year ago. His grandmother, Sarah, was Anita's sister, and he was definitely coming to the wedding with his entire family: He'd already e-mailed to plan some time together, in fact. She felt awkward about seeing him again. About the we-almost-did-but-didn't-so-have-you-done-it-with-someone-else-ness of things.

Plus she suspected—half hoping and half dreading—that her father was getting serious with a new, not-yet-introduced-to-Dakota secret lady friend. Not that she spent too much energy reflecting on that aspect of his life, and not that she relished the idea of having to share his affections. But she knew enough to recognize that—like Anita—her dad deserved another shot at love.

The holidays, it seemed, were all about celebrating love. Dakota wasn't sure how she felt about that emotion these days. And all her worries came back to the immediate moment in this kitchen, because Dakota was responsible for prepping a turkey dinner that Peri could use to impress her boyfriend's parents. It was her part of the bargain. In exchange, Peri would watch the shop during the week of Christmas so Dakota could do the thing she was truly looking forward to: a full-time internship at the V hotel kitchen over Christmas break. Sure, she'd miss out on a holiday dinner or two, but she was confident her dad would actually be relieved not to have to truck out to Pennsylvania as they did every year and eat a quiet holiday meal. Although her mother's younger brother, Uncle Donny, was congenial enough, her mother's parents were not big talkers. They were pleasant but taciturn. And her mother's absence at the holiday meal was palpable. Christmas had been a challenging holiday for everyone to get through since Georgia died.

So Dakota was quite delighted by her own initiative, having set up the internship on her own, even though it wasn't required at school. But she wanted to squeeze out every opportunity she could in order to reach success. She could hardly wait to tell her father about the internship, her gift to him this low-maintenance Christmas. She was even going to cook extra at Thanksgiving and freeze him a perfect holiday plate, with a generous helping of cranberry and mashed potatoes, an option if he chose not to go either to Pennsylvania or to see his parents on December 25. Dakota would, of course, delightedly be at the chef's beck and call in the V kitchen. Truly, she reflected with pride, she'd thought of everything.

Dakota stretched her arms, tired from carrying the groceries up the stairs, and then reused the tote bags to gather up the yarn, careful to sort by manufacturer. She scrubbed the counters and cupboards with a mix of warm water and white vinegar, and started a list of what else she might need for Peri's "home-cooked" Thanksgiving. Dishes, she thought, peeking back into the now-empty cupboard, hearing anew the same old creak she heard whenever her mom had rummaged around to find supper for the two of them. Dakota opened and shut the door several times in a row, mesmerized by the sound, before picking up her backpack and her handbag and readying to pop down one flight of stairs to the yarn shop.

She pulled out a compact for a quick look, peering intensely at the same self she met in her bathroom mirror every morning, her brown eyes, her café-au-lait skin, her hair in long curls. Did she half expect to see something else? Her younger self, her mother somewhere behind her? Dakota's body tingled whenever she entered the old apartment that had been her home until she was a teen, feeling the past and present rub against each other.

And yet her thoughts didn't feel as raw as they once did.

She saw more in her mind's eye than her mother lying tired on the sofa, than the moving men carrying her bed and boxes to her father's apartment after Georgia's death. Instead, she heard in the creaky old cupboard the sound of her mother, needles click-clacking as she knitted in the living room, pretending not to hear Dakota sneaking cookies. Or the two of them, exhausted after a tickle-and-laugh session, rolling in to grab snacks and watch TV movies, lying together under an old afghan Dakota's great-grandmother had sent in the mail from Scotland. Or surprising Dakota with a bowl of popcorn to turn into a garland as the pair set about decorating a very small Christmas tree with multicolored strands of leftover yarn. She heard all these things in the screech and whine of the old cupboard. The noise was loud, insistent. But then such is the sound of memory.

"Turn around," ordered Catherine, motioning with her hands. "Let's see the back."

Obligingly, Anita moved in a slow circle, her arms held out. She modeled the latest incarnation of her hand-knit wedding coat, an ankle-length ivory affair with a shawl collar that was as fine as lace.

"What is this? The third version?" asked KC. "I want you to know I bought one darn dress for your wedding and I plan on wearing it next month. You hear me?"

Anita cracked a tiny smile. She and her fiancé, Marty, had postponed their nuptials repeatedly—and each time she felt it bad luck to simply put her wedding outfit back in the closet. Instead, she took Catherine on a shopping expedition for a new dress and meticulously pulled out the stitches of the coat to start again with an updated pattern. Her sister, Sarah, who was doing part of the knitting, had gone along with the changes the first time. But this new coat was simpler and all of her own making. After all, Catherine had pushed her toward a dress that was dramatically more sparkly, and her coat—which she wanted for modesty and simply to express a bit of personal style—had a certain clean elegance to the drape of the open-closure front. No bulk. Just light, beautiful stitches.

"I adore the sheer effect," commented Lucie, fingering the sleeve.

"This coat is your best one yet," added Darwin, breaking into a wide grin upon seeing Dakota enter the shop from upstairs.

"It's beautiful," said Dakota, suspecting that Darwin's enthusiasm for her arrival hinged on a hope of treats. She closed the door of the shop behind her, subtly catching Peri's attention and letting her know with a raise of her eyebrow what she thought of the kitchen upstairs. Peri motioned toward the shop she had sweetly decorated for the holidays, with baskets and cornucopias of yarn on the table and at the register. Skein after skein—in harvest colors of amber and chocolate and rust—were threaded on strong cord to make garlands that swooped across the tops of the windows facing onto Broadway. Soon enough, Peri would replace the skeins with deep blue and brightest white, and then rich red and dark evergreen, the decor as lively and bright and interfaith as the members of the club itself.

As many Fridays as they could manage, this group of seven women pulled up chairs at the heavy oak table in the center of the room, a loan of furniture from Catherine's upstate antiques shop. The post-flood, pre-reno transitional knitting store was all about simplicity—wire shelves that were easy to put together and move around, a small desk (also from Catherine) for the cash register, and painted taupe walls to warm up the place. The business was lucky to have a loyal clientele, and the club responded by offering more classes during the week. Anita taught some days, and even Lucie offered to teach in the spring. But

Friday night remained sacred, and the shop was open only by invitation to the women who had banded around the late Georgia Walker, the shop's original owner.

It was the place where each one of the women knew it was safe to share struggles and dreams. There were always questions; they tried to avoid judgments. After all, they'd all made mistakes. And, of course, there was always time to knit. Especially with the holidays closing in, having a time-out for a little creativity and relaxation was a necessity.

Dakota tugged her new—old—find from her knitting bag and onto the table. It was not her usual type of project, and she paused to see if anyone would pay attention, or comment that she'd somehow managed to finish half a sweater since the week before.

KC sidled up to the table, leaving the rest of the women to covet Anita's wedding coat.

"Hey, kiddo," she said, picking up the half-sweater and examining it closely. She brought the yarn near her face.

"What do ya think?" asked Dakota, grinning, gleeful at the idea of finishing her mother's project. It made her feel as though she was doing important business, a private task she was finally mature enough to complete.

"I haven't seen this for a long time," said KC. "I might not have recognized it except for that terrible turquoise. A remnant from the 1980s, no doubt. From a sale bin."

"You know this sweater?" Dakota was excited. "My mom was working it. I just found it again, and I've done several rows.

There's not enough yarn left, though. I'll need to try and locate a match, guess the manufacturer."

Anita came over, her antenna ever alert to new and interesting knitting projects.

"My goodness," she exclaimed, looking to Dakota every inch the fairy godmother she always seemed to be, practically glowing in a cream coatdress and her ivory wedding coat. Silver hair framed her face, and her bangs stopped just above her eyes, which were narrowed with concern. "Your mother was doing up this sweater. That very fall."

"I know," Dakota said triumphantly, gesturing in the air with a rosewood needle. "And I'm going to finish it for her! I can handle it."

Anita nodded, relief flooding her face. "Good," she said. "I think that's very good."

"Even *I* know this sweater," said KC. "It's from before you were born. Your mother used to knit this at the office."

Dakota well knew that KC worked at the publishing house where Georgia had started her career, that Georgia had initially turned to KC as a mentor, and that the two had remained friends after Georgia left her job, became a mother, and transitioned to her career as a knitting mompreneur. Dakota remembered all these facts and yet was shocked that KC could find a connection to the piece. To get an inkling that the sweater was a UFO from before Dakota was born. Why would her mother pick it up again the summer before she died?

"You saw her making it?"

"Oh, hon, she loved to work it at lunch, always going on about her boyfriend. Blah, blah, blah." KC leaned forward so both elbows rested on the table and flashed a wicked grin. "You know. Your father?"

Dakota instinctively dropped the sweater as though singed. Even though she loved her dad. Lived with him part-time. Even still. This sweater was from . . . before. Before he left her mom pregnant and alone, before he came back and was forgiven, reunited with his family.

She wasn't so sure that she wanted to finish it anymore. There was much more history in these stitches than Dakota had anticipated.

"Let's get this meeting under way officially, ladies," shouted Lucie, breaking Dakota's thoughts. "Dialing Miss Ginger . . . now."

She hit the speakerphone function on her cell phone and winked at Dakota. Once, what seemed like not too long ago, it had been up to tweenage Dakota to call the evening to order. Now Georgia's daughter was a gorgeous woman of twenty, and Lucie's spirited seven-year-old daughter, Ginger, stayed up a little bit late to do the honors via telephone.

"Mommy!" bellowed Ginger, before launching into an up-to-the-minute description of her evening. "Uncle Dan made ice-cream cones, and Stanton spilled his on Grandma and then the cat tried to eat it off her sleeve and Cady farted into her diaper."

"So, it's a good night, Ging?"

"Oh, yes," exclaimed Ginger. The sounds of Velcro could be heard. "Are you ready for attendance? I have my pencils out."

"Shoot," said Dakota.

"Okay," said Ginger, shuffling a paper. She cleared her throat dramatically. "Attention, please. Dakota Walker?"

"Here," said Dakota, still close enough in age to remember the excitement of being allowed that special privilege of spending time with the ladies.

From her earliest days, she'd been at home in Walker and Daughter, her namesake shop. The long evenings spent hanging out, learning to knit or doing her homework, while her mother totaled up the day's sales. Georgia had been a single mother focused solely on her daughter and her business, until she finally connected with the women who now sat around the table. Since her death, they formed a tight unit around Dakota, overseeing her through her challenges with her father, James, her summer looking after Ginger while Lucie worked in Italy, her two years at NYU, and her recent switch to pursue her passion for baking at pastry school.

"Anita Lowenstein," chimed Ginger. "Are you there?"

"I am indeed," said Anita. "And delighted to be here." Uncharacteristically preoccupied with her wedding plans, Anita—who looked a good twenty years younger than her close to eight decades—was accustomed to the club members coming to her for advice. Although she still had trouble with her own three sons, who couldn't bear the idea of their widowed mother marrying again, she made no secret of her maternal feelings for Georgia and, therefore, for Dakota. Her recent reunion with her estranged younger sister, Sarah, had renewed her energy. Combined with her invigorating romance with Marty, who owned the building and ran the deli below the shop, Anita was

more content than she'd been since the loss of her surrogate
daughter Georgia.

"Pretty Catherine Anderson," called out Ginger, her mouth
so close to the phone that her every breath could be heard. "I'm
drawing a picture of you in your gold dress right now. Say
hello!"

"Hello," said Catherine. She liked Lucie's daughter, had offered to babysit now and again in preparation for her upcoming
visit with her friend Marco, who was bringing along his grown
son, Roberto, and his twelve-year-old daughter, Allegra. In her
forties and still learning to be happily single after a tumultuous
divorce years before, Catherine often fell into relationships that
didn't quite satisfy emotionally—including a secretive heady fling
last year with Anita's almost-but-not-quite-separated son Nathan
(who promptly returned to his wife post-consummation, naturally). These days, she focused primarily on her antiques shop and
wine bar business in Cold Spring, while also making herself in-
dispensable as Anita's ersatz wedding planner. Late at night, she
tapped out pages of a novel loosely based on her teenage years in
rural Pennsylvania, when she and her best friend, Georgia Walker,
had worked part-time gigs at the Dairy Queen.

"Peri Gayle is next on my list. I'm copying from last week's,"
Ginger explained. "I'm putting you down in green pencil today,
plus a butterfly."

"Good choice," said Peri. "My new bags are all about being
green." What was supposed to be a temporary spot at the shop
before heading to law school developed, over time, into joint
ownership with Georgia (and now Dakota). Plus, she devoted

herself to the creation of a line of knitted purses, backpacks, and messenger bags, which, thanks to an Italian *Vogue* photo shoot, had transformed her business from a homegrown concern within the last year into a phenomenon. Peri Pocketbook, the company, was enormously popular—though Peri had trouble keeping up with demand.

And Peri Pocketbook, the person, was still taking baby steps as she remembered to leave time for a personal life; her yearlong online-dating experiment had yielded many dates and one very witty lawyer who might really have potential. Who knows what could happen if she managed to pull off this Thanksgiving-dinner thing? Which was why she'd let Dakota into the kitchen in the first place! And even though her best friend KC would be no help in the cooking department, she was relieved that she wouldn't have to face her boyfriend's parents on her own.

"KC Sliverman," said Ginger, tapping her pencil into the phone. "Please report in."

"Silverman, Sil-ver-man," cried out KC in mock astonishment. "I'm always telling you, kiddo, it's Silverman."

Ginger giggled. She liked KC. She found her kooky.

KC, a petite fiftysomething, had turned an unexpected layoff in her past into a successful exploration of a second act. While Peri gave up the idea of a law career for herself, she tutored KC, and the two women become close pals as KC completed law school in her late forties and, ultimately, ended up working back at the same publishing company where she'd once been an editor. She'd tried marriage—twice, in fact—but announced (loudly and regularly) that she just wasn't the committed kind.

Brash, child-free, and bursting with energy, KC always shared whatever was on her mind. Though she'd promised Peri she would go easy with her boyfriend's family on Turkey Day.

"Auntie Darwin Chiu, whose name is different than Uncle Dan Leung," singsonged Ginger.

Darwin was the mother of twins Cady and Stanton, who lived next door to Ginger (and her mother, Lucie), all under the care of her physician husband tonight. ("It's not babysitting," Dan often said. "I'm parenting.") Once a grad student who ambled into Walker and Daughter to do a research project about the dangers posed to feminism by knitting, Darwin was now a champion of the power of craft and a full-time professor of women's studies—though, much to her frustration, still without tenure. She juggled research, writing, mothering, and following through on a concept she and Lucie had about creating intelligent, appropriate television for girls. Though the change in the world around them had resulted in some problems gathering funding. Not everything had gone as fluidly as they'd hoped, though Lucie had scaled back on her outside work in the hopes of making progress.

"And are you there, Mommy?" yawned Ginger, clearly exhausted from the hard work of taking attendance with colored pencils and drawing pictures.

"Yes, and Lucie Brennan says it is to bed with you, young lady," said Lucie. She never anticipated nearing fifty and being a parent to a seven-year-old as well as caring for an elderly mother fighting dementia. But that's what every day meant for Lucie, a video and film director who made everything from documentaries to music videos to commercials. An avid knitter, she poked into the yarn shop one long-ago day to pick up a skein of beige merino (during her fisherman-sweater phase) and ended up sitting down at a table much like the one they all sat at now, to work on her stitches. And she, like all of the women, just kept coming back. Friday after Friday.

What she discovered here, in this small shop one floor above Broadway and Seventy-seventh, was the true and absolute friendship she needed to make sense of who she was. Her life had lacked a certain something, but she hadn't understood what was missing until she found it: community. Smart, strong women who backed her up when she needed support and called her out when required.

Lucie tucked in her daughter over the phone as the members of the Friday Night Knitting Club—Anita, Catherine, Dakota, Lucie, Peri, Darwin, and KC—assembled around the table and began, as they so often did, to talk all at once. Everybody listened, but nobody heard a word. No matter. They'd start over again, one at a time, in a few minutes. But for now, it was enough just to relish this safe haven.

chapter two

A hush fell over the dining table as, one by one, forks stopped scraping and mouths stopped chewing. Half-empty platters of turkey and cranberry and sausage dressing rested after being eagerly passed back and forth by the entire twenty-four members of the Foster family, grandparents and aunts and cousins all crammed into the rectangular living area of James's two-bedroom apartment. The large TV remained on the wall, but much of the furniture had been removed or repurposed, such as the blue armchairs and a small wooden bench, now being used as dinner chairs at the table. James had approached the project with an architect's eye, using graph paper and measurements the Sunday before to map out a way to fit his entire family in his home.

Spacious by New York City standards, the place was barely large enough for such a party. His technique was borrowed from his parents' approach to the holidays back when they squeezed in all the cousins and grandparents they could. He had loved those big gatherings when he was young, the sense of power he felt at belonging to such a magnificent, boisterous, connected family. He wanted to create something like that in his own home for Dakota. And so he considered and rearranged, abutting several folding tables on either end of his glass-and-steel table, using wooden shims and thin books to create a level area, then covering the entire contraption with a tremendously long yellow linen tablecloth that he'd special-ordered over the Internet. His daughter, Dakota, had been knitting for weeks to create a felted table runner in harvest colors, and they'd borrowed dishes and platters and wineglasses from Catherine and Anita. (No point in buying all the extras when they'd never be used once the guests had all gone home, he thought.)

James rarely entertained in his home, preferring to keep it as quiet and private as possible, a habit from when Dakota had initially moved in with him after Georgia died. He'd hardly become a monk but had managed his private life around his family life, bringing none of his female friends into his daughter's life. He had decided early on that it wasn't beneficial for Dakota to see him with anyone other than her mother. James hadn't thought far enough into the future, however, to have built a plan for what he ought to do when he did meet someone he truly cared about. It was almost, he thought, as though he was slinking around, nervous that Dakota might find out he had real feelings for another woman. Frankly, it left him a bit confused as well. And besides, it didn't feel proper to broach discussion of a new relationship now that the holidays were here. Best for things to remain as usual.

Tonight, however, his apartment had been anything but its usual quiet. And he'd enjoyed himself immensely.

James sighed, though if he was honest with himself, he really felt like burping. Maybe make some more room down there. Dakota's Thanksgiving meal had been delicious. Too much, of course. But that was part of the tradition as well.

"Food coma," Dakota announced with satisfaction, observing her father leaning back in his chair and her grandfather's head beginning to bob as sleep tugged at his eyelids, though he still sat at the table. "I can't think of a better compliment."

She'd cooked the dinner by herself, managing on only a few hours of sleep after doing all the prep for Peri's big night with her boyfriend's parents. She'd taped detailed reheating instructions inside the cupboard and the fridge at Peri's place, replete with warnings not to use tinfoil in the microwave and to check the oven for yarn before turning it on. She had even left two fresh pumpkin pies on the coffee table in the living room, and then, exhausted, she flagged a cab to carry her back to her dad's house. During the week, Dakota had a dorm room at school, but she still crashed in the city on the weekends, coming in for club meetings and to work several hours at the shop. It was a grueling pace but worth it to get her own café running. She knew her upcoming internship would really kick-start her career. Of course, she'd just whipped out a meal for her hungry relatives.

Arriving too early on the Thursday morning was Catherine, who set the table with James and disturbed the cook, who was trying to sneak a nap on the sofa after peeling all the potatoes and starting to roast the turkey.

Catherine was the only non—family member at the Foster-and-one-Walker Thanksgiving, something she hadn't realized when she gratefully accepted the invitation. Everyone in the club had plans: Marty felt that he and Anita should spend Turkey Day with his niece at the family brownstone, and Lucie and Darwin were out at their duplex in New Jersey, hosting Lucie's older brothers and their families. One good thing for those two was that Lucie's mother Rosie may have lost much of her mental functioning, but she maintained a strong ability to remember old recipes. They'd planned a turkey, of course, with a side of Rosie's lasagna and homemade marinara. Ginger, she'd been told, would drag in a comfy chair so that Rosie could rule the cooks, demanding more salt, less pepper. Inspired as she remembered Lucie talking about food prep in their house, Catherine pulled out a stool in Dakota's kitchen and sat down to offer commentary. But both she and Dakota knew she didn't have much insight to offer. Catherine's food experience was limited to ordering and eating.

"Did you do tomato in the salad? Love the tomatoes in Italy," said Catherine, lost for a moment thinking of a memorable picnic with Marco overlooking the fields, how she'd ended up with tomato juice in places unmentionable. "You know what I liked most, though? Eating outside."

"Uh, they don't have outside in New York?" asked Dakota,

her mocking tone muffled as she leaned forward to smell the aroma from the simmering cranberry-and-orange sauce. She was quite accustomed to Catherine's rants about why Italy was more wonderful than anywhere else. Love had softened Catherine's edges, made her occasionally gush. "C'mon," chided Dakota. "I'm pretty sure they do. Though I never have time for such luxuries."

"You're just grumpy because you have your nose to the grindstone," said Catherine, opening the fridge and hunting for something tasty. She lifted a Tupperware to the light fixture to see what was stored inside. "What you need is a vacation."

"In Italy, no doubt," said Dakota, frowning with concentration as she stirred. "What I actually need is a hell of a lot more baking." She turned away from the stove to offer Catherine a taste, observing her every reaction.

Catherine made a sour face.

"What's wrong?"

"Nothing, it's delish," said Catherine, pinching Dakota's cheek because she knew it annoyed her. "I was just teasing you. You're getting so intense."

Dakota got a new spoon and stirred her sauce. "I have a lot to get done in my life," she said, leaving unspoken the rest but knowing that Catherine understood. Her mother had died before she turned forty, leaving Dakota with a feeling—no, a fear—that nothing could wait. Everything had to be now, now, now. Her college friends might pop off for skiing holidays, but she'd much rather be learning and working. That was something else her mother had given her: an appreciation of the value of effort. Of dedication. Of knowing that sometimes, sacrifices were necessary and appropriate.

"Guess what?" she said, trying to act lighter. "I have lucked out: The chef at Rome's V hotel hooked me up with a spot in the kitchen here in New York over the holidays."

"Not for Christmas, though," said Catherine.

"Yeah, for Christmas," scoffed Dakota. "That's a huge chance, to get in there. I don't march over with my schedule and see if I can fit them in. It's the other way around."

"What did your dad say?" asked Catherine, getting out a knife to slice into a pie that was cooling on a rack.

"That's for dessert!" Dakota shouted, then dropped her voice. "I haven't told him. Not yet. But we're doing a big dinner at Thanksgiving today, so no need for another next month. Right?"

"Right . . ." said Catherine, sounding unconvinced. "That's why a huge part of the country does two massive suppers practically back-to-back. Dakota, everybody knows the holidays are for family. That's the whole point."

She'd been crossing off the days on her own calendar, in fact, because she knew Marco was bringing his entire family in for Hanukkah, and for Anita's wedding.

"Well, somebody has to cook the food," said Dakota coolly, reaching into the fridge and rearranging a shelf to reveal a pumpkin pie that had already been cut. She pointed out the half of a pie (since her father had already enjoyed some for breakfast) to

Catherine and scooped on a huge dollop of vanilla whipped cream. "Otherwise, how would skinnies like you get your year's supply of calories?"

Dakota savored the way Catherine closed her eyes in delicious rapture as she gobbled up the slice of spicy pumpkin filling, the way the crust flaked at the touch of her fork. Dakota liked to knit. She liked to travel. But she positively loved watching other people tuck into her food, loved the way they sighed and relaxed after just one bite. This was her gift. Her magic.

Of course, it would be nicer just to laze around this coming Christmas, to hang out with her dad and her uncle Donny. He'd always made the trips to Pennsylvania memorable, picking them up from the shop for the trip to the farm. Later, after Georgia died, he put together a giant ball of softly packed snow far out in the fields, giving her a baseball bat and offering her some privacy to whack away her frustrations. To scream and cry and choke out all her rage at, well, everything. Uncle Donny, her mom's younger brother, was just that sort of guy. He noticed stuff without making a fuss. He kept to the background, and yet he had his role to play as well.

Still. Spending Christmas in Pennsylvania wouldn't get her any closer to reaching her career goals, Dakota knew. Some folks had the luxury of taking things slowly. Not her. She couldn't wait. She knew better than to take those kinds of chances. Than to make assumptions.

"I really do need a nap," Catherine said now, blotting her lips with a napkin and placing it beside her plate at the Thanksgiving table.

"And I am more than impressed," said James's mother, Lillian. "Wonderful job, Dakota. And to you, James, a wonderful job as well. I am pleasantly surprised."

"Thanks. I rearranged the furniture about seven times to get things just right, get enough chairs, put the extra tables up," he said, nodding. "It was a lot of effort. But I've been working out." He winked.

"That's not what I meant," said Lillian, inclining her head almost imperceptibly toward her granddaughter.

"I worked on that, too," said James, delighted by his mother's approval. Dakota was too preoccupied with thoughts of whipping cream to pay much attention.

"I guess now we'll have to do all the dishes," pointed out James's father, Joe. His face was lined and his hair grayer, but he continued to take good care of himself and remained active. Both he and Lillian were retired after full careers teaching high schoolers but still used their skills to tutor students during the year. Work, they told their children, kept their minds in shape.

"I'll wash if someone will dry."

"Let's just move to more comfortable chairs and fall asleep," begged Catherine.

"I put most of the comfy chairs into the storage room in the basement," explained James. "What you see is what you get. We can fight over the sofa, sit on pillows, watch football standing up, huddle up on the floor . . ."

"Or go for a walk," interjected Lillian. "The dishes will wait. They never seem to go anywhere else if you don't do them."

It was clear to Catherine that Lillian ran the family, because the entire troupe of Fosters rose from their chairs to immediately gather coats and scarves.

"No sleep, then?" she murmured before being handed her own jacket by Dakota, who shook her head.

"The grandma has spoken," said Dakota good-naturedly. "You come to a Foster meal, this is how you have to play it. Come on, I'll lead you by the hand. You can sleep and walk at the same time."

Catherine didn't mind, having missed time with Dakota since their schedules often conflicted. Certainly Dakota was on the run with her hectic school calendar in Hyde Park, and with trying to still make up time in the yarn shop, even working on several knitting projects from her mother's designs.

"How's the pattern stuff?"

"Ah, it's slow," said Dakota, stuffing her hair into a red newsboy cap she'd knitted so many years ago that it was a bit fuzzy in spots. "I thought we should do all the projects, so I split it up with everybody—you know, the good knitters, I mean . . ."

"I know, I know," said Catherine, who had never advanced very far in her abilities. She didn't mind not being a tester.

"And so it takes as long as it takes," Dakota explained, then took a deep breath, as if confessing. "I'm swamped. Totally bagged."

"You just knocked yourself out to feed an army of cousins."

"Yeah, but it's other stuff," she said. "The internship. The knitting café. I don't know." She knew Catherine's parents had passed away many years before, and yet somehow Catherine didn't seem overwhelmed by the holidays. By their absence. Dakota envied her this peace.

"Oh, right, the dreaded I-don't-knows," said Catherine. "Guys, the holidays, too much pressure, not enough sleep."

"Pretty much all of that," Dakota admitted. "It's a funny time of year. All a big countdown, you know. And to what?"

"The wedding!"

"Okay, yeah," agreed Dakota. "But don't you feel everything else is just over the top? Or that there's a huge rush to do something monumental by New Year's? To achieve some milestone, accomplish something huge? Make this year better than last year. Perfect, even. And we have one month left. Ticktock."

"I'm fine." Catherine shook her head a bit too vigorously. She was fibbing, and Dakota knew it.

"So, I imagine the visit from the family Toscano isn't fazing you one bit?"

"Well," conceded Catherine, tilting her head to the side. "Maybe half a bit."

In the previous year, the forty-four-year-old blonde flew to Italy for a week every other month simply to let life on the vineyard wash over her. Oh, there were weeks when she and her friend Marco Toscano would drive the coast, or spend a day or two in Rome, but most often they made their way to his family vineyard, the aptly named Cara Mia. My beloved.

On occasion, Marco—her boyfriend, if such a phrase made sense for such an attractive grown man—would make the return trip with her and stay in the city. Sometimes he brought along his mother-in-law to see her sister Anita, as they continued to get to know each other after decades of estrangement. Marco enjoyed puttering around in Catherine's antiques-and-wonderful-things store in Cold Spring. They took turns cooking meals on Catherine's rarely used stove, and he would read her latest chapters.

"You know what would be interesting?" he once commented. "If these two best friends grow up to be spies for enemy countries."

"Well," said Catherine. "We kinda did."

All in all, it had been quite an atypical courtship, with lots of heavy-duty . . . talking. Unlike her usual romances, where things moved quickly to the bedroom and then just as quickly out the door.

Everything about this relationship was different from her unhappy marriage to wealthy investment banker Adam Phillips and from her multiple failed romances following her very welcome divorce. And yet she'd uncharacteristically spurned Marco's advances during the summer trip to Italy last year, when she was preoccupied with finally rediscovering her independence and sense of self, Anita was desperately trying to track down her sister, Sarah, to apologize for breaking ties years before, Lucie was directing an Italian pop diva in an avant-garde music video, and Dakota was nannying Ginger and dating Marco's son, Roberto.

After Catherine came back to New York, she initially insisted on communicating with Marco only through e-mail. It was some kind of test, she supposed, a means to ferret out if he was interested in her heart or just her body. And Catherine, not one to be shy about putting her toned hips to good use, wanted something she hadn't had before. She wanted a relationship that was real. Of course, sometimes she gave in to the urge to hear Marco's voice, but mostly she held firm to her commitment to build a friendship. Through the e-mail letters she learned about Marco's late wife, Cecilia, how they'd met when he was in his twenties and rushing a wine delivery, accidentally bumping her with his slow-moving Vespa. He shared his deep concern for his mother-in-law, Sarah, as she and her husband, Enzo, aged, and he revealed the difficulties he felt raising his children alone.

"Every hour they grow older," he wrote to her, "and I question myself constantly. Have I said enough? Done enough?"

In droplets of details, she revealed—slowly—how she'd hurt her best friend and taken her placement at their dream college, how she'd made a bad marriage and stayed rather than try to make a go on her own. She spared the specifics but told him about the important flings, though she hadn't quite brought herself to admitting her tryst with Anita's son Nathan. Not yet. (It was ooky enough to consider that Nathan was actually first cousins with Marco's late wife. Not that she'd known that when she screwed him. No. But she'd known he was married, had believed he was going to leave his wife for her.) Coming off that bad business had left her wary of Marco as well. All of it was strange, building a romance in the absence of her two old friends, sex and drink. But somehow it became a more effective approach. Laying a foundation.

Though a woman who wears leopard-print panties doesn't change her spots. On her initial two-week trip back to Italy, Catherine expected nothing but making up for lost time, packing the sheerest and tiniest of baby-doll nightgowns. Instead, she found Marco battling a crop-destroying group of bugs in the vineyard and spent candlelight dinners practicing her Italian with young Allegra, who patiently repeated words and then giggled as Catherine said them incorrectly. There were caresses and furtive kisses, but Marco was beyond exhausted and she left Italy as untouched as when she arrived. And she didn't mind. Well, okay, she minded. But just enough to make her want to go back. To a visit that made it clear that Marco was worth the wait.

Catherine hadn't even packed her slinky nighties on that journey. She expected it to be similar to the previous visits, with Allegra, on break from boarding school, awakening with a fever in the night or another emergency in the vineyard. Catherine was frustrated, but she was still patting cool cloths on heads and borrowing a pair of boots to tramp down to the vines and nod sagely as Marco talked through his problems.

Her affairs, she realized, had never taken place with kids, dogs, and workplaces in the scene. She was used to being whisked away to cozy bed-and-breakfasts, to luxury hotels with crisp sheets, even just to the bedroom of her charming bungalow.

"What is this between us, anyway?" she'd grumbled to Marco one afternoon.

"It's a love match," he said. "Butting heads with the real

world." He kissed her deeply on the mouth and then said the words she was longing to hear.

"There's a trip to Rome coming up," he said.

"When?"

"As soon as Allegra's grandmother arrives," said Marco, a half-grin on his lips. "They're going. We're staying. In all weekend."

They skipped dinner, waving at the door as Allegra departed, and then, racing up to Catherine's third-floor guest bedroom, found themselves laughing and kissing and making love on the stairs. During a picnic. In the wine cellar. On the kitchen floor.

How powerful, afterward, when Marco told her he loved her. How natural it seemed to tug on those boots and tramp through the vines.

She assumed she'd feel disappointed when Allegra returned. But instead, she felt a giddy joy rising up as the car pulled forward, and the most magical melting feeling in the pit of her stomach as Marco's beautiful young daughter hugged her first.

And that was when she really, really knew. She was in love. With all of them.

Catherine wrapped her arms around herself as she slowly followed everyone out to the street, lost in thought as Dakota was called ahead to chat with a cousin.

Lillian fell back from the group to wait for Catherine, who continued to absentmindedly pull up the rear.

"You're in love," said James's mother straightforwardly. "It's all over your face. Kind of a goofy grin going on there."

"Yeah," admitted Catherine, reflexively reaching up to touch her face.

"I don't know why I'm always the last to know," said James's mother, crossing her arms. "Not like I want to go through that again. The surprise girlfriend. So just tell me: Are you and my son an item?"

Catherine looked at her sideways before laughing. She opened her mouth to speak, but only giggles came out.

"Well, come on, he's not that bad," said Lillian. "He's quite good-looking."

"Oh, I know that," chuckled Catherine. "And it's been suggested by more than a few people that we would make a good-looking couple."

"So, then you're together?"

"Whoa, no," said Catherine. The light changed, leaving them stranded across the street corner as the rest of the crew waited on the other side. She turned to face James's mother.

"James and I are not—never have been—romantically involved," said Catherine.

"I see," said Lillian, not looking entirely convinced.

"Sometimes it makes sense to fill in that gap with someone you know. But for us, we're more like family," said Catherine. "Good friends who have always known there's a line we ought not to cross."

Lillian nodded. "You mean Georgia, don't you?"

"It's always been Georgia for him," admitted Catherine.

"And I think I've found my guy. Finally. Maybe. I don't know. But probably. Though it depends."

"Of course."

"Because I'm not ready to make things permanent," she said. "Not that we've talked about it in so many words, because we haven't, but his mind is probably there. And I'm here."

"Right."

"So, when he asks—and he will ask—I'm going to say 'not yet,'" Catherine said emphatically. "I've thought about this a lot. Don't worry."

"Not worried," said Lillian, though not unkindly.

"He has a little girl, Allegra. She's always away at school, but I like spending time with her."

"And I'm sure she likes you," said Lillian, offering a string of neutral comments.

"I'm not," confessed Catherine. "It's hard to know. You can't really ask. Don't want to seem needy. Or weird. Or have Marco think I'm weird. His first wife was practically a saint, and I'm more of a sinner, if you know what I mean."

Lillian had met Catherine only a few times over the years and wasn't quite sure she needed to hear the ins and outs of Catherine's love life if it didn't involve her son. Still, she nodded politely as Catherine rambled on about grapes and jet lag and sipping prosecco overlooking the fields. Then Lillian steered the conversation back to what was on her mind.

"I worry about my son. He wears his grief like a shield. Oh, and I remember well every second of that day I met Georgia," said Lillian. "When these two strangers walked through my front door and suddenly I had a new granddaughter. I was so angry with my son and so tickled by Dakota. But Georgia surprised me with her strength. I told James she had spunk, but it was more like grace."

"Funny, isn't it," said Catherine, "how you think about height and looks as what is passed down. And the most important gift Dakota got from her mother was that mysterious bit of something. A powerful sense of self."

"Dakota is lovely and doing well," agreed Lillian. "But with her growing up, it's James I am concerned about. He can't go on like this forever. Comparing other women to her mother."

"He may be getting more serious," said Catherine. "Dakota thinks he has someone interesting this time around."

"She hasn't mentioned that to me." Lillian did not like to be left out of whatever was going on.

"She hasn't actually met her yet," said Catherine. "But she's dropping hints to James that she suspects."

"Then he's not serious enough," said Lillian. "The holidays won't make it easier. All about marking time and where you were last year and how long since Georgia. All the 'remember whens.' It's tough."

"Of course, it's also happy, like today." Catherine smiled, indicating the entire group on their way up the street. But she was really thinking about Marco. About a Thanksgiving in some fantasy future when she wouldn't be the stray guest—albeit a welcome one—but an integral part of a family.

The group clambered along the park side of Fifth Avenue, past the Plaza and FAO Schwarz, to stop in front of one of Catherine's favorite haunts. The rest of the gang wasn't as pleased.

"You brought us to Bergdorf's?" Joe asked his granddaughter.

"No," said Dakota. "I brought you on my architectural tour of New York. We're going to imagine this building as it was over a hundred years ago, when it was a Vanderbilt mansion. In fact, the entire city was different. This wasn't the heart of the retail district but of stately homes."

"Just like your father," said one of Dakota's aunts. "Always dragging us around to see buildings and tell stories."

"No," whispered James under his breath, marveling at how Dakota had taken command (with Lillian's tacit permission) of all of them. He'd once taken her on this very same walk, poking into art deco lobbies of corporate buildings and telling her anecdotes about the newer construction in midtown Manhattan. No, he felt she was so much more like her mother, the way she moved so gracefully when she pointed out a detail, or how she opened her mouth too wide when she laughed, showing teeth and tongue. She had her mother's build, slim and athletic, and her seemingly endless zeal for work. What Dakota needed was a vacation.

The city itself had already made the transition from workaday to holiday, the Christmas season emerging in the form of garlands and bows on store windows. No doubt Dakota was leading them to Rockefeller Center to eat chocolate and watch skaters circling the ice rink. He checked quickly to see if his mother was flagging, but she and Catherine were utterly enchanted by each other's company. He considered making small talk with one of his older sisters but, in the end, allowed himself to get lost in the joy of simply watching his daughter entertain the family. Telling jokes and slipping her arm through her grandfather's. Although she was the youngest, she was clearly a leader.

He'd never known her as a truly little girl, but it remained stunning how she'd quietly, thoroughly, turned into a woman. Just last year she'd seemed unreasonable and immature at moments. Now she focused on school, on the shop, on taking that binder of her mother's patterns and creating a book that captured her mother's talent. He felt pride but also something more: a growing respect for his daughter and the manner in which she approached her life. She seemed to be relaxing into herself. Confident in her choices. As much as he'd fought her decision to leave a traditional college, he could see that it had been the right move.

"Dad?" she'd asked last night, as he sat on the floor, wiped out from moving a good chunk of the living-room furniture, the stainless tables and the oversized leather chairs. She offered him a warm slice of apple-and-cinnamon pie.

"Yeah?"

"Thanks, you know. For just, you know, being cool with stuff."

"Don't work too hard," he noted. "You look like your mother, but I wouldn't want you to make your father's mistakes. You need to make time to live. To spend time with your family. Your old man!"

"That's worked out, too. Right?" Dakota bit her lip, then caught herself and stopped. James understood. What had always been most difficult were the big events, the birthdays and holidays. For years they had focused on re-creating the traditional Christmas in Pennsylvania, and each year emotions ran high. "Christmas can be a lot."

"True," he agreed. "Holidays make you remember, but that's okay. Everyone feels this way. It's normal. It's good, even."

"We don't always have to do the same traditions," she said. "We can do new things, shake it up a bit."

"Absolutely," he said.

That's when he knew his plan for a different kind of Christmas had been the right choice. Even in the current economic climate, even since he'd left his comfortable position at the hotel to begin his own architectural firm, he was glad to splurge for surprise plane tickets for Dakota and her maternal grandparents and even her uncle Donny, who maintained the family farm in Pennsylvania. Because watching her tonight, concentrating wholeheartedly on playing hostess, he could see how much she needed a break. Also how much she seemed lighter being around her family. And how, in the not-too-distant future, life would be different. She would be more than his little girl, she would want to do her own thing, marry, maybe even move away. Now was the moment to do something special, to bring all of Georgia's family together for Christmas, just as he brought his entire family to Thanksgiving. For her.

"I think I'm hungry again," shouted Joe from the back of the group.

"Well, Grandpa, then my plan has worked," announced Dakota, tugging onto her hands a pair of purple fingerless gloves that she'd made during her commutes on the Metro-North train to the city from culinary school in Hyde Park. "Because I made five kinds of pies yesterday and I expect you to try a piece from every one of them!"

Everyone laughed and started making their way back to the apartment.

"Dakota," said James, falling in step with his daughter and Catherine, "I have something to tell you."

Dakota tossed Catherine a now-he-is-going-to-tell-me-about-his-girlfriend look.

"A Thanksgiving surprise," exclaimed Catherine. "Is it an ice-cream maker?"

"No, no," said James, grinning from ear to ear.

"Well, I have great news, too," said Dakota. "About my budding career. But you first. What's her name?"

"Umm," James said, thinking deeply. "Glenda, of course. I always forget because I just think of her as Gran," he explained to Catherine.

"Huh? That's really weird, Dad. TMI!"

James shrugged. "I thought about keeping it a surprise but knew you'd want to tell everyone in the club."

A look of comprehension dawned on Catherine's face. "I hate surprises," she said. "They always interfere with plans. People ought to just talk about things. Out in the open. Maybe you two could have communicated about your ideas for the holiday season. Hmmm?"

"Oh, no," said James. "It ruins the thrill of telling you that we're going to Scotland for Christmas. I know how much you've wanted to go visit, and we've been so busy. So I booked!"

"This Christmas?"

"Of course," said James, a quizzical expression on his face. "When else? We're bringing all the Walkers together at Gran's."

"Dad! Why now?" wailed Dakota, thinking all at once about her internship and seeing Roberto and how much she missed her ninety-seven-year-old Scottish great-grandmother, practically one hundred but as sprightly and no-nonsense as ever. Her mother had always talked about how much she wanted to go to Scotland, as she'd done when she was a girl, but Georgia was able to take Dakota only the summer before she died. She'd always had to put work before fun. And now Dakota truly understood how hard some of her mother's decisions must have been. Because here she was, facing her own dilemma.

But James, taking her high pitch and general confusion for excitement, gave her a big hug. "It's extravagant, for sure, but I knew you'd love it," he said, walking with his arm around his daughter. "I won't let anything take away from our special trip. And we'll be back for Anita and Marty's wedding, of course."

Dakota swallowed, looking at Catherine in panic. What about her internship? What about Gran?

If only she knew what she should do.

chapter three

Peri had always suffered a love-hate relationship with storewide sales. Thanksgiving night was the
worst: She was unable to sleep, sneaking down to the shop in
her sweatpants and tee to get things ready for the massive Black
Friday hordes of committed knitters. Sure, it cleared old inventory and got some new foot traffic in the door, but all the same
it was exhausting. She'd be spent when it was all over. For now,
she was just trying to dash ahead of the fray.

"Do you have more of this light cotton?" *Somewhere in my
kitchen,* thought Peri.

"Is this the only yarn you have in this roasted-squash color?"
Yes, and I'm thankful for that.

"Can I return the final-sale items?" *Where does that ever happen?*

And on and on. Questions that Peri typically answered with
patience grated on her nerves.

All she could see today were the difficulties of running a shop—the long hours, the challenge to take days away, the ever-present fears of cash and flow that permeated her thoughts.

She'd been caught off guard by the woman who came into Walker and Daughter two nights before as Dakota toiled in the kitchen upstairs over pies. Peri had been closing up.

"So, this is the famous place," said the woman, who was extremely thin and had a shock of platinum hair over one eye. She was exquisitely dressed in a nubbly figure-skimming tweed jacket, wide-leg trousers, and tall leather boots. Peri knew her *Vogue* well enough to calculate the many thousands of dollars spent on this one single outfit.

"Welcome," said Peri. Word had spread among area knitters that Dakota had recently rediscovered a pattern book of her mother's original designs, and more than once, people had come asking for a look. Especially since the issue of Italian *Vogue*, with the singer Isabella (whose music video Lucie had directed) posed on the cover in the pink gown that Georgia had made for Catherine long ago.

These knitters who came by the shop were eager to see the outline of that Blossom dress, the variations on The Phoenix, Catherine's favorite gown designed by Georgia, or simply to look at the imaginings of a fellow knitter, her boundless creativity and interplay of color and texture. Dakota spent hours, Peri knew, imagining how best to highlight her mother's ideas.

She paused, wishing this woman was a friend so she could just try on those killer boots, and then asked again if she could help her pick out something from the shop.

"I'd like . . ." said the woman, scanning the shop. "That blue Peri Pocketbook clutch, please."

"Oh," said Peri, delighted. "I haven't even put it on my Web site yet."

"I know," said the woman, handing over a credit card. "I know all of your bags, and I want them."

Peri laughed, "All at once?"

"Absolutely. And I'd like you to make more, just for me."

Peri stopped laughing. Was this woman a bit off? she wondered. Buying her entire collection was definitely pricey.

"I officially came to the city for Thanksgiving with my elderly aunt," explained the woman as Peri swiped her card. "Though I had other motivations: I also wanted to come to this shop. Maybe see you." The woman offered Peri an oversized business card but held on as Peri went to take it.

"Peri," said the woman, the business card between them. "I can make Peri Pocketbook huge. All you have to do is come work for my label in Paris. Let me explain who I am: My name is Lydia Jackson."

"Oh my God," said Peri, recognizing the woman's name immediately. She was the chief designer for a cutting-edge French fashion house. "But you don't do knits."

Lydia Jackson let go of the card. "But I want to," she said, lightly tapping the Peri Pocketbook she'd just purchased. "And that's the key detail. I can make you a household name in the world of fashion. Bigger than when your bags were in Italian *Vogue*."

"You saw that? It was a huge boost," admitted Peri, her fingers tingling as they clung to the business card.

"And working with me will be like clinging to a rocket ship." Lydia Jackson spoke with absolute confidence. "The dress on the *Vogue* cover got fashionistas talking. But we're going to put our money where our mouth is—and our plan is to start whenever you call me at that number."

So, there it was. A most tempting offer. Two years ago, she would have accepted that card and walked right out the door. Well, maybe not.

But she would have wanted to.

Now she felt a stronger connection. She was very near having her own boutique, once the knitting café was completed following Dakota's graduation. A few years away. But getting closer.

Not to mention that it was Dakota who'd arranged for the *Vogue* photo shoot to come together. There was that little detail as well.

"Peri," said Dakota now, as she also struggled to keep up with the Black Friday rush. "Can you ring up Mrs. Jones?"

"Sure," Peri replied, remembering to smile. "Did you find everything today?"

The shop was busy enough that it felt warm inside, and Peri had opened the windows earlier, even on this cold November day, to let in some fresh air and lower the temperature. There were more folks popping in than usual: Business had been down in recent months and, clearly, knitters were waiting to stock up.

Part of the mini-boom, she thought, was due to Dakota's idea to offer casual lessons. She put a sign on the shop door earlier in the week, and then all during the afternoon of Black Friday she demonstrated how to cast on at the top of the hour and how to knit on the half-hour. She and her best friend from NYU, Olivia, were alternating "classes" with Anita. Which left Peri to run the till all day. Punch in the SKUs, deduct the discount, and hit the total button. Cha and ching. She knew she should be encouraged, especially as several customers were looking carefully at some of the marked-down Peri Pocketbooks. But the lack of sleep, guilt for even considering the job offer, and her general sense of frustration left Peri confused. She didn't want to have to make hard choices. Not now. What she wanted was to feel magically in love and whistle while she worked, like some storybook princess. (Who was probably not in her thirties, overworked, and crammed in a tiny apartment. But not everyone starts out in a castle, right?)

Instead, she felt as though her love-life ambitions were being thwarted. She'd dried out the turkey the night before. What a rookie mistake! Dakota had left such detailed instructions, but Peri figured turning up the heat might speed along the meal. Not so. And Roger's mother had made quite a show of spreading cranberry sauce all over her bird.

Then she chewed and chewed and chewed.

Peri wished she'd never bothered making the effort at all,

hadn't fallen into the hope that displaying a bit of domestic talent would make Roger decide if he was in or out. She feared she'd grown desperate, that her near decade of living in the city, of passing thirty, had forced her hand. Should she wait for someone just right or someone who would do nicely? She liked Roger well enough. He was attractive and successful. Had a fun way about him. But clearly he danced to his mother's tune: He'd barely eaten, and when he praised the pie—Dakota's delicious maple-sugar pie that Peri was pretending was her own—he backtracked upon seeing the narrowing of his mother's eyes.

KC ate two slices, staring down Roger's mother bite for bite.

"Think of it this way," KC had said as they did the dishes last night. (Dakota had ensured that Peri didn't have only yarn on which to serve.) "Better to find out now than to marry the beast—and have to live with her son all the same."

"You're just anti–settling down," said Peri.

"No, I'm just anti-settling," said KC. "Don't do it, hon. Divorce sucks, even if you don't love the guy anymore. Better not to make a wrong choice."

Peri cringed at the word "choice." She hadn't told anyone about meeting Lydia Jackson.

"I just figured that *this* would be the year," admitted Peri. "I made a New Year's resolution that I'd find love and marriage . . ."

"And push a baby carriage," interjected KC, piling up the dry plates by the sink. "I know the rhyme. But what's with the artificial agenda? So, you decided. What puts you in control?"

"I don't believe in letting life just happen, and you know that."

"Sometimes the right thing just comes along," said KC. "If it makes sense, you just gotta do it."

"He's the one?"

"Oh, hon, that's not real," said KC. "There's about one hundred guys out there just perfect for you. Depends on timing and if you're both in the same place mentally and—let's be honest—if you ever cross paths."

"So, it could be anyone, then?"

"Not anyone," said KC, munching on a few odd green beans in the bottom of a dish. "An anyone that's right for you in your life as it is. Not what you want it to be. But who you are. Because you don't know how you're going to change, and, hopefully, the guy can change right along with you."

"Your life experience would indicate I shouldn't pay attention to you," teased Peri.

"On the contrary," said KC. "My advice is because I tried to do it your way. It's taken me to my fifties to accept that I'm not the marrying kind."

"Sure you are," said Peri. "You just married a company."

KC tossed a damp dish towel in Peri's direction. "So, okay, somehow I've worked my entire career at Churchill Publishing," she admitted. "It's outlasted both marriages—and I even reconciled after it had layoffs and dumped me."

Peri rolled her eyes. "They love you there."

"Love. Roger. Connection?" asked KC.

"Roger's okay," said Peri, wavering. "He's a nice guy."

"There's a ringing endorsement," said KC. "Look, is the sex fantastic?"

"KC! Come on, now," said Peri. "I'm not spilling details."

"I'm serious. If you're going to marry a so-so guy, he better blow your freakin' mind," said KC. "That's all I have to say."

"And now we know why you're single."

"Damn straight," said KC. "I don't care if it takes until I'm ninety; I'm going to find my G-spot."

As much as KC was fun to have around, Peri knew they were fundamentally different. They could shop, share books, talk about work, try out new restaurants. But KC seemed never to have had a biological clock, while all Peri could hear was her own, keeping her agitated late at night when the distractions of the day had faded and she lay quietly in her bed, hoping for sleep. What if it didn't happen? What then? Could she pull a Lucie and do it on her own? And if not, what would it mean to redefine her life after spending most of it under the assumption that for all the adventures of her career, she'd eventually acquire the traditional trappings of a house and family? Sometimes she felt as though she were choking on her own disappointment. And whenever she tried to tell KC, she heard in reply that she was young and not to worry. But potential isn't always realized, she knew. Peri might simply not find what she was looking for personally or professionally. And that's what left her frightened. That's what left her sneaking looks at Lydia Jackson's business card.

She knew that not every woman felt this way. But she did— and that made it difficult, sometimes, to smile at the customers and bag up the yarn and just be content with what she did have. Because she still wanted more.

"No school today!" shouted Lucie, using a hand on Ginger's oversized backpack to steer her in the door of Walker and Daughter. Thankfully, the rush of shoppers had calmed somewhat by the afternoon: The hardcore knitters knew that the best buys were always when the shop opened and had likely returned to their homes to gloat over the latest additions to their stash. Lucie had avoided the frenzy because she knew she'd be right in the thick of it, fighting over the cashmere bargains.

"Hey, I didn't think I'd see you guys," said Dakota, as Ginger squeezed her around the middle.

"Well, we have played video games, and drawn pictures, and chased Grandma around the house for tag, and then Cady and Stanton had to go down for a nap. So we decided to trek into the city."

"Auntie Darwin suggested it," offered Ginger. "Her homework is late. So she's grumpy."

"And she's in a funk that the twins' second Thanksgiving has passed and it will never come back," whispered Lucie.

"That's the weird part," announced Ginger. "She took pictures all during dinner."

"Oh, I remember feeling that way," said Anita. "Babies grow up so fast. You feel as though you can barely capture the moment, let alone relax and savor all your feelings."

"Did you make any cookies?" asked Ginger.

"No, we're teaching knitting today," Dakota explained to

Ginger. "But all the customers have gone home now. Maybe more will come soon."

"Well, I'll be the teacher, then," said Ginger, clambering into a chair.

"And what will we learn from you today?" said Dakota, playing along.

"Reminds me of you," mouthed Anita, standing behind Ginger but looking at Dakota. She'd known Dakota all of her life and, on occasion, found herself surprised to see a twenty-year-old where her senses told her a toddler should be. She didn't blame Darwin one bit.

"I'll show how to knit a bookmark," Ginger announced matter-of-factly. "My mother gave me a pattern, and I know it by heart. Almost." She struggled to lift her backpack onto the table, then unzipped the main compartment and began rooting around. Within seconds, she had dumped out a turkey sandwich, a bag of baby carrots, a hairbrush, two mismatched socks, her stuffie Sweetness in a doll-sized multi-striped knit poncho with matching hat that was clearly made by Lucie, and a chapter book with a bookmark sticking out of its pages.

"Here," she said, opening the carrots and popping one into her mouth.

"A carrot?"

"No, the book," crunched Ginger. "Inside." She turned to a page in the middle and dangled a pink ribbed rectangle with a fringe. There were several holes where stitches ought to have been.

"Pretty, right?" asked Ginger.

"Gorgeous," Dakota replied.

"It's something to keep her busy," said Lucie. "And you're getting really good, honey."

"I know," said Ginger, rifling through her backpack again and coming up with a square pair of needles and some inexpensive yarn. "You wanna see me?"

"Sure," said Dakota. "I even remember making my very first bookmark. I think I was five."

"You were four, in fact," said Anita. "If I recall correctly, you found it most frustrating."

Dakota tilted her head, looking in the distance, thinking. "I kinda remember selling them or something? In the shop, I guess. Do you ever have those can't-quite-recall thoughts? It's as though they press on your mind but it's hard to put together all the details."

"Well," said Anita, settling into a chair to watch Ginger counting off her stitches. "You were far younger than four when you went with your mother to sell her knitting. At the flea market."

"Seriously?"

"Before there was a Walker and Daughter, there was a committed young mother raising money to bring up her daughter through knitting commissions and street-market sales," reminded Anita.

"And the bookmarks were sold for three bucks," said Lucie. "I know because when I was pregnant with our knitting wiz over here, I asked Georgia for advice. I was afraid about making ends meet. She told me what she did to raise funds and assured me that anything is what you'll do to provide. Absolutely anything."

Some days Georgia didn't even bother to get the mail. After all, she'd have to bundle up the baby, schlep down several flights, and who knew what she'd discover in the mailbox after all that bother?

"Bills, bills, bills," she muttered to herself, purposefully glancing away from the large pile of white envelopes practically multiplying on her coffee table whenever she left the room. She'd hidden the bills that were past due underneath the bathroom sink, where she could pretend to herself they'd gotten lost in the mail. Some nights, after finally getting eighteen-week-old Dakota to sleep, she'd wash that same bathroom floor and take tiny peeks in the door of the vanity cupboard, hoping the bills really had gotten lost. After all, winter was starting. Surely bad weather led to delays with the mail? Even with items sent in October?

Georgia simply hadn't realized just how much the hospital bills would be. Her health insurance was the cheapest plan and therefore had all sorts of loopholes, leaving her on the hook for much more than what was in her savings account. Oh, she'd anticipated a whopper or two, but she assumed her income would be rather more robust by her baby's arrival. Not so. Although Mrs. Lowenstein—she couldn't imagine ever getting used to calling her Anita, even though the older woman insisted—bought several sweaters after Georgia made her the first, it was obviously going to be impossible to make a living on knitting commissions. Even though she didn't waste, using the odds and ends to fashion bookmarks she could sell at the uptown flea market on Saturdays, the baby in a Snugli. Still. She could make all the bookmarks possible, eat all the ramen noodles in the world, and it still wouldn't leave her enough left over. At this rate, the baby—gorgeous little

Dakota, all crinkly nose and soft skin—was going to have to live on breast milk for the rest of her life. It was the only thing around here that was free.

There was a lot to be angry about, she thought, as she unwrapped a cold turkey sandwich she'd purchased from Marty's Deli the night before. The editorial job she'd quit, the apartment she could barely afford to heat, the Thanksgiving she didn't really have. Every second a choice between difficult options presented itself. And only in the future would she be able to look back and know whether she'd made the right decisions. For now, all was risk.

"I wonder what James ate in Paris tonight," she growled, taking a huge bite out of her sandwich, and then another. She was tired and afraid and frequently woke up in a panic at three a.m., but still she knew she had the better deal. She had Dakota, who smelled kinda good, even when she smelled really, really bad.

It was obvious that she needed to revise her strategy to make a life for the two of them, Georgia Walker and her daughter. That's what we are, she thought, Walker and Daughter.

She peered hopefully into the paper bag that had held the sandwich. Sure enough, hidden under a jumble of napkins, was an oversized black-and-white cookie tossed in the bottom. He was nice, that guy from the deli, in an old-uncle-you-see-once-in-a-while kind of way. He offered Georgia extra food for free, and when she protested, he'd find a way to sneak it in somewhere.

Earlier, she'd taken a breath to soothe the butterflies in her stomach and told him, straight out, that she was knitting on commission. Without hesitation, he'd ordered two sweaters and another for his brother Sam, offering a deposit.

"*Already getting cold,*" *he said.* "*I might even need more soon. Do you think you could add a Yankees logo, or is that too hard?*"

"*Of course,*" *she told him.* "*Though it might cost a little more.*"

"*Naturally,*" *he'd replied. And that's when she'd sprung another idea on him.*

"*I see you get awfully busy here in the mornings, and I'm close by . . .*" *She faltered, lapsing into silence.*

"*Sure, I could always use a little help around here in the mornings,*" *Marty'd said easily.* "*The bagel crowd can get rowdy. How's Monday? We can probably find a drawer around here for the baby.*" *He grinned to let her know he was joking about Dakota, then handed her the bag with her turkey inside.*

Georgia smiled into her sandwich. She was still nervous—Would that go away anytime soon?—but it was a good Thanksgiving, after all. Because if spreading a little cream cheese on bagels meant her baby had a chance, then she was more than ready to pick up a knife. The knitting? She'd just have to work that in somewhere else.

"I don't think I ever knew that stuff," Dakota said thoughtfully. "It's weird to realize how well I knew my mom, and yet she had all these other parts to her. Hiding bills like a crazy person."

"No, it's right," replied Anita. "Necessary, even. You're not a little girl anymore. You said so over and over, of course. But it seems to me that you're ready to learn the different sides of Georgia Walker. Beyond the mom and business owner."

"We all knew her in different ways," added Lucie. "She taught me a lot about courage."

"And about believing in impossible dreams," said Peri, across the shop by the register.

"For all of us, certainly," said Anita. "But maybe we focused so much on protecting you through your teens that we didn't help you see Georgia's many facets."

"Like what? Tell me everything," insisted Dakota.

Ginger put down her bookmark and looked at the women. "Yes, everything!" she echoed.

"No, what I think we ought to do is not censor ourselves so much, perhaps," murmured Anita, gazing at Ginger.

"Not like every story about Georgia is racy, either," said Peri.

"Is that a reference to my father? Because that is *waaay* too much information."

Lucie chuckled. "Perhaps what Peri meant is that Georgia was real. She had bad days. Sometimes really bad days."

"She even had days when she was ticked off at you," said Peri.

"Come, now," said Anita. "I wasn't thinking those types of stories."

"Like when?" asked Dakota.

"The bike thing," Peri said with enthusiasm. "When your dad bought those bikes and you were so excited."

"See, that wasn't me," said Dakota, and then gazed around. "Okay, a little bit me. I finagled getting that bike. But it was a damn good bike, you know!"

She laughed, reflexively looking out toward the stair landing, where the bikes had once been stored.

"This is what we don't do enough," announced Anita. "Telling happy stories. Or just remembering in a way that makes us laugh."

"Because Georgia was not a saint," piped up Lucie. "She was so genuine. That's what drew us all to her. We got her, and she got us. She made mistakes. Nobody's completely got it together in the Friday Night Knitting Club. It's a condition of membership."

"I'd like to hear the secrets," said Dakota. "Or just stuff I didn't know."

"Sometimes we all cling to a belief that we must make our lost ones perfect in our memory. It's a dangerous game," said Anita. "But from now on, I'll make it a point to call up some stories about Georgia. And you, Dakota, can make it a point to ask the women in the club. Your father. You see, there's something magical about the way you can get to know someone better even after they're gone."

Just then Peri left the till to sit down with the women at the table.

"Hey, Dakota," she said with forced casualness. "Can I talk to you later? I've had something come up."

hanukkah

Eight nights to recall an exhilarating triumph over adversity, a stubborn persistence when belief overtook logic. What a philosophy for life! Imagine bringing that same approach to knitting. Taking chances, risking challenges, hoping breathlessly that it will all work out. Consider the folly of tackling a stitch too far advanced, the welcome rush of satisfaction when you see it come together and hold. The victory of accomplishment.

chapter four

Everything ought to have been done already, thought Anita, for a wedding that had been on and off for more than a year: a zigzag of joy and frustration that was wearing her out. Was she silly to want to get married again at almost eighty years old? The New Year's party was going to be their last effort, Marty warned her, before he was tossing the big wedding idea out the window and eloping with her. He didn't care whether it was Las Vegas, Mexico, or New York City Hall: She was going to be Mrs. Marty Popper by the beginning of the New Year, and that was that. He had waited patiently for seventy-five years, he explained, and that was darn long enough.

Anita sighed, sipping coffee as she sat on the cream-colored couch with her feet tucked up under her and waited for her wedding planner—aka Catherine—to bring over a pair of shoes that she insisted would be perfect with Anita's latest dress.

She'd purchased two new outfits, a sparkly silk sheath with Catherine as well as a two-piece combo on the sly, with a cowl-neck top and pants that were so wide they looked more like a split skirt. Either one would work with the redesigned wedding coat, though Anita was careful not to let Marty know she'd bought a spare. It would probably send the wrong message, imply that she was already thinking ahead to the next rescheduling. Truth be told, Anita found it easier to doubt that the wedding would come together than to risk yet another disappointment. And did marriage really matter if they had each other?

"It matters to me," Marty had said when she tried that argument.

Funny how she'd have blown her top if her sons had lived with their girlfriends before a wedding, she thought. Then again, she'd certainly reached an age when she could make her own rules. She ought to write that down and remember to say as much to Nathan.

Anita put down her cup and began to make a list, trying to focus on her upcoming Hanukkah party. It was an ad hoc plan that had popped into her mind just this morning: have the members of the club come over for the candle lighting, perhaps give them each special gifts, like new needle bags or cable-hook necklaces. The timing worked also because her sister, Sarah, was coming two weeks before the wedding, so she'd have a chance to combat her jet lag. Anita knew she was looking for distractions, trying to keep her mind off Nathan. That boy knew one song, and getting her away from Marty was all he could sing.

"I just don't think your heart is in it, Mother," he told her over the phone last night, his voice calm and smooth. "If it was, you'd be married by now."

"Ha!" Anita paused, not wanting to have yet another shouting match with her oldest son. Those always left her awake most of the night, pestering Marty with endless ". . . and another thing . . ." insights as she re-argued with Nathan in her mind and used Marty as a sounding board for her imagined debates. She used to be sharper, she knew. But she felt weary these days, and her best lines came to her hours after the conversation ended. She tried to save up her smart retorts, but the moment to use them never seemed to come around again.

"I've been rescheduling out of sensitivity to you," she pointed out to Nathan on yesterday's call. She might be exhausted, but she wasn't out of the game yet, she reminded herself.

"But Mother," he insisted. "I never asked you to do that. The show must go on, as they say. You could have left me in the hospital room. I would have understood."

She loved him, yes, but on occasion she really didn't like Nathan all that much. Even when he was a small boy, he could lapse into manipulation. Stan had been immovable; she wanted to compensate by giving in. Now his ego led him to believe she was easily fooled.

The last wedding, the event that would have taken place two months ago in October, would have been a gorgeous affair, with burgundy calla lilies and yellow gerberas in high center-pieces and a whimsical cake, chocolate-fudge frosting with polka dots of buttercream. Those nuptials were canceled only a few hours before she'd been due to walk down the aisle, as Anita—in her previous version of her wedding dress and knit-ted coat—and her boys rushed a breathless, grimacing, chest-clutching Nathan to Beth Israel hospital only to find out, after multiple tests and hours of white-faced worry, that he had sim-ply experienced a massive case of anxiety. Faked or genuine, it was hard to determine.

The similarities to her late husband's fatal heart attack—coupled with the fear of losing her oldest son, whom she loved in spite of his antics—left Anita hysterical. Marty held her for days as she relived Stan's death, purging her system of the ter-rible shock, talking through regrets and concerns as she knit a vest of the type she'd made for Stan years ago. It took her al-most a week to recover.

What that man needed, Catherine had pointed out to his mother at the club meeting after the non-wedding, eating vigor-ously along with all the women to polish off the giant leftovers of wedding cake, was a dose of Valium, a few years with a shrink, and a good, swift kick in the ass.

"And I offer my foot if it's required," Catherine had said, stuffing a huge piece of cake into her mouth. "Or both feet. Whichever will hurt more."

The doorbell rang in the apartment now, and Anita stepped back as Catherine blew in, her cheeks pink from the cool

December air, dragging a giant shopping bag in one hand and a small bakery box in the other.

"Here," she said, handing off the box to Anita. "Before we do shoes. I brought you samples to try, since the last baker had such a hissy fit about his cake not being able to be admired."

Anita grimaced. All these shenanigans were tremendously embarrassing, from being left with a giant (and expensive) cake, to putting deposits on ballrooms, sending out invitations to friends old and new, then having to reach all concerned to postpone. Again and again. She felt bad for the other, probably young, brides who could have been able to use the dates and venues she'd reserved. Oh, and the travel arrangements that guests were making and breaking, from Marty's brother to Anita's other boys, David and Benjamin, to all the guests from Italy. Extra fees and penalties for everyone. Only Nathan paid his own with a smile.

"I thought we were going to forgo cake this time," Anita said glumly. "I can't believe I'm on my fifth wedding and I only made it to the altar once—in the 1950s."

"We are not going to forgo anything," Catherine replied, stepping into the kitchen and then coming back with a knife and the coffeepot. "Let me cut you a little taste of hazelnut and of lemon."

Anita took another sip of coffee, peering over Catherine's side to see inside the bakery box. The bite-sized cakes were topped in smooth icing stripes of yellow and cream. "Nathan called again, and Marty was none too happy about it," she admitted. "It's kind of set the tone for the day."

"Nathan." Catherine paused. "Strikes me as a man who doesn't always know what he wants. So no reason to pay attention."

"It's hard, as a mother, to simply ignore your child when he's clearly upset," explained Anita. "No matter that he's in his fifties."

"Wouldn't know," Catherine said briskly.

"Oh, it's not too late for you," reassured Anita, who well knew how Catherine had, on occasion, wished for a family. "Hollywood stars are having babies until they're seventy, it seems. You're barely forty."

"Closing in on forty-five, and you know it," Catherine said, focusing intently on slicing up the little cakes.

"Numbers, all numbers," said Anita, rummaging in a drawer for napkins. "If not Marco, then someone else."

"Not Marco?"

"So then it *is* Marco," said Anita, nodding. "I wondered why you've been so quiet recently. I decided it was either because you'd gone off him or because you were really sure."

"I wouldn't say I'm sure, Anita. I like him, but I don't know," said Catherine. "I've made it clear I'm not looking to make it all permanent, of course. I'm trying to be a leader, not a follower, anymore."

"If you say so, my dear," said Anita. "But in good relationships we have to play both roles, the leader and the follower."

"So, why don't you elope, then, as Marty suggested?" said Catherine, wagging her finger in the air. "It's because you're not much of a follower."

"Sometimes I am," Anita said softly. The two women stood,

coffee cups in hand, nibbling at petit-four-sized tidbits of deliciousness.

"They're scrumptious," said Anita. "But the wedding is too close. And then there's the holidays. No baker would take it on."

"Not an issue," said Catherine. "I've already arranged a meeting."

"When?"

"How about now?"

"You?" Anita tried to hide her shock.

"What a vote of confidence," said Catherine. "But no." She walked over and opened the front door. Dakota jumped inside.

"You don't have time," Anita started before Dakota could even open her mouth. "You have school, and holiday hours at the shop."

"And your dad is taking you to Scotland," interjected Catherine.

"Fabulous," said Anita. "Just what you need. Back for the wedding?"

"Yes! And no, I'm not going," said Dakota.

"What?" Anita was stern.

"It's not like that," said Dakota. "No doubt I want to go and see Gran. But I have an amazing opportunity to intern in the V kitchen. No one else from my class has anything like this lined up. I have a life plan here."

"Are you sure? Choosing work over the holidays . . ." Anita smoothed Dakota's cheek. "What did your father say?"

"About that," said Dakota. "I haven't told him yet. No need to stress him."

Catherine covered her ears. "Don't want to know," she said. "I'm having coffee with James tomorrow."

"I'm a big girl," said Dakota.

"Well, big girls make big mistakes," said Anita. "Trust me on that. Because I've had it up to here with interference in my own affairs."

"So, how about the cakes?" asked Dakota, her eyes pleading.

"Too much," said Anita. "I'll say no simply to save you more work."

"I'm not doing it alone," said Dakota. "I have a team of class-mates who all want to pitch in. It's good practice."

Anita tasted another bit of cake. "Yes, it is very good. I think you're getting even better."

"Yup," agreed Dakota. "I am. And I've never been able to do something really great for you, Anita. So, this is my chance."

"Well, once you put it that way, I can't refuse," said Anita, leaning in to hug her surrogate granddaughter. "I will pay top dollar, however."

Dakota rolled her eyes. "It's a gift," she said.

"Nonsense," said Anita. "Your love and hard work is the gift. For the rest, I write a check. A large one."

"You know she's going to sneak money in somewhere," said Catherine. "So, you might as well share it with your friends and invest in pastry bags or something." She carefully unpacked the objects remaining in the oversized bag, including several shoe boxes, opening one to display the four-inch crystal-encrusted heels inside.

"Oh, I'll fall right on my head," protested Anita. "Who wants a wobbly bride?"

"All right, you can save those ones for your wedding night," teased Catherine, as Anita blushed and made a swatting motion in her direction. She didn't think she'd ever feel comfortable mentioning certain things in Dakota's presence.

"I brought something special for you," continued Catherine. "More special than shoes." She held up a tiny jewelry box. Once white, the paper coating had faded; the edges of the box had split long ago and been shabbily repaired with masking tape that was also yellowing with age.

"Yes, this certainly looks like quality," said Dakota, applauding. "I'm not sure this is going to match those pricey shoes."

Anita held her tongue, waiting. Slowly and carefully, Catherine eased the lid off the box to reveal the jewel inside: a sterling-silver butterfly pin.

"That's it? All this fanfare?" asked Dakota.

"Well, it's newly polished. I thought Anita could put this pin on her handbag," said Catherine. "This butterfly is what I wore at the winter formal in 1981. Your mother ordered us matching pins from a mail-order catalog for sixty bucks. That was a lot of ice-cream cones to serve up at the Dairy Queen, I'll have you know."

"You couldn't borrow my grandmother's pearls or something?"

"That was just the point," squealed Catherine. "All the other girls wore white dresses and borrowed necklaces. Georgia wore a cobalt dress with spaghetti straps, and I wore a red halter dress."

"And silver butterfly pins," said Dakota. "Forgive me for stating the obvious, but the two of you sound like a pair of fashion don'ts."

Anita picked up the pin. "Oh, I don't know," she said. "It sounds like two good friends making a statement of their uniqueness. I bet if you dug around in your mother's costume jewelry you might find her pin."

"Costume was all my mother had," said Dakota. "I wear the few things that fit my style, but the rest just sits there."

Catherine ambled over to the sofa and sat down.

"Anita, let's get crazy," she said. "You try on your dress with the shoes, and you, Dakota, listen up to one of the few times I ever saw your mother in a gown."

"I'm sure it was the only time," said Dakota. "She mainly wore jeans, you know. And she liked it that way."

"Not always," said Catherine.

Georgia secretly liked the crinkling. The crunchy swish of her skirt as she walked down the hallway away from the school gym, the way the boys who never paid much attention before were looking her up and down. Even Simon Hall, whom she beat by one percentage point on the history final. Even him.

She turned around to watch Cathy behind her, rolling her eyes at the retro disco song being played, then pushed the swinging door with her butt as the two made their way into the girl's bathroom to update their makeup and talk, their dates standing around anx-

iously in the hallway, uncertain if it would seem okay to ask other girls to dance while they waited.

It was nice to feel pretty, Georgia thought.

To be fair, the entire scheme had been Cathy's idea, which meant it would automatically be expensive. No one in Harrisburg would be wearing dresses from New York to the winter formal.

"It'll be the biggest thing we've done," Cathy had insisted. No matter that they had to figure out how to get there and back, and not tell either of their parents.

"We're old enough to know what we want," she'd said.

Georgia agreed.

Bess and Tom Walker would not approve of the waste, and Georgia knew she'd have to lie and say she found the dress at the local shop, hoping her mother would be too busy or disinterested to question. But Cathy was adamant that no other girl have the same dress she was going to wear. The winter formal was the biggest night of the semester, she'd said, and she wanted to make sure everyone—especially the guys—noticed her.

Not that Georgia didn't want to be noticed herself. But she had other things on her mind: She had her life all planned out, and nothing—and she meant nothing—was ever going to make her deviate from her schedule. College, New York, career. Maybe marriage and kids, someday, a long way away. But for now her goal was to leave this town far behind her. Cathy, for all you could say about her, felt exactly the same way. She was going to be a writer.

Oh, Georgia dated, for sure, but mostly it was the boys from the school paper, where she was the editor, and they spent as much time kissing as they did arguing over whether there would ever be a woman anchoring the evening news on her own. But Cathy was different, always preferring to be somebody's girlfriend. Oh, she was smart, especially if you could get her away from boys long enough to actually get her to share the thoughts forming in her head. But mostly it was all about boys. She wasn't any better hanging out at Georgia's house, enjoying the puppy-dog way Georgia's brother Donny made up excuses to sit on the beanbag in the rec room and pretend to chat with them. He'd even made Cathy a mix tape, spending hours choosing from his collection of records and cassettes of The Police and AC/DC and—just so she wouldn't confuse his intentions—a ballad or two from Journey.

"You shouldn't encourage him," Georgia told her. "He's two years younger than us. That's gross."

"Not when he's twenty-eight and I'm thirty," Cathy replied. "Then he'll be sexy."

"Still gross," said Georgia. "You have nothing in common with Donny anyway. And it's just plain weird."

She didn't say that she sometimes hung out with her brother in his room, listening to that collection of music on his stereo, or that he sometimes did her chores for her so she could spend more hours putting together the school paper. Instead, she made fun of the way he planted his own patch of garden, experimenting with new seeds and farm-fresh fertilizer. Even though, secretly, she thought it was kind of cool.

"Well, I don't need to have anything in common with guys," Cathy replied, as Georgia rolled her eyes. "I let my pretty smile do the talking." She showed Georgia an article torn from the pages of a magazine that advised her to do just that.

Still, Cathy could write well, and she was fun. Plus, she really knew how to make a person look good, managing to find blue stockings and blue shoes and even blue mascara to match Georgia's dress.

She liked the way she seemed different tonight, her eyes outlined in thickly glamorous eyeliner and her bangs finally—for once— staying high and in place. Note to self, thought Georgia, she ought to buy Cathy's brand of hair spray.

The excitement of getting dressed up had seeped into her system, and she'd splurged on a set of brooches to share with Cathy. It was either butterflies or turtles; she leaned heavily in the direction of amphibians but figured that wouldn't quite work with Cathy's interpretation of elegance.

"What a great idea," Cathy had said when Georgia showed her the pin. "No one will have them."

Georgia liked that idea, of being separate and special.

"I heard once that if you look at something and think, I will always remember, then you will," said Cathy. "We're like princesses today."

"We'll always remember the fancy pins I bought out of a catalog?" Georgia looked doubtful. "And we're hardly royalty."

"Noooo," said Cathy. "We'll always remember the night we looked so beautiful and sophisticated. Your hair looks really awesome with all that crimping. And who knows where we'll be in twenty years, right?"

"You'll be living in the suburbs and driving a station wagon, and I'll be editing The New York Times," said Georgia. She suspected that most of their classmates were likely not moving too far from home, and sometimes she feared she would end up right back there. She loved Bess and Tom. But it was as though their values belonged to some other world. Georgia had places to go and choices to make, and she wasn't about to let sentimentality get in her way. She made a goofy face; tonight was not the time for seriousness. "We might not even know each other," she said, attempting a clumsy British accent. "We'll be too famous."

"Even then we'll never not know each other, Georgia," said Cathy, as she stood only inches from the bathroom mirror, reapplying shiny pearlized lip gloss. "It's just something I know."

"Well, I can tell you for a fact that I won't wear panty hose." She lifted her skirt high enough to show Cathy the run in her prized blue stockings.

"A cinch," said Cathy, snapping open her purse to locate a bottle of nail polish. "Just put this on and let it dry."

"Thanks," said Georgia. "I'm glad you know what you're doing."

"Don't I always?" Cathy said, tapping her head. "Stick with me, G. I know how it's going to all turn out."

chapter five

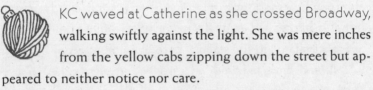 KC waved at Catherine as she crossed Broadway, walking swiftly against the light. She was mere inches from the yellow cabs zipping down the street but appeared to neither notice nor care.

"Hiya," she said, puffs of cloudy breath escaping from her mouth. The thermometer had taken a dip that morning, and snow was expected. Accordingly, KC had wrapped herself in an oversized puffy black coat and a pink-and-lime striped snow cap with the flaps pulled down over her ears and a pom-pom flailing around on top.

"You look ridiculous," said Catherine. "Did you make that hat?" Although KC had improved her knitting skills over the years, even making baby gifts for Darwin last year, she was hardly committed to the craft.

"You're just jealous," said KC.

"No, really," said Catherine. "You look like a ten-year-old stuck in a fifty-three-year-old's body. It's disturbing."

KC laughed. "I like it," she said. "But mainly it keeps my ears warm. Who cares? I'm not like you, sacrificing myself to frostbite just to show off my new hairdo."

Catherine instinctively put her hands to her head. "It's just a bit of color."

"Yes, you're going blonder for winter," said KC drily. "I can see that." She headed into the movie theater where the two had purchased tickets to a foreign-language film. Getting together for a weekend outing was something the two single women enjoyed, each finding in the other a welcome partner to check out a new exhibit at the museum or luxuriate at the spa. This afternoon, Catherine had made the movie selection, and the women rode an escalator to the screens in the basement level.

"I should have known." KC groaned as she looked at her ticket. "An Italian love story. What I could use is a good, bleak Swedish drama right about now."

"But KC, December is special," insisted Catherine, balancing her coat, gloves, and a small bag of popcorn without butter. "Now is when we feel love most of all."

"Not everyone, bucko," she said. "Did you read that in a greeting card?"

"Marco is coming in a few days earlier than planned," admitted Catherine, who'd made sure to get the goose-down pillows she knew he liked for her bedroom. Although he'd be staying at the hotel with the family, she wanted him to feel right at home whenever they found a chance to sneak off to her Hudson

Valley bungalow. She was eager to get physical, of course. But she was also as enthused to just be able to snuggle next to him, her feet in his lap, and have him listen to every thought she'd had—about the holidays, about her hair, about the state of the world's antiquities—since the last moment they'd spoken.

"That explains some of it," said KC, considering and then rejecting malted milk balls. "I wouldn't mind all this lovey-dovey agenda if it was Dakota: She's young. But the three of you are *Girls Gone Wild: Love-Sick Style.* Peri is moping around that her eggs are cracking or some ridiculousness, Anita's stuck on the wedding channel, and you keep mooning about like a puppy. And you want to know why?"

"I'm sure not," said Catherine, running through in her mind all the things she needed to do before tomorrow.

"It's the presents," said KC, plopping herself down in her seat without even unzipping her coat. "You've been seduced by consumerism."

"You're going to sweat to death with the heat on," observed Catherine. "There, that would be a different ending for you."

KC continued talking as if she hadn't heard a word.

"Everyone goes all shopping crazy in December, trying to find the just-right gifts for everyone, from people they like to people they work for to people they really, really hate. It's insane. It's shopping as punishment. Enforced, fakey frivolity."

Catherine continued to listen as she piled up coat, hat, gloves.

"But all this shopping has made *you* think about wedding gifts, and that's made you think about weddings. And there you go."

"Love as commercial enterprise?"

"Pretty much," announced KC, holding down Catherine's seat so she could settle in.

"I like the season," said Catherine. "That's all. No psychological analysis required."

What she liked, Catherine knew, was the possibility of reminding Marco just why he liked to be alone with her. Though she'd made certain when they talked last night to let him know she was all good with the status quo. No need for him to misunderstand her enthusiasm and think she wanted to take their commitment up a notch. He hadn't even asked her to marry him and she'd already said no multiple times. After all, communication was a good thing, she'd learned.

"You didn't used to like the season, Cat," KC pointed out in a low voice. "You used to be just as indifferent as I am."

"You call this indifferent? Whoa," said Catherine. "I have a feeling something else is afoot. Does our dear KC finally wish to settle down again?"

"No, absolutely not," she said, finally lifting off her earflaps and removing the hat to reveal her short, dyed red hair spiking up due to static cling. "All other months, I feel fine. I like my work, I like my apartment, I even like my friends. Present company excepted, of course."

"Naturally," said Catherine. "I *am* insufferable."

"But then whammo, the holiday season explodes and all around it's family this and family that," said KC. "No one celebrates the singleton holiday. No one writes a song about eating Chinese food and catching up on old magazines on Christmas."

"Uh, you're Jewish," pointed out Catherine, lifting a hand to smooth out KC's hair and then reconsidering.

"Precisely my point!" shouted KC, getting shushed by other moviegoers even though the previews hadn't even started. "Christmas isn't even my holiday. And it still overshadows everything. It's the soundtrack to the month of December, and sometimes, quite frankly, it can be a little much. Jingle schmingle."

Catherine sat quietly for a moment, glancing at KC, who sat with her arms folded. Not so long ago, she wouldn't have paid a great deal of attention to another person's distress. Now she tried to listen to what was *not* being said.

"Do you think something will change with the club once Anita gets married?"

"Anita? No," said KC. "She already has her rhythm with Marty, and it includes time for all of us. The rest of you? Well, you can see how hard it's been for Darwin over the last year."

"True," said Catherine. "She's hit-or-miss when we get together. Too much going on with the babies."

"And that's just the first wave. You're all in it, so you can't see," insisted KC. "Changes are coming for the group. They're already happening. I can feel it in my bones."

"So, you're psychic now? 'Cause, as you know, things have a way of being unpredictable."

"It doesn't take a crystal ball to see what's going on," said KC. "Already Lucie and Darwin live with their families out in the burbs. Peri is obsessed with that life, convinced it's going to answer some deep questions within her."

"Sometimes work doesn't fill every need," ventured Catherine, who figured KC would listen even less than Dakota on that subject.

"I'm not saying it has to," KC said with impatience. Some moments Catherine chose to ignore what she knew all too well, she thought. "But there's a lot of programming about what it means to be women, and not everyone is going to have *that* life. The absence of what you're taught to want can make it hard. Even when you're the one doing the choosing."

Catherine looked—really looked—at KC. Full on.

"Is it difficult for you?"

"I got over that business a long time ago," huffed KC. "I don't want to be responsible for anyone but myself. But it's as though we've been able to live in our own bubble, and now reality is closing in. Dakota is going to finish cooking school soon and get started on her knitting café. I'll be like the old sofa from the 1960s that your parents couldn't bear to throw away, the leftover furniture that doesn't fit the decor. The single friend among all the couples."

"Walker and Daughter isn't going anywhere," said Catherine. "And neither are any of us."

"You don't know what's coming," KC said as the lights went down, lowering her voice now. "Just when you think you do is when you'll be surprised. My fear now is that I'm going to lose all of my friends soon, as they desperately reinvent themselves as Stepford wives."

"No one other than Anita is getting married," reassured Catherine. "I don't even know if I'd want to get married again. Besides, I think the club can only handle one big event a year."

"Don't tell me you never fantasize about Marco and getting married and stomping on grapes together," insisted KC, crunching on a generous helping of popcorn. "You'd get two free kids thrown in the deal. With accents."

"Yeah, maybe, but I don't know," said Catherine, heat rushing to her face. Was she really so certain, she wondered? Because she had been dreaming about Marco often, and not just when she was sleeping. The point was that she thought about being with him, and almost as frequently she daydreamed about having tea parties with his daughter or playing video games with his son, Roberto. Even though she knew they were too old for that. She didn't just imagine romantic dinners but also boisterous family gatherings where all would sit around the table late into the night, telling stories and joking with one another, Allegra nodding off as the hours wore on. Content simply to be together.

Catherine had purchased all sorts of clothes and books for Allegra, wrapping them herself in shiny gold paper imprinted with red Santas and then tearing it all off and bringing down her gifts to the specialty paper shop to have them professionally wrapped and bowed. She purchased tickets to *The Nutcracker*, not sure if she should suggest an outing with only Allegra or with the entire family. In the end, she bought ten tickets. Just in case.

She'd set up a system with Marco recently, that he'd call her phone and let it ring once, and then they'd chat over the Internet, able to see each other. Some days—just a few—she didn't even touch up her makeup before switching on her computer to talk.

These were the things she liked about Marco: He liked to

watch her eat, lots and lots of food. He didn't think she was silly to pick up writing again after all this time, and then told her what he thought could be improved. (She'd been mad about that, at first.) He often told her she was beautiful and then would compliment her hands or her laugh. He once said he thought women looked better as they aged. He was smart. He talked about his first wife—Roberto and Allegra's mother, Cecilia—in a natural way, as though she was still part of the family, just in some different place. He didn't find it unusual that she did the same with Georgia.

"We shouldn't forget these parts of our lives," he often said. "We should celebrate our luck at having such wonderful people who have loved us."

Not to mention that he liked to kiss for hours.

Of course, Marco had flaws, possessing a bit of a temper and being sulky when things didn't go his way. But his moods passed quickly, and Catherine, he once pointed out, reacted in exactly the same way. They were simpatico, he said. And tremendously good-looking, he'd added with a wink.

But there were also the obvious problems, the main issue being that he lived with his family across the ocean in another country. And Catherine was finally comfortable with her independence; she had flirted with the idea of moving to Italy but held back, realizing she would once again be making sacrifices, would find herself on uneven footing.

"Oh," she said now to her friend, "I don't think it always works out quite so easily."

"No," agreed KC. "Real life never does." She leaned over.

"The holidays can make you feel left out. It's the dirty secret of December. I just don't want to be lost in the background, jumping up and down."

"Don't worry, KC, you're too loud to ignore," said Catherine, waving off the shushers behind her.

"Why do you think I make so much noise, then?" KC replied.

It was very possible, Darwin realized as she graded student essays while the kids napped, to have too much togetherness. Not with her husband, Dan—she felt she saw even less of him as they juggled their work lives to ensure that someone was always around to look after the twins. No, with her very best friend, Lucie, whom she adored. Problem was, she couldn't go a day, barely an hour, without running into her.

"Bye," she'd say as she pecked Dan on the cheek, before rendezvousing with Lucie on the porch of their duplex. "Morning, Ginger. Morning, Luce." The two women coordinated activities for the kids to minimize driving, and they even kept Rosie busy with just enough housework—folding laundry, emptying the dishwasher—that she felt she was contributing. They'd tried convincing her to relax after they'd initially moved in, but Rosie always tried to get up on stepladders and dust the tops of the cabinets when no one was looking. Now they'd convinced her that Darwin did the dusting (which she did not) and wrote out a lightly scheduled to-do list for Rosie. Keeping her occupied proved to be a safer option.

There were other quirks about their lifestyle as well. Rosie had become self-conscious about napping when Lucie was home, but for some reason, she felt perfectly fine about resting her eyes on Darwin's sofa. If it worked, it worked, and that's what mattered, Darwin always reminded Lucie. After all, hadn't that been the point when the two friends bought an attached house, with room for each family on either side of the joining wall? And Lucie was more than willing to take Cady and Stanton when Darwin wanted to work on a paper, or even to just let her get some sleep before a big presentation.

But they fed off each other's worst traits as well, with Lucie obsessing that each Sunday, each holiday, could be her mother Rosie's last. Even though her physical health was okay. And Darwin, even as she was exhausted, would chase Cady and Stanton around the house, recording and photographing every moment because she could barely remember one minute to the next. The sense of holding on tightly while it all rushed through their fingers loomed in their homes, and they rolled their eyes as much as Dan, overhearing them worry out an hour, shook his head and urged them just to enjoy life. It was difficult to relax when it was all going so fast. They could savor an experience only in the retelling.

Living so close, brainstorming together late into the night on plans for their TV channel Chicklet—in addition to their main jobs as professor and director—and trying to manage the needs of three kids and one forgetful senior was causing tensions to build. Each woman longed for a chance to be on her own. For at least fifteen uninterrupted minutes.

That very reason led Lucie to plan on attending Christmas at her brother's and Darwin to agree to pack up Cady and Stanton and fly with them solo to visit her parents in Seattle. Dan would arrive a few days later, on Christmas Eve, having little vacation time, since he was the junior doctor in the practice. For good measure—and to maximize time with her grandchildren—Betty Chiu took pains to invite Dan's mother, the formidable Mrs. Leung, for the holiday meal. Darwin's sister, Maya, would also be at the house, sleeping on the pull-out couch in the basement as Dan, Darwin, Cady, and Stanton stuffed themselves into the two single beds that filled what was once Darwin and Maya's shared childhood bedroom.

In spite of all of the inconvenience, Darwin looked forward to Christmas. She'd already begun packing, piling up diapers and plastic pants and toddler cardigans with matching hats made by Lucie, all stacked in neat, orderly piles on the sofa and the coffee table. She'd dragged down two huge suitcases, black and tattered, from the attic barely a day after Thanksgiving, placing them across the doorway to deny the twins entry into the space. Momentarily confused, the pair simply refocused their energies on pulling pots onto the kitchen floor. And Darwin simply pulled on a pair of noise-canceling headphones and continued what she was doing.

Thing was, she spent so much of her energy focusing on milestones that once she reached them, she simply looked past to what was coming next. She'd been that way when she struggled with infertility, desperate to share a baby with Dan, and then found herself horrified by the stress of new mommyhood.

In the same manner, Darwin had been convinced that sharing a home with Lucie would solve her concerns for child care. Which it did. What made it tricky was that it brought up a host of new challenges, including the fact that they all lived basically on top of one another.

If this, then that: an equation that had summed up Darwin's attitude many years ago. Now she knew there was no set way of parenting, of being married, of living a life. And for the first time since the kids were born, she wanted to slow down and really celebrate. Not just to tick off the twins' second Christmas as another line on her to-do list of life, but to step outside of her day-to-day to truly absorb the memory. To recognize that she would have this holiday only this one time, and as such, she ought to make it count.

chapter six

Last year she was different. Next year she would change again. There was no standing still, no letting things sink in. The girl she was, the woman she would be: Dakota felt as though being able to sort out her emotions would make her options clearer somehow. That understanding the past would help her rate the future. But all she experienced was confusion when she tried to think logically about what was the wisest course of action. She felt as though she'd been kicked in the stomach when Peri told her she'd been approached with an offer. Then she felt angry. Then panicked. How would it impact school? Dakota already worked as much as she could. What should she do about the shop? *If* Peri took the job. Which she might not, right?

The one fact she knew for certain was that she wanted to sort it out alone. Without running to her father, or to Anita, or to Catherine.

She'd texted, asked for the meeting. Peri suggested Grand
Central, making things convenient for Dakota—who was coming in on the Metro-North train from school in Hyde Park—
and avoiding the yarn shop altogether.

Dakota sat on the train, surrounded, as usual, by her pack-
mule accoutrement: a backpack of books, her purse and cell phone
tucked inside, the knitting bag stuffed with that damn unfinished camel-and-turquoise sweater, as patient now as it had always been. Waiting to be finished. She closed her eyes, almost
drifting to sleep with the rhythm of the train, and tried to sort
her thoughts.

It was troubling how at the beginning of last year she was
ready to walk away from the shop, and now she finally had come
to a concept—with the knitting café—that would allow her to
build on her mother's legacy and fulfill her own goals as well.
How finally everything was fitting. All that was required was
Peri's part-ownership and participation to keep things running
as Dakota completed her studies and James found a way to redesign the building in between trying to keep his business
afloat; the Walker and Daughter redesign was hardly his most
lucrative venture.

She'd thought of the obvious solutions of finding new people. But it wasn't as simple as replacing Peri with someone else.
Walker and Daughter wasn't just a store; it was a family. It felt
as though Peri was abandoning the whole enterprise. The whole
group! Just wait until they all found out; she could already imagine the outcry.

All this Dakota believed, and yet she wished the status quo could remain. Just a smidge longer. Just until she was ready.

But then, that had been the problem with the club's plan all along. It had all been about Dakota.

Dakota marched up the stairs to the restaurant overlooking the lobby of Grand Central Terminal, surveying the painted stars overhead, the gleaming gold chandeliers, the hordes of shoppers and commuters scurrying across the grand hall as they arrived and departed.

"Hey, lady," said Peri, waiting in a booth with a cup of tea. "Nice to see you outside of the store. When was the last time that happened?"

"Yeah," said Dakota. "Too long."

When Peri was twenty-four, she recalled, she'd disappointed her family by avoiding law school. Her plan had been to break into the designer-handbag industry, but instead she spent seven years of her life running a business that, although partially hers technically, was not exactly hers emotionally. Everyone thought of the shop as Georgia's and Dakota as her chosen successor. What a terrible role for Peri, Dakota realized, looking at the slim, serene black woman she'd admired as a young girl (and could now call a friend as well as a colleague), to be expected to always be the regent, never the monarch. To always be in the wings. Even the handbag business, which initially benefited from the exposure in the shop, was now growing more slowly than it might be because of Peri's commitment to Walker and Daughter.

The balance was shifting.

"We're hurting you," Dakota said quietly. "Managing the store is holding you back." Even as she said so, her stomach tied itself into knots, knowing that drastic changes would occur if Peri wasn't there. What if they couldn't find the right manager? What if business continued to slow down? What if she needed to literally buy Peri out with cash? What then? It didn't seem right to expect other people—such as Anita, such as her father, such as Marty—to continually make Walker and Daughter their pet project financially. But after two redesigns in as many years, the shop was running with a tight cash flow.

"No, I'm doing fine," said Peri. "So many designers don't get the chances I've had. The shop means so much to me. And this was such a crazy idea."

"Working with Lydia Jackson in Paris? You couldn't get better exposure if you got your bags on *Project Runway*," said Dakota, ordering a tuna burger and sweet-potato fries.

"But there is so much unknown," said Peri, sipping from a cup of tea. "I've worked in a knit shop for almost a decade, and suddenly I'd be whisked away to Paris. What if it didn't pan out? What about Roger? And what about you?"

Dakota knew that when Georgia Walker was twenty-four, she was pregnant and frightened, having abandoned a potential career in publishing to flee back to her parents. Her chance meeting with Anita resulted in an unexpected life as a knitting entrepreneur. And that's all it was: an opportunity to which she said yes, even as it scared her. This was her mother's great legacy, Dakota knew, more than the physical existence of the shop. Her great gift to her daughter. The ability to dare.

"You have to decide what's best for you," she said now. "Not me. Not the shop. Just Peri."

"But I don't know," admitted Peri, her lips trembling just slightly. Like all the members of the club, she had spent many years trying to soothe Dakota's loss of the only parent she'd known for much of her life. The result being that most business decisions were made based on what was in Dakota's best interest. Not Peri's. It was an unspoken requirement of all of the women, and an expectation that had made Peri feel resentful and generous by turns. And yet, in the instant she was offered the chance of a lifetime, the chance to walk away, she hesitated. Freshly aware that her connection to the shop—and to Dakota—was about much more than business. Something she'd forgotten too often.

"I was so mad at you," said Dakota, laughing as she sampled her dinner.

"When I told you last week about the job offer?" Peri looked startled.

"I was referring to when you redesigned the shop," said Dakota. "Didn't want anything to be changed."

"Oh, well, you were difficult," agreed Peri. That redesign had been the result of an ultimatum.

"Yes," said Dakota. "Peri, I was riding the train here, half thinking about a dough that wasn't rising properly, and I just knew: This whole situation hasn't been fair to you. It *has* to change."

"I'm no victim." Peri stood up straighter in her chair. "I have always had a choice in my life, whether I believed it or not. And I've made quite a success for myself."

Dakota nodded.

"With help from friends, I know," said Peri. "In that respect, we're even."

"No," said Dakota firmly. "We're not. You've thrown your soul into your career and made sacrifices to honor promises from long ago. How could you know what chances were coming? I've been given a huge gift: love and support and the space to grow up on my own terms. I've suffered, I've lost my mother, but I've never made sacrifices for anyone. I receive, but I rarely give."

Peri frowned, troubled. Dakota had had many personalities as a teen—mainly petulant—but recently she'd become quieter and more focused than ever before. More, Peri had observed on more than one occasion, like her mother.

"Dakota, don't you understand that I've decided?" said Peri. "It's too much, weird timing, cold feet. I'm going to turn the job down. Nothing is going to change at Walker and Daughter."

"Please don't," said Dakota. "Just think about it. Wait until the New Year. Then decide."

"And what are you going to do with the shop if I'm not around?"

"I haven't figured out that part yet," Dakota acknowledged. "But I'm working on it."

⊂━━━━━⊃

The weathercasters were calling for a blizzard, but the snow was just drifting down lightly as Dakota trudged from Grand Central to her father's apartment. One down, one to go. She'd avoided her father lately, not wanting to tell him about her internship, not ready to let him know she was not going to go to Scotland. After speaking with Peri, she felt more certain than ever that work had to take priority. Maybe later she'd have a moment to slow down and take a trip. But here, in December, she had to be like her mother. She had to look after business. She had to develop her skills in order to reach her potential.

Dakota said all that and more to James, who sat impassively listening to her reasoning, the only clue to his feelings revealed in the manner in which he clenched his jaw tightly.

"I know it seems selfish, Dad," she finished. "But it's what I need to do for my future. This internship is beyond huge. Sometimes we have to make sacrifices."

"Having an inch of self-awareness doesn't make your decision any less selfish," spat out James. "You are taking something away from me here. From your grandparents, your uncle, your great-grandmother. You talk about sacrifices, Dakota, about finally—what was your phrase?—'understanding the power of decisions,' and yet the main person you're thinking about here is you. Only you."

Dakota paced the living room of the apartment, weaving around the furniture that had been put away on Thanksgiving. "Sometimes you have to choose work over fun," she said.

"I agree," said James, his voice controlled. "But what a mistake you make when you choose work over family."

Dakota looked up sharply, the smart retort on her tongue, before James interrupted her.

"It's what I did, Dakota," he said softly. "We all lived with the consequences. And it's a regret that never goes away. There will be other internships, other restaurants, other opportunities. But there will only be this one Christmas, this one December, this one moment to enjoy these holidays with your family." He'd half convinced himself that accepting that Dakota was now an adult would make his life easier, but all at once he understood that his powerlessness would frustrate him always. If only she would believe he'd learned a thing or two!

"I can make my own decisions, Dad," Dakota said, as calmly and quietly as her father. The two faced each other, both tense and uncertain.

"I know," said James, leaning back in his chair and bringing his hand to his forehead. "But that doesn't make them smart decisions. Or the right ones."

chapter seven

The plane was delayed by weather. Catherine didn't know what to do as the arrival time moved farther and farther away. At this rate, it would be tomorrow before they finally got here. Should she stay and wait for the Toscanos and for Sarah? Go home for a few hours? Throw out the box of bagels she'd brought with her as a welcome-to-New-York gift?

She was certain airport security was about to arrest her any minute for acting suspiciously, as she would make up her mind to leave and march to the automatic doors, wait for them to open, and stand there. Then she'd circle back to stare at the arrivals board, hoping to see something different. Sometimes she did: The flight was coming in even later than first suspected.

There was only one bar left on her phone's battery indicator, too, having been depleted as she spent the better part of two hours calling everyone. The plane is late, she told Anita. And Dakota. And KC. And James. She called him, trying to soothe herself with some last-minute tips.

"Of course you're on the phone with me," boomed James into his cell. "I'm known the world over for my successful romances. You know, how I walked out on the love of my life for over a decade. That's my first tip: Don't do that."

"James, quit being an idiot," hissed Catherine. "Marco and his kids are going to be here any hour now, and I'm a bit jumpy."

"Just be yourself," said James. "Isn't that what they say?"

"No," said Catherine. "The point is that I want to be better than myself. I want the children to fall in love with me."

"You can't replace their mother," said James.

"I'm not trying to," said Catherine. "But you said so yourself, you just waltzed back in and Dakota loved you anyway."

"Pure luck," said James, chuckling. "And okay, I bribed her. That's no secret."

"I told Marco only about half of what I'd bought for Allegra and Roberto, and he said I should return most of it," said Catherine, her voice rising. "He said it would be too much."

"Well, maybe you should listen," said James. "I did annoy Georgia a lot by spoiling Dakota. Made her look chintzy in comparison."

"So, what you're telling me is . . . not really anything I can use?"

"Essentially, yes," said James, his deep voice breaking into a laugh. "It's all good, Catherine. If it wasn't, you wouldn't care so much."

"Speaking of caring, Dakota told me about her intention to skip Christmas," said Catherine.

"Oh, yeah, that," said James. "It's awkward all around. I promised Georgia's Gran that I'd bring her family to her, and she's counting on it."

"You're not really going to go on your own, are you?"

"Have you met Georgia's Gran?"

"I have, actually," mused Catherine. "So I hear what you're saying. As for Dakota . . ."

"We're agreeing to disagree," said James. "She seems to believe becoming an adult means always choosing work."

"I've never quite had that mind-set," admitted Catherine. "But Georgia did."

"And so did I," said James, the frustration evident in his voice. "But sometimes you have to realize there are more important things, dammit." He was frustrated.

"Dakota thinks you have a girlfriend," Catherine blurted, trying to change the topic. "A serious one. But I told her I didn't think so."

"Umm, she does?" asked James. "Did she say anything else?"

"*Do* you have someone serious, James? Are you in love or something? Why haven't you said anything? I tell you about Marco."

"And where that's concerned, Catherine, you'll be fabulous," said James, talking quickly. "Take a deep breath and don't give Marco a sloppy, wet kiss in front of his kids and you'll be fine. Talk to you soon. Bye."

Catherine let her hand that was holding the phone drop to

her side. Apparently, Dakota was correct in her assumption about her father. It felt final even to consider the idea that he might fall in love—real love—with someone other than Georgia. Would he marry her? What would Dakota call her? What would Georgia think?

If this is how I feel about James finding a girlfriend, she thought, *I can only imagine how strange this holiday will be for Marco's children.* Hanging out with her when they'd rather be with their mother, if only she were still alive. Maybe this had all been a bad idea?

"I'm the girlfriend," she said aloud. "The girlfriend," she repeated to a stranger walking in the corridor. *I'm the person standing where their mother ought to be*, she realized. Catherine put on her coat, firm in her decision to go home and wait for Marco to let her know when he'd arrived. If he wanted to. If she wanted him to.

Unexpectedly, a person stood up and left a seat empty in the waiting area.

"That's mine!" shouted Catherine, practically hopping over the legs of random people to snag the available chair, sighing with relief at the sheer joy of resting her sore feet. *These boots are made for taking taxicabs*, she reflected, looking at her five-inch heels. She'd stood for hours, and now she squirmed as her feet tingled, the blood rushing back to her toes.

Never is when Catherine had waited to pick up someone from the airport. It hadn't struck her as something necessary. Her cheating ex-husband made it home on his terms, and she learned to accept that sometimes he took trips without her. Oh, she'd seethed, but she survived.

Now she wished she'd brought flowers. Catherine could

barely sit still. She wanted to see Marco the minute he walked off that plane. But thanks to the rules and regs of the new world, she had to content herself with toughing it out with the rest of the waiting hordes in baggage claim.

The arrivals board updated again; another forty-five minutes were tacked on.

"Hello," said Catherine, raising a hand above her head but careful not to stand lest someone dive for her seat. "Anyone here want a bagel? Seems like we could be here all night . . ."

Catherine had barely slept since the Toscano family arrived in New York, showing off her beloved city. Sarah's husband, Enzo, had been grateful to settle into a bed and recover from the stress of travel. The rest of the crew took on Manhattan, seventy-something Sarah included. An entire day at Central Park, beginning with carriage rides, skating at Wollman Rink, and finally warming up over dinner at Tavern on the Green, the restaurant decked out in garlands and Christmas trees, as they watched through the wall of windows the snow dusting the treetops. That was followed up with stops at the ballet, the theater, the museums, shopping, The Rockettes.

"Catherine, Catherine," said Marco, pulling her aside after a long day of sightseeing. "The schedule is very active. But didn't you plan any time for us to be alone?"

"No," she admitted. "I didn't want to take you away from your family . . ." She didn't want to tell him she was nervous, worried about how the children would feel to spend a holiday in New York. And that she was nervous, certain he was going to want to make things official, and that she was equally certain she wasn't ready for such a move. "I thought it would be better this way," she continued.

"It's good, yes," he said, bringing his lips close to her ear. "But Roberto is a young man now, with not so much interest in tagging along with his papa. And Allegra just needs a good night's sleep. She could go spend an evening with her nona Sarah and her aunt Anita while Marty and Enzo keep each other company. Then you and I could be together. Wouldn't that be nice?"

"Yes," agreed Catherine, feeling torn. "But then Allegra would miss the lunch I planned at the Russian Tea Room. Doesn't she want to have tea?"

"Oh, *bella*," said Marco. "You have all of tomorrow to plan another perfect day. Let's turn the children over to Sarah and take a walk, just the two of us." She agreed.

Hand in hand, they strolled down Central Park South, not even speaking for several minutes as they savored each other's company. Catherine didn't know what she wanted more: to take Marco aside and kiss him deeply or to pepper him with questions. But he seemed to be in no rush, content simply to be together on a crisp winter night.

Eventually they ducked into a hotel, stepping out of coats and scarves to enjoy a couple of dry martinis at the bar.

Marco looked over the wine list. "I wish they had Cara Mia," he noted.

"I know a great little shop upstate that carries it," Catherine purred. Marco smiled; Catherine's interest in his wine is what had initially brought them together.

"This issue has been on my mind often," he said. Catherine held her breath, certain what was coming next. She'd have to turn him down, of course, but that didn't mean the romance was over. Not in any way. She loved him. She hoped he knew that. She paused.

Marco cleared his throat.

"It's time to invest, you know," he began. "In something new."

Catherine nodded vigorously, taking a large gulp from her glass. Oh, this might be difficult. He looked so eager.

"So, I've made a decision, and I hope you agree," said Marco, stretching forward and placing his fingers lightly on her knee. "I hope you're as thrilled as I am."

"Oh, Marco, I know . . ." Her voice trailed off as Marco stared intently at her, politely waiting. He *was* such a gentleman. She did love him. Maybe she'd been too hasty after all, to dismiss outright the idea of marrying again. Yes, she could do it. She could be ready. No, she *was* ready. She was definitely going to say yes. Catherine swallowed. *C'mon, Anderson*, she thought. *Admit it. You've wanted this all along—the man, the kids, the marriage.* They'd sort out the details later. Oh, she hoped they had a very extravagant bottle of bubbly at this bar.

"Catherine, did you want to tell me something?" asked Marco. "You look like the cat that ate the canary bird."

"No!" Catherine practically shouted. "You first. Go on. Go!"

Marco's eyes widened with excitement. "Okay," he said, as loud as she was. "I am going to buy a vineyard in America."

"You're what?" Catherine began coughing, having swallowed her drink the wrong way. She began flailing her arms a bit as Marco patted her enthusiastically on her back.

"I know, I know," he said. "It's scary. But it means I can rationalize more trips here—and, above all, break into the American market in a big way."

"Anything else?" Her voice was still froggy from coughing. But she had to know.

"Yes," boomed Marco, as Catherine held her breath expectantly. "I'm going to try a new grape."

She managed a tiny smile. "I think it's a great idea. Just stupendous," she muttered, peeking into her glass in case there were any diamonds floating on the bottom. Perhaps she just missed the big moment? All she could see were two overstuffed green olives bobbing in gin, and neither of those would look very good on her finger.

Sometimes a walk is just a walk, Catherine, she reminded herself. *Sometimes a drink is just to discuss an exciting new business development.* She felt embarrassed and foolish.

"What?" Marco brought his face closer to hers. "I thought you'd be so happy. Enough with this going slow business! I did it your way for over a year, and now we do it my way."

"What does that mean, exactly?"

"We spend lots of time together. We take picnics. We have big, roaring fights, and we don't worry that it will be a big deal because we won't see each other for months," he said. "We get to love each other."

"But you'll still have Cara Mia in Italy?" said Catherine. Besides, she thought they loved each other already.

"Of course," said Marco. "Though I have another reason to want to be here as well. Roberto has been accepted at a school in Florida. He's going to get a degree in flying. He tried the wine business, and now he wants to do his own passion. He honored his end of our bargain, now I honor his. Don't let on that I said anything. He wants to tell Dakota first of all."

"Okay," said Catherine, though she suspected Dakota had moved on. "And what does your daughter think of your world-domination plan?"

"Allegra has gone to boarding school for so long that she looks at it as a second home," said Marco. "I'm always a jet away, no matter where I am."

"Sounds like you have it all figured out," said Catherine. "You know, maybe we should call it an early night. I think I'm as tired as your kids." She'd been referring to Roberto and Allegra as "the" kids for days now, but it didn't seem as though Marco noticed the difference.

"I'd like to go to bed also," said Marco, caressing her cheek. His touch felt very, very good, and as much as Catherine wanted to nurse her crushed hopes, she wanted to enjoy some private time with Marco much more.

"Okay," said Catherine, leaning her head to the right, an invitation for him to caress her neck.

"Bartender!" he said, gesturing animatedly. "Bring the check, and pronto!"

"Isn't it wonderful, Marty?" Anita beamed at her gray-haired fiancé, standing several steps back to take in the view.

She loved it when her living room was full of family, when the cushions were thrown off her neatly arranged cream sofa and piled on the floor so the kids could lean forward on their elbows and chat. It reminded her of when her boys were young, when she was young.

Anita smiled as Allegra yawned widely, her hand covering her mouth. Even though she'd visited with Sarah and her grandchildren in Italy over the past year, it was clear—from the long pauses in conversations and the formal way the children spoke to her—that they were still figuring out their way around one another. What was particularly special about tonight, however, was that there was no occasion, no party. The fact that Sarah called and asked if they could come by that very evening demonstrated to Anita how far they'd advanced. They were acting like what they were: a real family. And it was amazing.

Two days from now would be the last night of Hanukkah, and she had organized a catered buffet and a selection of wines from Marco's Cara Mia vineyard for that event. But this evening was a different type of celebration, a chance to light candles with Sarah as they had once done in their youth. Certainly, she knew that Sarah's life had diverged from how they were raised, but a family-only ritual was something she very much wanted to share with Allegra and Roberto. To show them their heritage and teach them to be as proud of their Jewishness as their identification as Italian.

Roberto and his younger sister listened politely to the prayers and watched with interest as Anita used the center candle to light six more flames on the menorah. But they smiled most broadly when Anita invited them into the kitchen to watch her fry homemade latkes.

As the night grew late, Allegra snoozed in the guest bedroom while Roberto sat at the dining table and texted his friends. Marty turned in early, with the intention of giving Anita and her sister the opportunity to talk. They sat, silver heads close together, murmuring in the living room.

"The children are happy to be in New York," said Sarah. "It seems so glamorous to them."

"Aren't you enjoying the trip?" asked Anita.

Sarah shrugged. "It's difficult to be back, in some ways," she explained. "A lot of what-ifs are still floating about in the air."

Anita placed her hand over her sister's and held on tightly. Sarah patted her lightly.

"We're long over feeling bad, Anita," she said. "But it's peculiar how a scent—the nuts roasting on the streets, for example—takes me back to another time. Remember how I used to watch Nathan all the time? I can't wait to see him at the wedding. He was such a special boy."

"Well, he's developed into quite a difficult man, I can assure you," said Anita.

Sarah listened as Anita ran through a litany of complaints about her eldest.

"Do you ever wonder," she asked Anita, "why it's so easy to see how someone else makes mistakes and so hard to see our own?"

"If you think I'm doing something wrong, then just tell me," she insisted.

"Who am I to say?" said Sarah. "But I do know how difficult it is to see another person where someone you love ought to be."

Anita felt a twist in her heart. How painful it must be for Sarah to see her son-in-law, Marco, courting Catherine. How difficult to be gracious while suffering inwardly because the new romance was a constant reminder that your own daughter had died, leaving her family behind. Reflexively, Anita thought of Georgia and Dakota and James.

"The holidays can make those things more difficult," she said.

Sarah shook her head. "It's not just Hanukkah or Christmas or New Year's," she said. "It's the birthday parties, the anniversaries, the Tuesdays you often got together for a glass of wine. It's all the small minutes you shared, the inconsequential stuff, that makes its absence felt most powerfully."

"Catherine is a good person," said Anita. "She's not without flaws, I'd be the first to say so, but she is very caring. She loves your grandchildren."

"This I know," said Sarah. "Otherwise, I would have chased her away a long time ago. But it doesn't change my loss. That's a constant."

"I understand," said Anita, wanting to share a story about an afternoon she and Georgia mislabeled all the skeins of yarn and stayed up half the night to get things in order for the grand opening of Walker and Daughter. But she held back, knowing that tonight was for Sarah and her memories.

"What will you do if things get serious with Catherine and Marco?" she inquired.

"Well, I'll do what any good grandmother would do," said Sarah. "I'll teach her how to cook properly. And who knows? Maybe I'll even find a way to love her like you do."

chapter eight

 There was a sari shop on the corner, its windows filled with mannequins enrobed in fuchsias and golds, in place of what had once been a butcher shop. More than forty years ago.

"It's so much to take in," said Sarah, a hand on Anita's arm. The two sisters had often talked about taking a trip to see the old neighborhood during their previous visits in the past year but one way or another had managed to fill up their days looking at old photographs, knitting on Anita's wedding coat, or simply swapping stories of all the events they'd missed in their decades of separation. "Next time we'll see the old home," they would say, "next time." And now it was next time. Anita had arranged for a car service to drive them around the area in Queens where their parents had lived and where they had grown up, weaving in and out of the streets where they played as little girls and were walked home on dates as young women. They rode in the backseat of the car for half an hour before Sarah was ready to dry her eyes, button up her coat, and stroll around.

"I can see it all in my mind as it was," continued Sarah. "And it's just . . . disappeared. Of course it has, why wouldn't it? That would have happened whether I was in New York or in Rome. And yet I rather expected to see what I left behind."

"You just held on to it as it used to be," whispered Anita, as she led her sister down the street. "I avoided this area all through the seventies and eighties, because every time a store-front would change I'd know that meant somebody died or moved away."

"I wanted to show my husband," said Sarah. "But there's nothing here to show. The homes have other families. The syna-gogue is a community center. The only thing left is the old public high school. But I doubt the girls are in bobby socks and circle skirts."

"I'm sorry," said Anita. "My actions . . . I . . . That's what took it away. Your home. Your birthright."

Sarah leaned in close to her older sister; two silver-haired beauties huddled against the chill of old pains.

"There's no use to come of that," she said finally. "So, I was away. And now I'm back. This is our strange journey together. But even if our neighborhood is now for another generation, at least we are together."

"Do you believe Mother and Father know?" asked Anita.

"I don't see why not," said Sarah. "And I don't think they'd think much of the sari shop."

She squeezed Anita's hand as they ambled past street vendors selling books on tables or putting together food from carts, and a guitarist playing classic rock songs in front of an open guitar case. Sarah threw in five dollars, then five more.

"Who knows?" she said. "Maybe he's just raising money to get home for the holidays."

———

Ginger was intrigued, Anita could tell, by the display of dreidels on the coffee table. She reached out to touch them, was reprimanded by her mother, and then tried to spin again when Lucie wasn't looking. Darwin was having a similar issue with the twins, who were more interested in tasting the colorful spinning tops than playing with them.

"It's nontoxic paint, right?" Darwin kept asking. "Or did you have these when your boys were small? Because there might be lead. Have these been tested?"

"All new for tonight," reassured Marty, still limber enough to get down on the floor with the kids. "Here, let me show you." He sent a wooden top whirring right off the edge of the table, to enthusiastic applause from Ginger and her glamorous new hero, twelve-year-old Allegra.

"Looks like you've been replaced," said KC, poking Dakota with her elbow. "That's a sure sign of adulthood. When kids no longer find you as interesting."

"Uh, thanks," said Dakota. "I think."

"Is that a wrinkle I see?" teased Catherine, peering close to Dakota's face. "Methinks you look almost twenty-one."

Anita had invited all the members of the club, as well as James, Sarah and Enzo, the Toscanos, and several friends and neighbors, to her Hanukkah party. It seemed the perfect way to visit with everyone before the various families went their separate ways, dashing off for Christmas celebrations and trips to Scotland and eating Chinese food by themselves (à la KC), before reuniting for what Marty had taken to calling "the wedding of the year." Yes, Anita worried that something else might go wrong, that Nathan might have more shenanigans up his sleeve, but she had a trick for making it from here to there: She was going to turn off all of her phones and stitch together a pair of light, lacy wraps in a silvery thread for her two attendants, Catherine and Dakota, to coordinate with their strapless dresses.

Anita looked up to see the two having an intense chat in the corner.

"Mingle, ladies, mingle," she advised, coming over to join them. "Looking for Roberto?"

"Kinda." Dakota hesitated. "It's been a while, you know. We're in different places in our lives."

"My goodness, you sound like you're getting a divorce," said Anita. "I think just saying hello might be the simpler approach. He's going to be here with his father any minute. Allegra came early with Sarah."

"It's uncomfortable," said Dakota. "It might be hard for you to understand."

"Of course, dear," said Anita, turning to Catherine. "And what about you?"

"Where did you say Sarah was?" asked Catherine, craning her neck to look around the apartment.

"She's on the phone in the guest bedroom, talking to someone in Italy," said Anita. "Why don't you go in and check on her? Here, take her this glass of wine." She handed Catherine a glass of white and a napkin.

"Oh, I don't know," said Catherine. "I wouldn't want to interrupt."

"Just see how she is," advised Anita. "Have a conversation about something other than Allegra."

*

"Hi," said Dakota, her gut tied up in knots. She put a hand on the back of her neck and rubbed.

"Are you sore?" asked Roberto, who had been ushered over by Anita the moment he stepped into the party.

"No," said Dakota quickly, blushing. "I mean yes. All the kitchen work can tire my muscles." Seeing Roberto was too weird, almost as though he was crashing her real life. Not the fun summer in Italy—he fit right into that scenario—but here, back in New York, where she had real work to do, he was out of place. It was fun to text or whatever, but she was quite sure she didn't want him around. She wanted to put him in a corner of her past and keep him there.

"So," said Roberto, his hands in his pockets, bobbing up and down on his heels. "This is quite the big party. I've never been to Hanukkah before this trip."

"It's cool," said Dakota, who'd spent many years celebrating Anita's holidays with her.

"You look pretty," said Roberto, changing the subject.

"You, too," said Dakota, her face feeling hot. "This sucks," she blurted.

Roberto laughed nervously. Then he leaned in, like a conspirator, and whispered. "It's strange seeing you here," he said. "I used to show you all around in Rome, and now I'm the lost boy in your city."

Dakota decided to take a page from her mother's book and get straight to the point. "Do you have a girlfriend now?" she asked.

"No, well, sometimes, but not now," said Roberto. "I'm moving to Florida for school."

"Florida?"

"I'm going to become a pilot. Finally." His face erupted into a dazzling smile, and Dakota could finally see the confident guy she'd fallen for in Rome. He hadn't changed that much. He was still very cute.

"Good for you, Roberto," she shouted. Dakota was delighted. She continued to be confused by what she felt for Roberto—it had been a hell of a long time since Rome, she decided, and there was another fellow at school who'd caught her eye—but no doubt Roberto was still a good guy.

"It's not so bad having you here," she admitted finally.

"I think maybe so, too," said Roberto, raising his glass in salute.

The doorbell rang as more guests arrived, and Anita bustled over to let them in, a tray of her latkes in hand.

"This party is simply fabulous," she cried out to no one in particular as she made her way to the door. "I haven't thought about my wedding more than once an hour all day." Then she dropped her delicious potato pancakes all over the floor.

"Greetings, Mother," said Nathan Lowenstein, standing on the other side of the threshold and helping his wife off with her coat. "Happy Hanukkah."

He stepped inside and glanced to his right and then, just as quickly, to his left. Always important to know who he was dealing with.

As Nathan's mother had neither invited nor uninvited him to the Hanukkah party, he decided it was appropriate to take matters into his own hands, and made arrangements to travel to New York anyway. Naturally, he brought his wife, Rhea, and his children, who always loved to see their grandmother.

He did, briefly, consider the high probability of encountering his mother's promiscuous acquaintance, Catherine, but remained committed to his plan. He was going to appeal directly to his mother's conscience by enlisting the help of his aunt,

Sarah, to talk his mother out of her doomed marriage. She'd thank him later. Of that fact he was certain.

Anita's face went white. "It's Nathan," she called out to Marty, though he could plainly see that fact for himself. She fluttered about as KC and Darwin brought paper towels to help scoop up the smashed potato pancakes, making faces at each other over the shared loss of such deliciousness.

"Welcome," said Marty, his broad smile never wavering as he strode briskly to the door. "What riches of family we have to-night." He hugged Rhea and the children in turn, then shook hands with Nathan.

"Marty," said Nathan crisply.

"Nathan, hello," said Marty. "My darling Anita's unpredict-able son. Why don't you help me with the drinks?"

"Where's Sarah?" Nathan said curtly, nodding vaguely at the pretty young girl waving at him.

"Remember your young cousin Allegra? You met her at our spring wedding, I believe?" asked Marty. "Well, she's never been to a Hanukkah party before. I do hope tonight will be pleasant for all." Not for a millisecond did the smile leave his face.

"Oh, dear," breathed Anita, jumping as the doorbell rang again. "Who could that be now?"

But it was only Peri, bringing along her boyfriend, Roger, ready to join the festivities.

"Just have to calm down," said Anita, kissing Peri. "I've had more than enough surprises in my lifetime."

Quietly the door to the guest bedroom opened, and Sarah

glided into the party, her eyes crinkling with delight when she recognized the face of her favorite nephew from long ago.

"Anita didn't tell me," she said to Nathan. "Your arrival must be a surprise for me. I love seeing you so."

Nathan thought of telling her he hadn't been invited, but he didn't want to upset Sarah. He didn't, actually, want to upset his mother. All he had to do was get things back to how they were supposed to be and all would be well.

"I have to talk to you," he whispered now. "It's important."

"In a minute, darling," assured Sarah, pinching his cheek as though he were still a little boy. "I must find Marco." She stepped over to whisper in her former son-in-law's ear and watched him as he made his way to the guest room, then returned to Nathan's side.

"Catherine has something to ask him," announced Sarah. "And I have given my blessing."

"She's a slut," hissed Nathan, though only his aunt could hear.

Sarah angled her body to appraise Nathan fully. "How would you know?" she asked, her eyebrows arched. Although it had been ages since she'd reprimanded him for some ridiculous infraction against his younger brothers, he suddenly felt defensive and outwitted. Like a small boy. Sarah had always been devoted to him, but she had never fallen for the tricks he pulled on his mother. She was never intimidated by him. "I know," she used to murmur as she tucked him in at night more than forty years ago, "that you are scared sometimes. And I will protect you."

"Your mother will always love you, Nathan," she said now.

Firmly. "But I don't think your wife would understand you speaking of Catherine on such familiar terms. And so we'll let that all be, won't we?"

"Sarah!" Nathan was shocked but wary. "I thought you would help me. You, of all people, should understand."

"All too well. Nothing can be guaranteed more than history repeating itself," said Sarah, her gaze firm. She didn't seem so sweet right now. "Your mother can't see that you are just like she was when she threw me out. Self-righteous and silly. But I loved her anyway. I never stopped wanting my big sister. And your mother adores you. Even when you . . . make a fuss. When no fuss is needed."

"Why not?" spat out Nathan.

"Because it makes them happy. Anita, Marty, Catherine, Marco," explained Sarah. "All the other issues are of no consequence. And something you should think more deeply about: The only worthy goal is love."

———————

Catherine suddenly felt shy when Marco entered the room. She'd sat on the bed, waiting, then stood to straighten her violet cocktail dress, then checked her teeth for lipstick stains in Sarah's mirror, then sat again. Then stood. Then pretended to watch idly out the window at the cabs navigating through the piles of snow. She would turn around slowly, casually, when Marco was there, she'd decided. As though she hadn't been watching the red minutes tick away on Sarah's clock radio.

"Catherine?"

"Oh, Marco," she said, dashing across the room at lightning speed and wrapping her arms tightly around him. "I had a big talk with Sarah, and she's so lovely." Catherine began to cry. She made a feeble attempt to speak but only cried harder into Marco's shoulder. His burgundy silk shirt was covered in tears, a big splotch on the right side.

"*Bella*, what is it?" Marco, genuinely confused, reached out to lift her chin. "You are very American. You talk, talk, talk all the time about how you feel. 'I'm the independent woman.' No shutting up. And then when something is clearly upsetting, you keep your mouth shut and all you do is the tears. Help me."

She needed to take a risk. That's what Catherine had decided over the past few days. What was she waiting for anyway? Why was it up to him? If all of her energy getting to know herself, understanding what she truly wanted out of her life, was to mean anything, then she had to get over some old-fashioned notion of a man getting down on one knee. She didn't need a gallant knight. She didn't need rescuing. What she needed was a family. And she'd found one. With a man and children she loved.

"If your daughter was still alive it wouldn't be like this," she'd said to Sarah just moments earlier. Catherine hadn't done her usual approach and polled Anita and the club about her decision. She simply waited until she could speak to Sarah alone. "I feel as though your loss, their loss, made the room for me to learn what love is."

"It did," agreed Sarah, sighing. "We know sadness together. But maybe Roberto and Allegra will know the joy of having two very different, but loving, mothers."

"How can you be so gracious?"

"Because I'm a pragmatist," said Sarah. "I play life as it comes. Besides, you're very clever."

"What do you mean?"

"You knew enough to come to me first!" said Sarah. "But enough stalling. Perhaps we've arrived at the moment when you should ask the man directly."

Now Marco was staring at her, worried. It was hardly the confident pose she had planned to strike.

"Marco," she breathed, a bit ragged from her weepy spell. "I'm not so big on traditions anymore. But I'd like to do something significant. I want to make a speech. I want to say how I feel."

"At the party? About Anita and Marty?"

"No, about us," said Catherine. She stepped back, solid on her own feet.

"Marco, I love you. And Roberto. And Allegra. I want to share my life with you."

"You are a big part of our life," said Marco. "And it's *fantastico*."

"Marco," shrieked Catherine, suddenly panicked. Was he purposely not getting it? Was it a language thing? What the hell, it was time to get straight to the point.

Catherine dropped to one knee. "What I'm saying is that I want to marry you. Marry you!"

"Well, *bella*," said Marco, pulling her to standing and stroking her sleek blond bob. "Why didn't you just say that in the first place?"

There were no secrets where Anita and Sarah were concerned. Not anymore. No sooner had Marco left to talk to Catherine than the two sisters were hovering outside the bedroom door, pretending not to listen. They discreetly looked the other way and pretended to pass around napkins to nearby guests when Marco stepped out of the room to collect Roberto and Allegra, and then rushed to the door, napkins in hand, when he closed the door with his children and Catherine inside.

Marty tapped his fiancée and her sister on their shoulders.

"Ladies," he said. "Shouldn't we offer a little privacy here?"

"It's private," said Anita. "It's not like we're in the room with them. Now shush, I can't hear."

"Go get a glass," said Sarah. "That's how we did it in the old days."

Marty shook his head.

"Stop that," said Anita. "Now, do you think they would want to do New Year's? We're all together."

Marty sighed, not really offended that his bride would want to share their wedding day. He knew her all too well.

"I can barely breathe," said Dakota. "This is the most tense eavesdropping the club has ever done."

Ginger was hopping around from foot to foot, charged up by the energy in the room but uncertain what was happening.

She held hands with Dakota and chatted animatedly to Lucie and Darwin and the frowning man by the desserts.

"Are you excited?" she asked Nathan, bouncing up and down. "Everybody's excited! Wanna jump with me?"

"No," said Nathan, biting off a large hunk of doughnut and chewing rapidly. "And I am most certainly not. Excited."

Roberto opened the door as his father and Catherine exited the guest room. Catherine's face was puffy and wet.

Sarah twisted the napkin in her hand nervously.

"Well? Well?" said Anita, leaning forward so much she was almost on tiptoe.

"We're going to be married," said Allegra, dashing out around her father and Catherine and into the living room. "And I will be the flower girl." She threw up her arms in triumph, as though she'd just won a great prize.

A cheer went up among the party guests, even from the folks who didn't know Catherine well.

"Everyone loves a wedding," said KC. "Even me. If it's someone else's."

"Double wedding?" asked Anita. "Is this going to be a double wedding?"

"Why not," agreed Marco. "She spends months telling me 'Don't get any ideas, buddy,' and then she knocks me off my socks. So I better get it done before she changes her mind." Catherine hugged her friends, and Sarah, and Ginger, before being introduced to Anita's daughter-in-law, Rhea.

"Oh, my," she exclaimed, face-to-face with a very pleasant-seeming woman in her fifties who congratulated her warmly and introduced her children. "How . . . nice to meet you. I am truly, truly glad to meet you. And Nathan. Here *you* are."

"Catherine," Nathan said evenly. "It would seem some sort of felicitations are in order."

"Indeed," she said smoothly, giving no indication she had once—foolishly—imagined herself in love with Nathan. Imagined herself ousting Rhea and that such behavior would somehow be okay. *Oh, Catherine*, she thought to herself. *You really used to be a mess, now, didn't you?*

Nathan leaned in to shake her hand, his mouth close to her ear as he pecked her cheek. She was surprised by the inviting scent of his cologne, had expected it would somehow smell different because of his boorish behavior.

"Get my mother to call it off," he growled, his voice low. "I'm sure Marco would be very interested to know, shall we say, more about your behavior last summer."

Catherine's eyes flashed.

"Isn't this something, Nathan!" squealed Anita, giving Catherine a big squeeze as she came alongside Rhea. She was delighted for Catherine but also relieved for herself, hopeful that her son would have more respect for another bride.

"Oh, it's something, all right," grumbled Nathan. He narrowed his eyes at Catherine. She'd inserted herself into his life at a weak moment, he thought, and now she was caught up in his mother's wedding drama. But that didn't mean his fight was over. On the contrary. It was just getting started.

"Let me fix you a drink," said Nathan, practically shoving

Catherine toward the cocktails and leaving his mother and wife blathering on about the wonderful turn of events.

"I'm not thirsty," said Catherine, though in reality her throat was dry.

"I don't hate you, Catherine," said Nathan, pouring a full glass of Cara Mia pinot and sipping it himself.

"How reassuring," she replied, waving at Darwin and Lucie as they beckoned her to come over.

"Act however you want," said Nathan. "But it looks like we're going to be kissing cousins, of a variety. And I'd hate to have to tell Marco a few details, *hmmm*?" He drained his glass and set it down loudly.

"You know, Marco is wonderful," hissed Catherine. "He understands everything. My past. My present. Which means we have no secrets, Nathan."

"Certainly not," he said.

"Push me," said Catherine. "I could shout out anything. Right here. Right now. It's not going to affect *my* relationship."

She indicated Rhea with a tilt of her head, hoping he wouldn't call her bluff. She wasn't about to embarrass Anita, upset her daughter-in-law, or devastate her grandchildren. She'd already mucked around in their life quite enough last summer. Still. Nathan didn't need to know that. She threw him a hard look.

"How nice for you," Nathan replied, glancing quickly in the direction of his wife, who caught his eye and flashed him a stunning, happy smile. Almost imperceptibly, Catherine could sense Nathan relax and then stiffen as he turned back to her.

"You wouldn't . . ." he said.

"I'm just saying," said Catherine. "I'm sure you'll agree that this double wedding is going to be problem free. Come January, both Anita and I better be newlyweds."

She took the bottle of wine from Marco's vineyard right out of his hands.

"Excuse me," she said with confidence. "But I'm pretty sure this belongs to me."

christmas

Somewhere, under the flurry of tearing gift wrap and devouring of chocolate bells, is a day about family and connection and thoughtfulness. Just as every hand-stitched item—every knit, every purl—encodes a secret message about devotion. Knitting is simply an expression of love.

chapter nine

"Nothing is stopping you from making the trip to Scotland. Everything—work, school, the shop—will all be here when you get back."

That's what her father had said last night, making his case as she arrived late from the final club meeting of the season, and James's simple statement continued to ring in Dakota's ears. Everyone else who celebrated Christmas was gearing up to spend time with family, Dakota knew, and she'd spent all night listening to their plans and brushing off their insistence that she reconsider and go to Scotland.

"The world is filled with kitchens, Dakota," Darwin had said. "But there's only one Gran. Your mother adored her."

"I do, too," said Dakota, feeling ever more uncertain. *Be tough,* she told herself. *Do what is best.*

Darwin was off to Seattle, Lucie to her brother's house with Rosie and Ginger in tow, Catherine caught up in the idea of her first Christmas in which she would be responsible for filling the stockings, and even Peri, with the shop closed on Christmas and the day after, was scheming for a now-you-see-her-now-you-don't mad dash to see her parents in Chicago.

"Just long enough to eat some chocolate, hand out some presents, and leave before my mother and I start arguing," she explained.

Only Dakota was bravely sticking to her goal of interning in the V hotel kitchen.

"Because it teaches skills, responsibility, and the value of hard work," she told her mirror as she dressed carefully in a black suit and red pumps. Conservative was one thing, but no need to go boring, she decided. She wanted to impress general manager Sandra Stonehouse, let her know she was serious about becoming a pastry chef. Who knows? Maybe this gig would lead to other internships, perhaps even a job after graduation. Then again, she didn't have the luxury to dither around, what with Peri's job offer floating ominously on the horizon. Her mind swirled constantly with the potential challenges. She absolutely had to sharpen her skills and open the café. Her only other choice, in order to keep her mother's shop going, was to give up her passion altogether and leave school to run the shop full-time, and try to sneak in college somehow over the years. Not, she knew with absolute certainty, what her mother ever intended. And she'd fought so hard to make her father support her culinary dreams. She wasn't ready to give up now. Not yet.

She spritzed on a perfume, applied some lip gloss, and put on her mother's gold hoop earrings.

"Wow," said James, upon seeing the newly outfitted Dakota. "You look just like your mother did when she worked at Churchill Publishing. Sharp and professional."

He was upset that she wasn't coming to Scotland, it was true, but although he'd made his feelings known, he hadn't made things too tense around the house. Although she had found her plane ticket in various locations—tacked to the fridge, on the coffee table, where she often studied. Just enough to remind her of the options. She imagined James and Bess awkwardly making small talk over coffee as Gran insisted on making good Scottish oatmeal and Tom and Donny surveyed the garden, discussed trimming hedges and if the place was getting to be too much. She imagined microwaving the holiday plate she'd tucked away in the freezer after Thanksgiving, heating it up late on Christmas night after a day on her feet in the kitchen. Er, make that an actual *restaurant* kitchen. Dakota twirled around.

"I'm going to see the general manager at the V," she told her dad now.

"What?" said James. He seemed startled.

"It's standard practice," Dakota explained, toasting a slice of wheat bread. "The chef chooses the interns, but the general manager interviews everyone who comes to the hotel. You should know that, you worked there long enough."

"Uh, yeah," said James, slurping up his last sip of coffee. "Guess I just forgot. So, when's your interview with her?"

"Ten," said Dakota, wiping toast crumbs off her suit jacket as she munched. "Any tips?"

"Be yourself and sit up straight," said James, placing his dishes in the sink. "And don't forget your grandparents and your uncle are coming over. We fly tonight. Your ticket's still good."

"*Daaad,*" sighed Dakota. "Sometimes I just gotta cut the cord, you know?"

"You don't," he said. "That's just a rumor about adulthood. But most of us still rely on our mentors, and for some of us, our mentors are our parents. Spend some time in Scotland. You might learn something you never knew."

"Okay, I'll use that in my interview," said Dakota, rummaging through the knitting bag she took everywhere, part habit, part security blanket. She wished her mother's red journal held explicit instructions on what to do when faced with two amazing choices.

"I left a stack of little presents on your bed. Can you pack them, please? A little something for everyone. Do you think Grandma Bess likes potpourri? And these. I just finished a pair of new slippers for Gran."

"Of course," said James. "She can add them to her one-a-day collection."

Spontaneously, Dakota leaned in to her father and gave him a hug. "I wish I could go, but I just can't," she said. "But you're still my favorite guy in the world."

"Yeah, tell that general manager how impressed you are with your old dad," said James, proud of himself for not meddling as he watched his daughter stroll out the door for an interview with the woman he'd been secretly dating for months.

"You came highly recommended," Sandra Stonehouse said, as she glanced at Dakota's résumé, one hand on her lime-green reading glasses as she read. A dark-skinned athletic-looking woman in a navy pantsuit and tiny gold earrings, nothing on her person—or on her desk, with its row of stapler, tape, and pencil holder—seemed out of place: Ms. Stonehouse exuded professionalism. And yet, Dakota wondered if those glasses meant there was more to her. She certainly seemed like an interesting woman to know.

"That's unusual for someone of your age," she continued. Her neutral expression was difficult to read, thought Dakota, who had never before been in this type of meeting. Except at school, she was typically in on the decision-making. Another reason, she realized, why it was pretty amazing to inherit a family business. Even if it did cause headaches!

"I hung out with the chef at the chain's hotel in Rome a summer ago. He's been very encouraging," said Dakota, before opting for full disclosure. "My father used to be the chief architect of this hotel chain. James Foster."

"Yes, I do know that," said Ms. Stonehouse, without looking up. "I once worked with your father in Paris, though I didn't know him well then."

"He's a good guy," said Dakota. Ms. Stonehouse raised her head briefly, a tiny half-smile on her lips. "And now he's started his own business. It's extraordinarily successful. Turning clients away right and left."

"Impressive," said Ms. Stonehouse, who knew that James, like many entrepreneurs, had experienced a few hiccups getting going. "The hotel industry's been suffering, too. So there's a lot to be said for marketing and just trying to ride things out. But let's talk more about you, Dakota. What's your background?"

Dakota filled in the details of the knitting shop as it was, and how she hoped it to be, with the café and all that. "And that's why I need some real-life experience," she concluded. "I'm good, well, more like I'm not bad. I want to learn."

Ms. Stonehouse nodded. "You're a very serious young woman," she said. She wanted to say that she was tremendously curious about Dakota, had heard James boast and complain about her, and had spent a fair amount of time imagining this first meeting. She hadn't expected it to be at the hotel, hadn't realized until she looked at her day's agenda that Dakota would be coming through the door. Had freaked out, in fact, even considered having her assistant do the interview. But ultimately, she put the needs of the hotel above her own. And at the V, this general manager always had a personal meeting with every new employee.

"Not always serious," said Dakota. "But I'm figuring it out. I'm figuring life out."

After being silent for what seemed like ages, Ms. Stonehouse stood up and came around her desk.

"It's a big deal to work through the holidays," she said. James had broached the trip to Scotland with Sandra months ago to ensure that she was comfortable with him being gone over Christmas. Later, he mentioned that Dakota was going to work over Christmas and that he wasn't pleased about it. Not once, however, did he say Dakota was coming to the V. She had to admire his restraint. If it had been her, she'd have called in the favor and gotten Dakota's job canceled. The least she could do, she decided, was give the most important man in her life the gift he most wanted this Christmas: time with his little girl. All the same, if the romance with James continued, she didn't want Dakota to accuse her later of manipulation. *They didn't prepare her for this at Cornell*, she thought. Interviewing your lover's child.

"I'm going to be straight with you," she continued. "Most of our staff are fighting to earn days off. And we do have an opening for an intern after the New Year. You could help out on weekends and prepare for Sunday brunch. It's one of the hotel's highlights."

Dakota nodded very slowly. *Think, think, think*, she told herself. She was pretty sure she recognized this type of trick question from that book on being an engaging interviewee.

"I'm ready to accept the challenge," she said now. "I may miss my family, but I know how to work hard and believe I have valuable skills to offer the V."

"Such as?"

"Such as . . . a willingness to work on Christmas?" said Dakota weakly. She attempted a bright smile, showing lots of teeth.

"Okay, Dakota Walker," said Ms. Stonehouse. "You're in." In truth, the kitchen staff could use the extra help. But she hoped to God she wasn't out when it came to James.

Catherine was beaming as she sat inside the city's least swanky coffee spot, Marty's Deli, waiting for Anita and Dakota.

"You look stunning," said Marty, finishing up his morning stint behind the counter. He intended to work until the deli was transformed into the knitting café, which meant that he had a few years left until retirement. He brought a plate of cookies over to Catherine, who gobbled two chocolate chippers immediately.

"I am freakin' starved all of a sudden," she said. "Ever since the proposal, I am damn hungry."

"Maybe you've got a case of nerves," said Marty. "Anita's been cool as a cucumber since this turned into a double wedding. Now that you're involved, she can stand up to Nathan because she's fighting for you. It's not about her anymore."

"What's he doing now?" Catherine contemplated another cookie.

"Oh, the usual," said Marty, taking one himself. "Jabbering on in long, rambling speeches about the meaning of family. Claiming he won't attend. Throwing tantrums, in a manner of speaking."

"And his wife?" asked Catherine.

"She lets him rant," said Marty. "Then again, they hit a bad patch a while back. So, maybe this is a good sign."

"So, will I technically be related in some way to Nathan now?" mused Catherine. "Will I have to see him regularly now?"

"Your mother-in-law-to-be is his aunt," said Marty, considering. "And your stepkids are his cousins. But don't worry. Marrying into this family is A-okay. Only Nathan is loco."

"I actually think he's just a troubled guy," said Catherine. "Needy, acting out. He acts the jerk, but he has more potential."

"Sounds like the description of a teenager," said Marty, standing up as Anita entered the shop, her arm around Dakota, their breath surrounding them as they exited the chilled winter air.

"Guess who got her first real job today!" announced Anita, her eyes crinkling.

"It's the internship," explained Dakota.

"So, you're really not going to Scotland then?" asked Catherine. "I mean, are you sure?"

"Of course she's sure," Anita said swiftly. "Otherwise she'd turn it down and go with the family. This isn't just any restaurant, you know. Besides, the holidays come every year." She settled into her chair as Marty went off to get drinks for all.

"You're just revved up because it's your first Christmas with your new family," said Dakota, piling up her winter outerwear on a nearby chair.

"Right," agreed Anita. "All the other holidays over the years will pale in comparison."

"Like getting the entire family together in Italy sometime," said Catherine, finally synching with Anita. "That might be fun, but Roberto would probably have something better to do. I'm sure Marco would just get over it."

"Such as an internship," said Anita. "Family is important, but an internship is much more crucial."

"Could never get another one of those," said Catherine. "But a ninety-seven-year-old grandmother? Better to make her wait until you can fit her into your schedule."

"All right, all right, you tricked me," exclaimed Dakota, as she took the mocha that Marty offered. "I thought you were actually excited for me."

"Dakota, I am truly proud of you," said Anita. "But what will make you happier when you look back? That you spent a memorable Christmas at your Gran's with all the Walkers and your father, or that you finally learned how to keep your soufflé from falling?"

"I already know how to do that," said Dakota.

"See what she means," said Catherine. "Holidays may come every year, but each year is once in a lifetime."

"Don't invite regret where you don't have to," said Anita. "We all make our own choices. Your internship might lead to wonderful opportunities—or you might just learn a thing or two and move on. But you'll never stop wishing you had made this trip."

"I wasn't expecting to be in this position," Dakota said finally. Honestly. "I feel inundated by dilemmas."

Anita, sensing her fatigue, changed the subject to the upcoming New Year weddings. Dakota finished her mocha, grateful to lose herself for several minutes listening to myriad descriptions of Catherine's dream wedding dress, and was sorry she didn't have the freedom in her schedule to help her select it. But Anita was more than prepared to return Catherine's favor and become her pseudo wedding planner, offering suggestions and ideas to color-coordinate.

How funny to think back to Catherine, as superficial and difficult as she once had been, and to know that now this caring, confident woman was soon marrying into Anita's family, thought Dakota. Strange, also, because once she and Georgia had been the closest thing to family Anita had when Stan was gone and her sons were so far away. And now the family was bigger, and more complicated, and interconnected in ways none of them ever would have dreamed.

Dakota thought of her mother's dreams for the shop, and for Dakota's future. And how quickly everything could fall apart. One autumn afternoon they sat around, all the club, her mother recuperating, and mere days later they held a memorial service. Circumstances could change swiftly. Perhaps, she wondered, she was letting her head run over her heart. She might have trouble keeping the shop going without Peri, without the café being ready—this she understood and feared—but she might also get to next Christmas and discover she'd missed the best chance to spend a holiday with Gran. Too much could happen.

She looked at Anita and Catherine, planning their weddings, and thought about her grandparents and uncle arriving at her father's apartment, with tidy rolling suitcases they'd probably purchased just for the trip.

"Life changes," piped up Dakota. "Families change." And that's when she knew the choice she wanted most: She didn't want to miss out on whatever shifts might be going on with her

Walkers. Not this Christmas. Because that's all she had right now, this one holiday. This one moment. And she wanted to be part of that dynamic. Not separate. Not ever.

Dakota grabbed her coat, pecked Catherine and Anita and Marty, and ran to the door, looking back quickly. "I'm going to see Gran," she shouted. She ran up to the store to touch base with Peri, loaded up on some yarn for the flight, and then, on her way to pick up some dry cleaning, she called Gran.

"I'm going to come for Christmas, Gran," she shouted into the phone, trying to hear over the din of the honking cars on Fifty-seventh Street.

"I know that, Dakota, my dear," Gran replied. "I've been making up the rooms all morning."

"But I almost didn't make the trip, Gran," Dakota said. "I was going to stay in New York and focus on my career."

"Oh, pish," said Gran. "I knew you'd reason it out. We're going to have a grand visit. All my family together . . ." Her voice caught mid-sentence.

"Are you all right, Gran?"

"Of course, my dear," she replied. "It's just that the cats are very pleased about the way it's all turning out. Hurry and get to the airport now. Don't you dare miss that plane."

"But, Gran, the flight doesn't leave for eight hours," said Dakota.

"Exactly right, then," said Gran. "You better get there soon."

Dakota ran through her packing list in her mind as she made her way over to the hotel. She wasn't delighted about telling

Sandra Stonehouse she'd changed her mind, not after making such a case for getting the internship. But the sacrifice she needed to make, she realized, was not skipping the holidays for work. It was sacrificing a cool opportunity for the higher priority of honoring her family.

———

The doorman waved as Dakota entered the lobby of her father's building. She strode briskly through to the elevator, glancing at her watch. Her Gran's travel worries rang in her ear and, combined with the realization that she needed to do laundry before she could pack, she figured she had three hours to be ready before Bess and Tom and Donny arrived. Maybe a quick stir-fry for supper, a bit of rice and veggies before a Christmas overload of carbs? Or maybe just order pizza? She fumbled around in her bag for her key, unlocking the door with one hand and using the other to dial up Sandra Stonehouse and prepare to plead for the internship after the New Year.

She stepped through the door, held her breath, and hit send to connect the call. She walked the few feet into the living area, startled to hear an unfamiliar ringtone.

"Dad! What are you doing?" Dakota was stunned to see James standing in front of his desk, his arms wrapped around Sandra Stonehouse, the jacket of her navy suit casually tossed over the back of the sofa, her handbag vibrating from the ringing of her cell phone.

"Dakota!" James jumped back but kept an arm on Sandra.

"Hello, you have reached voice mail for Sandra Stone-house . . ." Dakota heard through the phone. "Guess I don't need to leave a message now," she said drily.

"I'd like you to meet my friend. My good friend. My girl-friend." He cleared his throat. "Dakota, this is Sandra."

Sandra smoothed out her clothes and made mad swiping motions around her mouth, certain she'd smeared lip gloss on her chin. She didn't feel anywhere near as in control as she had that morning. Sandra managed a small wave in Dakota's direction.

"Hello again," she said quietly.

"Hiya," said Dakota. "I was calling your office, but, apparently, you make house calls." She avoided looking at her father, certain she could guess his expression.

Sandra reached over to pick up her jacket, but James shook his head.

"Dakota, I invited Sandra over to my home," he said. He hadn't wanted to interfere, so he'd waited until Dakota's interview should be completed, and then, hearing Sandra's voice, realized just how much he was going to miss her, even being away for just a few days. Spontaneously, he'd asked Sandra to join him for lunch, packed in between throwing together two salads. "I didn't want to spring anything on you. Believe me, I would have preferred a nice get-to-know-you at a good restaurant. But you said you wouldn't be home until the late afternoon."

"Well, I had an epiphany," said Dakota. "About Christmas."

"Let's hear it," said James, sitting on the sofa and beckoning to Sandra to join him. She perched herself on the arm, her back stiff.

"This is awkward," said Dakota, not wishing to sit down with the happy couple but not leaving the room, either. Even just a few months ago, she knew she'd have bolted out of the room, devastated to see her father kissing a woman who wasn't her mother. Not that she actually wanted to see him kiss anyone, quite frankly. That was just too much.

Of course, she'd noticed how much happier James had seemed lately, even if the economy had thrown a few obstacles at his business plan. In fact, Dakota had suspected that a new romance might have something to do with his new-and-improved demeanor. So, she'd already made up her mind, theoretically, to be happy for him when he finally came clean. Doing so wouldn't alter the truth that she'd have preferred to see James with her mother. An impossibility, of course. Which meant it was cruel and selfish for her father to be lonely all the rest of his life just so Dakota would feel fine about it all. More than anything, she just wanted him to be happy. He deserved it.

She'd reasoned out all of these issues in her mind recently, and yet it took her by surprise how her stomach lurched to see her father kissing his girlfriend. And why did that girlfriend have to be Sandra Stonehouse? Dakota wanted to work for the woman! She still needed that internship at the V after the New Year, dammit.

"I was calling to take you up on that internship-after-the-

New-Year thing," she said. "I lost sight of a family commitment I had in Scotland."

"Okay, we can arrange that," said Sandra, inwardly delighted for James and yet desperately trying to tap her professional persona. It was hard enough to date a man who was haunted by memory and even more difficult to be gracious as he planned a holiday with all of his beloved Georgia's dearest relatives. But she was holding on. Though now she'd just lost the lovely, long afternoon alone she'd been anticipating.

"What I just have to know," continued Dakota, her arms folded in front of her and her oversized knitting bag causing her to lean over to one side. "Was hiring me something to do with my dad?"

"Hiring you had nothing whatsoever to do with your dad," Sandra explained briskly. "I think you have some decent potential. Though there will never be any special treatment."

"All right," said Dakota. "I can live with that. By the way, it's very nice to meet you." Remember to be polite. That's what her mother always said.

"Thank you," said Sandra, slipping her suit jacket over her wrinkled white blouse.

"This is great," said James, visibly relieved. "I'm so glad the two of you have met."

Dakota gave her father a look, briefly concerned that he might lose his mind and invite Sandra to Scotland.

"By the way, Dad, Gran doesn't think seven hours is enough time to catch our flight. So, we better get a move on," said Dakota. "I'll be in my room packing. No need for me to relive the horror of your good-byes. Some things are best left unimagined and unobserved." Dakota picked up her knitting bag and flopped down on her bed. Part of her wanted to cry. Then again, as she stuffed jeans and sweaters into a duffel, she knew Gran wouldn't permit her such self-indulgence. After all, she had a plane to catch.

chapter ten

So, this is how insomniacs feel, thought Dakota, as she shuffled behind her father, grandparents, and uncle in Edinburgh Airport. From rushing around to get her warmest clothes stuffed into her suitcase, to being sandwiched between her snoring father and her uncle, whose head kept rolling onto her shoulder, Dakota hadn't been able to sleep on the flight at all. Not even when she closed her eyes and counted to five hundred.

Instead, she knitted, stealthily, always careful not to wake anyone else up as she worked her stitches. She had a lot of extra gifts on the go, thanks to the yarn she'd picked up from Peri, and only a few days to finish before Christmas.

Dakota yawned as they waited for luggage, and as her father and Donny rented cars, paying only vague attention to her grandmother Bess listing out all the must-do chores as soon as they put a foot inside her mother-in-law's house. The truth was, although

Dakota had spent every Christmas of her life in Pennsylvania with her grandparents, and several visits over the years to see her grandfather Tom's mother in Scotland, she'd never actually been in a house with Bess and Gran at the same time. And everyone— from Gran, to her grandmother, to her mother when she'd been alive—made no secret of the fact that Gran and Bess merely tolerated each other. Barely.

"We'll likely have to clean from top to bottom," Bess was saying to Tom now. Her face was stern, as usual, which made it easy to overlook her wide eyes and high cheekbones. She was an attractive woman, Dakota's grandmother, if ever she thought to relax. "I packed some Clorox wipes in case she follows me around and makes things difficult."

"Now, now," said Tom. "We've not even got there yet. If there's a need to tidy, fine. But let's not just rearrange for its own sake."

"Are you implying something, Thomas?"

"Isn't this fun, Grandma Bess?" Dakota jumped in, hoping to stop her grandparents before they launched into one of their mini-feuds. Bickering was such second nature to them that they no longer noticed. In a few minutes, she knew, her grandfather would make a joke and Bess would be amused and giggling. It was just their way.

Her uncle held up a set of keys and twirled them on his finger.

"You're with me," he said, pointing to Dakota. "Mom, Dad, you can ride with James."

"Oh," said Bess, taken aback. Although she'd grown fond of

James during his many trips to bring Dakota to visit them, they'd never actually spent very long together. He'd always helped Tom with a chore or two, eaten his holiday dinner, then left Dakota to stay with them for a few days. She liked that, felt he understood how much she needed that space. It was awkward, in its way, this nagging resentment she felt about how hard her daughter, Georgia, worked at the yarn shop, about how alone she had been. All because James had left.

Georgia may have forgiven, thought Bess, but this mother had made it a point never to forget.

Half asleep, Dakota didn't argue. She let her uncle grab her suitcase and roll it toward the cars as she followed. "See you later," she mumbled, looking forward to the moment when she could sit down and get a little shut-eye.

Cold air blasted her face. "Wake up, sleepy," said Donny, powering up the car window he'd just lowered to let in some fresh Scottish oxygen. "This is my big chance all week."

"Huh?" Dakota was groggy, her face creased from balling up her coat to use as a makeshift pillow.

"Hanging out with my only niece," said Donny, smoothly following the curve of the road, driving past compact cottages nestled a sprinkle of inches away from the road. "I'll never get a minute alone with you if Mom and Gran get ahold of you."

Dakota's uncle Donny was her mother's only sibling, a

younger brother who long ago followed after his sister or waited at the front door until she came home from first grade, selling penny tickets to the puppet shows he rehearsed in the dining room.

"And then Mom would come along and be all anxious about some ladies coming over for tea," Dakota's mother once told her as they rode in the car to Pennsylvania for a Christmas visit. "Everything had to be just right in the house, didn't it, Donny?"

Back when Dakota was a girl, Donny drove in to pick them up in his newly washed blue pickup every Christmas Eve. Until Georgia died and James was on the scene, and then Dakota no longer had her annual chitchat with her uncle in the car. She looked forward to those moments, knowing that Donny wouldn't mind that she'd overloaded her suitcase with too many clothes and toys, unaccustomed to traveling. Before their trip to Scotland during the summer she turned thirteen, Dakota had hardly ever taken a trip other than to see her grandparents.

"Oh, you know," Donny had said to whatever was at issue, shrugging. He was always the one trying to make the peace, Dakota remembered, sticking up for Georgia when Bess became fussed, and defending their mother when Georgia launched into complaint. "It all worked out in the end."

He'd explained how the two Walker kids spent days constructing a not-so-sturdy outdoor headquarters away from their mother's house, a lean-to consisting of sheets of plywood propped up against a tree and covered with an old tarp they found on a shelf in the barn.

"No doubt Dad had plans to use it again," Donny said then. "Can't afford to waste on a farm. But he didn't say anything, even came over to watch us do our shows."

"Sometimes," Georgia had agreed. "But he was almost always working."

"You're always working, Mom," Dakota had said that trip, when she was eight or nine. "And I don't mind." Her comment had killed the conversation for a bit, but then Donny found some other topic, and the chatter just started up again.

They'd made out okay. That's what Donny always said on those car trips, clearly impressed with Georgia's shop—he would stand in the shop, as Georgia collected paperwork from the back office that she'd catch up on the day after Christmas, and marvel at all the colors of yarn along the walls—and delighted by every joke Dakota made.

"Did it not used to be okay?" young Dakota would ask in reply, and wait patiently for a response that never came quite directly.

Dakota enjoyed her uncle Donny, admired his easygoing, quiet way. "If your father hadn't come along," he'd said to her one holiday, "I'd have wanted to raise you myself." Donny Walker hadn't strayed far, returning after college and a year tree planting out West, to help manage the family farm in Pennsylvania. He had never married, confiding in her during the last visit that there weren't a lot of women vying for a chance to be a farm wife. He'd purchased more and more land next to her grandparents, experimenting with organic crops, and had a series of local restaurants as clients. But as Dakota well knew from the yarn shop, being innovative didn't always equate with financial success. The Walkers were far from poor, to be certain, but they were far from rich.

"So, spill it," said her uncle now. "Tell an old farmer all about the life of a twenty-year-old in the big city."

Dakota grinned. That was one good thing about being an only child: She was always voted most popular.

"I love school," she began. "Stressed about the shop. Business could be better. Plus Peri's got a job offer in Paris, of all places—don't tell, okay?—and I just saw that guy Roberto I dated in Rome. He's still cute! So, that was weird. Then Catherine got engaged, to that guy's father, so we'll be seeing each other maybe a lot. Or not. But definitely at the wedding, which is now a double wedding with Anita, on New Year's. Oh, and I discovered that the woman who was almost my boss is actually Dad's secret girlfriend. But she insists that has nothing to do with it."

"I think I need you to write this all down for me," said her uncle, winking. "You're a born storyteller. Just like your mom. She was good at making up stories when she and I were kids."

"Like what?"

"Oh, fun stuff, sometimes, when I was scared," said Donny. "About an invisible frog who lived at Gran's and ate bad dreams. I liked the idea of him, that frog. Georgia invented lots of adventures for him, told me he lived in the pond out back. But her cleverness wasn't just make-believe. She was also smart about getting us out of scrapes."

Albums, T-shirts, and a Walkman were all on Donny's Christmas list, taped to the outside of the white refrigerator in Bess's tidy but tiny farmhouse kitchen. And the top item—on there almost as a joke—was not something that could be bought in the store.

LEARN TO DRIVE!

That's what her little brother wanted in his stocking. True, he'd been around farm equipment all his life, but he'd never actually been out on the street. Didn't know how to parallel park, for example. Not that Georgia was very good at that part of driving, either, having been at the wheel for only a year. She'd had some near misses, almost hitting a cyclist who was biking along the side of the road. Good thing she'd been going about ten miles an hour, agitated by the sudden appearance of snow.

She'd had an errand after school, to pick up some supplies for the farm at the hardware store, and her father let her borrow the truck to drive to school, taking Donny along, of course. The car would have been even better, because it had a cassette player and she'd just borrowed the new John Cougar album from her friend Cathy. But wheels were better than the bus any day. Of course Cathy, waiting for her at the side entrance of the high school with her typewritten column for the school paper, immediately begged for a ride home upon seeing Georgia in the truck. Georgia felt cool about it until Cathy began shrieking as a man on a bike got closer.

"Be careful!" she shouted, then sighed loudly as they passed him. "You should think about moving to the city, like Philly or New York. Nobody drives there at all."

"I think Georgia's a great driver," said Donny, as Georgia flashed him a thumbs-up in the rearview mirror.

Sometimes Donny was annoying, but other moments he was useful to have around, Georgia thought. That was part of the reason why she decided she'd grant his Christmas wish, even though he was barely fourteen. Besides, she had to watch her budget, and this gift was free. A girl had to watch her pennies, she knew, especially if she hoped to afford Dartmouth.

The problem was that Georgia and Donny would have to run their lessons on the sly. That was made all the more challenging because it always seemed like her mother was hovering about, listening in on conversations and trying to noodle her way into everything.

"She just wants to be involved," her dad had insisted more than once, when Georgia took her complaints out to the barn.

"She just wants to criticize," Georgia would insist.

"You don't know quite everything," Tom said. "Not yet, anyway."

Well, what Georgia did know was that Donny wanted to learn how to run a car, and she was going to teach him. Their plan was to pretend to go to bed at a normal time, then sneak out at midnight.

"What if mom hears the engine?" asked Donny, who was then conscripted to tiptoe into their parents' bedroom and put a pair of earmuffs on Bess. Tom was well known in the family for being able to sleep through any sound, then awaken at precisely four a.m. every day.

The two bundled up quickly in boots and hats, slipping out the kitchen door, the keys gripped tightly in Georgia's hand. They opened the truck door, Georgia sliding across the seat and Donny positioning himself behind the wheel. It took several turns of the ignition to get the old truck to start.

"Yeah!" shouted Donny, as the truck roared to life, before getting a dig to his ribs from his older sister.

"Shut up," she said. "You'll wake everybody up. Now push down the clutch, put it in gear, and give it some gas. Just a little!" The truck lurched forward. Donny hit the accelerator again, and the truck moved forward in fits and starts.

"Promise me you'll never be a truck driver," Georgia said.

"Nah," said Donny. "I'll be a veterinarian. I'll look after the sheep at Gran's."

"They have cars there, too, you know," said Georgia, using her arms to brace herself from hitting her forehead. "You're going to have to get better than this."

And so the entire week before Christmas, Georgia and Donny escaped out of the farmhouse, with its rules and order, and drove around the farm from midnight until four a.m.

"It's totally beautiful in the dark," Donny said, gazing at the fields, their house in the near distance and a light or two farther away, probably marking a front step on their neighbors' homes. He swigged some hot chocolate from a thermos, he and Georgia becoming more bold about sneaking the makings of a midnight picnic from the kitchen. Their mom, noticing the missing pantry items, put it up to the holiday week.

"It's desolate," said Georgia. "Suffocating."

"It's just a farm," said Donny. "Just land. Crops. Besides, you love Gran's."

"That's different," she said.

"How?" He wiped a drop of cocoa with his sleeve.

Georgia was silent for so long that Donny thought she'd nodded off. "I don't know," she conceded. "It just is."

"You're nice now, but you're not always. You give Mom a hard time," said Donny, stuffing three cookies into his mouth all at once. "The two of you are a lot alike."

"We're not," insisted Georgia. "I'm nothing like her. And you won't say that again if you want to drive."

"I could do it without you now," he said, offering her a cookie.

"Maybe," said Georgia. "But you won't."

No one enjoys being told their limits, not Georgia by Bess and not Donny by his sister. So, on Christmas Eve, after the entire family had returned from a service at the Presbyterian church, enjoyed a plate of tarts and shortbread, and said their good nights, he decided to go on his driving adventure earlier than usual, leaving his big sister back at the house. Not yet asleep, Georgia heard the rumble of the vehicle and ran outside with just enough time to see him motor his way down the long driveway and over to the empty road beyond. Georgia had never let him drive off the farm.

"It's too icy tonight," she half yelled, glancing quickly back at her house lest her parents hear and then taking off running down the driveway, her coat still undone and her hands and cheeks pinking up rapidly. Dammit, she thought, Donny's going to drive himself right off the road. Mom and Dad are going to freak out! And Donny will probably be dead. And then I won't have my little brother anymore.

Ahead of her, she could see the flash of headlights, on and off, off and on. The little bugger was showing off, she thought. Or spinning on black ice. She ran faster, imagining a middle-of-the-night trucker zooming by, rushing to get a load of Cabbage Patch Kids to the toy store before Christmas, smashing her brother to smithereens.

She ran the full mile and a half, squeezing her hands tightly, until her sides cramped and she began coughing on the chilly air. Still, she seemed to be gaining on the truck, with her stupid brother inside. How? she wondered, drawing closer, hearing the sound of the engine being turned. And turned. And turned.

The car was stalled. Donny had flooded the truck's engine, and the vehicle was stuck in the middle of road, perpendicular to the lanes. He was cutting off the entire road.

"I'm so going to kick your ass," she huffed, as she drew the door open, her lungs painfully frozen with cold and her teeth chattering. To his credit, Donny wasn't crying, but he looked damn scared.

"It won't go," he moaned. "I'm freezing."

"Move over, dim bulb," she said. "And quit pressing the gas. Sheesh! What have I been teaching you?"

"I can't remember," said Donny. "I'm too cold."

Georgia looked over at her brother, who, in his haste, had left the house without a proper coat, hat, or gloves.

"Are you even wearing socks?" she asked.

"No," he whined. "I was in a hurry."

"Maybe now you'll know better than to go it alone," she said, peeling off her jacket.

"I'm not going to wear a girls' coat."

"Put it on or I'll tie you to the front of the truck and dump you in Hansen's field," she growled. "Now, I've got to wait for the engine to clear. You'd be stupid to wait in a car on the middle of the road, so you might as well run up to the house. And be quiet!"

"What are you gonna do?"

"I'm going to wait to start the car, return it home, and crawl back into bed, dummy." She stuck out her tongue. "Go home, Donny." Later, the truck back in its usual spot outside the farmhouse, Georgia locked all the doors and checked on her little brother, snoring slightly in his bed, his ears still red from the cold. Exhausted—and relieved— she crawled under her blankets without taking off any of her clothes.

"Hey, Georgia," said Donny, pinching her toe to wake her up on Christmas morning, her mother wondering loudly downstairs why she was sleeping so late. "If ever you need a ride, just give me a call. I'll always come pick you up."

chapter eleven

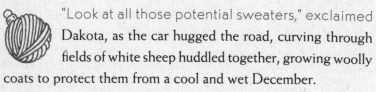"Look at all those potential sweaters," exclaimed Dakota, as the car hugged the road, curving through fields of white sheep huddled together, growing woolly coats to protect them from a cool and wet December.

"We're coming up to town," said Donny, slowing to make a turn as the highway curved into the main street.

Dakota drank in the sights of Thornhill, the tea room and the church and the dress shop, reveling in the comfortable familiarity of the town where her Gran lived. The air was a bit foggy and overcast, and although technically still daylight hours, the overall effect felt like evening. Holly wreaths decorated doors here and there, twinkling lights glowed on several windows, a string of festive bulbs crisscrossed the high street, and all around the side of the road lay a good coating of snow. Southern Scotland was kitted out for the holidays.

There were two places in the world where Dakota felt most

content: Walker and Daughter, and Gran's cozy little bungalow in this rather tiny Scottish town. "My second home," she said to Donny.

"Mine, too," he replied, turning up the driveway toward Gran's home, the heavy wooden front door open and Gran already standing on the step, waving with her right hand and holding a pair of needles and what looked to be a checkered scarf in the other. Dakota rushed out the door to hug her great-grandmother, who wore her Gran uniform of black oxfords, red cardigan, and a head of freshly permed white curls.

"You look just like yourself," exclaimed Dakota, as her uncle began unloading suitcases from the car. "Though I think you've shrunk, Gran. You're quite shrimpy."

"I shan't listen," said Gran, who, although she was in her late nineties, liked to play coy with the facts of aging. "I'm as tall as I ever was. Taller, even."

Dakota whispered in Gran's ear as Gran listened and nodded. James pulled up with Bess and Tom, and after a moment of warm greetings, Gran launched into issuing instructions about who was to go where.

"We've a full house, no doubt about it," she announced, leading them into the lounge. The house hadn't changed in years, with its coal-burning stove and navy love seats, the rose wallpaper, and the tiny, sunny kitchen with its compact white appliances and the nook that looked into the back garden and gave a peek of the farm fields farther still. "You're with me, Dakota," she said. "I've put Tom and Bess into the good guest bedroom, and James and Donny will have to fight it out in the sewing room. There's a daybed that neither of you will quite fit on and one of those blow-up airbeds. Nancy Reid picked it up for me at Jenner's in Edinburgh."

Bess frowned. "Nancy said to say hello to you, Tom," said Gran, a twinkle in her eye. "And to you as well, Bess."

"Old girlfriend," whispered Donny to James and Dakota. "Gran always likes to stir the pot."

"Wouldn't she have been his girlfriend, like, forty-five years ago?" asked Dakota.

"At least," said Donny. "Plus, she's married and lives a few farms over. Gran's just needling Mom."

"I never knew," murmured Dakota, widening her eyes at her uncle.

"Gran's an angel, Dakota," whispered Donny. "But that doesn't mean she won't play the devil sometimes."

"I can hear you talking, Donald," said Gran.

"I think we're about to have quite a Christmas," James said to his daughter, dropping his voice very low. "And I want to talk to you about Sandra. I spent all afternoon discussing the sale of farmland for housing developments and what I really wanted was to spend my drive with you."

"We'll get some time, Dad, I promise," said Dakota, lugging her suitcase down the short hallway to Gran's bedroom, with its flowered bedspread, white pillowcases with colorful embroidered edges, and green afghan tossed over an old armchair that had probably been moved to the bedroom during a redecorating spree in 1957. She unpacked speedily, knowing Gran would never stand for her living out of a suitcase, hanging a dress in the wardrobe next to Gran's row of five collared white blouses, black slacks, and light-blue suit with ruffled edge. She put her sweats in the drawer in the space Gran had made, next to her cardigans stacked neatly in piles of red, green, or blue, and she put her extra pajamas next to Gran's pale-pink full-length long-sleeved nightdress. The drawer smelled of gardenias from a sachet tucked in the corner. All in all, it was cozy, just as a great-grandmother's home should be, thought Dakota.

"I just pulled out the shortbread." Gran poked her head in the doorway just as Dakota was tucking her suitcase—empty except for a few gifts—underneath the high double bed. "Good job, young lady. Come on now for a bite."

The group, faces and hands washed per Gran's edict, crowded around her kitchen, extra chairs brought in from the dining room. Biscuits and cheddar and bowls of canned fruit dotted the same scratched old wooden table where Dakota had sat with her mother and Catherine and had her first Scottish tea, and where she and James had enjoyed many a chat during their trips to see Gran over the years. It was also, she thought, as she looked around the crowded room, where her uncle Donny had eaten breakfast with his older sister when they flew over after harvest season every few years, and most likely where her white-haired grandfather had eaten his supper after a long day of learning sums and helping with the sheep and the fields.

"I suppose I should have just brought everything to the dining table," said Gran. "We don't fit properly."

"No, Gran," said Dakota. "This is good. It's perfect."

"Good," said Gran. "It's early supper and then to bed." She

pointed a finger at James and Donny. "No staying up late talking, either. You two will have to chop down the tree in the morning. Dakota and I will select it."

The entire committee trooped after Gran, who'd popped out of the car as soon as it was stopped and began leading the way to the old bog called Flanders Moss.

"Should we really be cutting down a live tree, Gran?" worried Dakota. "Don't you have an artificial one in the attic?"

"Pish," said Gran, pursing her lips. "The town needs to clear the bog, and the trees are going begging. Besides, I thought we'd decorate both trees this year, do a boys' tree and the girls' tree. Get a little posh by having two trees. I've never done that in all my years."

"Dakota and I decorate the tree every year when we're in Pennsylvania," said Bess, a few steps behind but not out of earshot. "Don't we, Dakota? It's very special."

"Yeah, Grandma," said Dakota, feeling strangely caught between the two women though no one was doing anything specific. It was just that everyone seemed to want her attention or to tell her a story. Gran had told her that just because the boys had to go to bed didn't mean she couldn't have a little chat with Dakota, snuggling in bed with her and sharing stories about holidays during the war. When everything was rationed and she was nearly out of sugar, making the tiniest shortbread to put in her boys' stockings, empty and waiting at the foot of the bed.

"I took an old sweater of my husband's, undid all the stitches, rewound the yarn, and made slippers and mittens for my boys," she told Dakota. "And then my neighbor came over and helped me fix up an old bicycle Tom and his brother could share. She was mechanical, and I had the green thumb, and between the two of us we kept our farms going while the men were overseas."

The bicycle overjoyed Tom, she said, who declared he was going to cycle to Germany to bring his father home for Hogmanay.

"That's Scottish New Year," Gran had said. "It was a big deal back in the day, when we used to drink to the chime of the bells and sing 'Auld Lang Syne.'" Dakota had hunkered down in the covers and drifted off to sleep listening to her Gran's slightly reedy voice sing, "Should old acquaintance be forgot, and never brought to mind . . ."

Now, this morning, she was as in charge as ever.

"There's the good one, Tom," yelled Gran. "Chop that smart-looking Scots pine, the tall one there."

"That'll never fit in your front door, Gran," insisted Dakota. "It's twelve feet tall."

"Aye, it'll fit," she said. "We'll find a way. Because that's the one I want now. We'll do it up grand. Chop, chop, boys."

"Glenda," said Bess. "I'd like to go to the store this afternoon so I can make some tarts."

"I have mince," said Gran. "That should do nicely, I think."

"No, I always make butter tarts," said Bess. "It's *my* tradition."

"Those were Mom's favorite," exclaimed Dakota, looking away from the men playing lumberjack. "Uncle Donny used to bring up an entire tray in the truck when he'd pick us up."

"Yes, I know," said Bess matter-of-factly. "I always sent those especially for Georgia."

Summer was nice, too, to be out of school, but good weather just meant a lot of chores to do. Since she'd officially become a big girl by entering kindergarten, her list of chores got bigger as well. So winter was much better because the farm was all quieted down, and because Donny was on his very best good-boy behavior in case he got caught doing something naughty. Which was all the time, she often pointed out to her mother. Santa ought to be notified.

"Are you going to bring over the chair?" asked Mommy, and Georgia was more than glad to oblige, puffing out her cheeks as she used all her arm muscles to move the furniture a few inches, then rested, then dragged it a bit more. This was their special time, girls only, when Donny was down for his nap—she suggested to Mommy that she ought to lock the door to keep him in there—and the two Walker girls raced to the kitchen to choose recipes from a big book on the counter. And then they could make it up together. Mommy was very particular, everything had to be done in just the right order, and all the cups and spoons had to go back to their very right spot, but Georgia didn't mind. She liked to see the big smile on her mother's face when she did something just right.

"One day you'll have a little girl all your own, and she can

make butter tarts with us every Christmas," said Bess, as she helped her daughter stir in flour, not even minding as Georgia spilled some on the counter. It was nice to have a chance to relax and just linger a bit with her daughter. Most hours she was running around to do all she could to keep the house tidy and meals well-rounded, and still help Tom with the outside chores. Her own home life had been different, her mother disorganized and forgetful, meals not always getting to the table in a typical fashion and the kids fending for themselves. Bess hadn't wanted to repeat that kind of life. But the concept of marrying a farmer had never entered her imagination when she was single. She had always envisioned a life in town, maybe even in an apartment in the big city, riding the trolley car to run her errands. Instead, she fell in love with a handsome Scotsman with big hands, who'd known only life working the land and intended to do the same in rural Pennsylvania. He kissed well. That's what had done it. The way he kissed. That's what led to the marriage, and to Georgia and Donny who'd followed.

"How many tarts can I eat?" asked Georgia, her ringlet curls gathered up in two pigtails. She was stripped down to her undershirt underneath her apron, to save on the washing, and the white blouse and cardigan her grandmother had sent from Scotland rested on an arm of the sofa. Georgia loved the knitted trinkets her grandmother was always posting over from the U.K., the soft-faced dolls and the multicolored mittens on a string.

Bess had never learned how to knit, didn't want to sit down with her mother-in-law and get a lesson. She preferred her own company, her own house, where she was the one in charge. Where she kept things so she could manage.

"One tart now, and one later," said Bess, gazing at the beautiful child that was all hers. She'd given birth to an angel. Two angels. And she wanted to say, "Eat as many as you want," but she wanted, even more than that, to be a good mother. She wanted to do the right thing, set an example. "Tomorrow is Christmas, and we'll have goodies then also."

"Maybe two now?" asked Georgia, watching the oven with longing.

"I don't know," said Bess. "We'll see." She heard the sounds of Donny getting restless in his room and knew she'd better act quickly or he'd be screaming. A good mother wouldn't let all the peace and quiet get ruined.

"I know," said Georgia. "Let's just bake them every year. Then I'll always get some."

"Yes," said Bess, leaning forward to surreptitiously smell the sweet scent of her daughter's hair. "That's what we'll do, then. We'll bake together every year."

chapter twelve

The smell of cinnamon coaxed Dakota awake, and she opened one eye to discover that Gran's side of the bed was empty. The room was still dark. She took a deep breath, imagining the gingerbread or scones that might be in the oven, and stretched, then tiptoed down the hall in her pajamas. The door to the sewing room was ajar, and she could see her father on the daybed, his feet hanging over the end, still deeply asleep.

"Gran, what time is it?" she asked, as she stopped in the kitchen, bending down to glance through the oven window to see rolls rising and browning.

"It's morning," said Gran, who was still in a housecoat and knitted slippers. "Even though it looks like twilight outside. No time to waste on Christmas Eve. We're having the cousins over tomorrow, and we'll need fresh baking."

Dakota yawned, wishing she could crawl back under the

afghan at the end of the bed, but the sight of her elderly great-grandmother washing dishes made her trudge to the sink to help. She reached over to hug her, practically resting her chin on the top of Gran's fluffy white hair.

"Here's a cuddle, then," said Gran, giving Dakota a squeeze in return. "What's on your mind, love?"

"Nothing," said Dakota, pouring herself some tea from the pot she knew her Gran would have made before anything else. She dropped in a healthy spoonful of sugar and a dash of milk. Leaning against the counter, she took a long sip and then another as Gran put down her dishcloth and stared at Dakota over the rim of her glasses.

"Nothing?" she prodded.

"You and Grandma sure don't get along," said Dakota, trying to change the subject. "Always grumping at each other."

"Ach," said Gran, as if waving off a fly. "We're just two old bats, that's all. Set in our ways. I thought we'd rather mellowed over the years."

"Not so much," said Dakota.

"She's a bit of a fussbudget," admitted Gran. "Probably mad because she likes things to go her way, and we're in my house now."

"She's always nice to me," said Dakota.

"As she should be," said Gran, filling up Dakota's cup and then her own. "Is that what's on your mind?"

"Oh, Gran, I'm stressed out," said Dakota, who didn't need much more prompting. She'd been bursting to talk ever since she'd arrived. "There's too much going on. Peri has a job offer and I don't know what to do about going to school and keeping Mom's shop successful. Then Dad got a new girlfriend—a real one, somebody serious—and I'm trying to be cool, but it's really bugging me. Why now? Why Christmas?"

"Why not now?"

"Because, because," sputtered Dakota. "I don't know. On the one hand, I want him to be happy. In my imagination. But I walked in on them, Gran, and they were kissing. It was . . . highly disturbing. I mean, not like you ever married anyone after your husband died."

"Married? Is your father getting married?"

"No, not that I know of," confessed Dakota. "I just meant it's not like you dated anybody after you were widowed. You just knew you had the one love, and that was that."

"Oh, is that so?" said Gran, sitting up straight in her chair. "You dated somebody?"

"Ach, no, not one man," said Gran, making a face. "And staying home alone never made me any less lonely. See now?"

Dakota got up to remove the rolls from the oven, signaling for Gran to stay put. Then, seeing that the flour was already out, she fished out a clean metal bowl to do some pastry.

"Mince pie?" she asked, knowing Gran was planning to make the very same this afternoon. But she'd been looking a bit worn down since her guests had arrived, and no need for her to stand on her feet all morning. Dakota would do the pies and then move on to sugar cookies, her father's favorite. And then, she hoped, there would be the chance of a nap.

"How do you think Mom would feel about it?" she

asked cautiously, her back to Gran as she cut in the flour and butter.

"If she was alive, she'd be mad as heck," said Gran. "But since she's somewhere else, she'd understand."

"Can I tell you something strange?" asked Dakota. "Lately I've been feeling mad at Dad for all that stuff from long ago. Like breaking up with Mom and leaving us alone." She stopped mixing, her hands covered with flour. "And I don't know why."

"It wouldn't change anything that happened after he came back, you know," said Gran. "Your mother's illness was what we used to call 'one of those things.' But it seems to me that the older you are, the closer you get to your mother's age, the greater your understanding of how she might have felt. Perhaps you can appreciate her perspective, and her hurts."

Dakota moved nearer to Gran.

"So, now what?" she said.

"Who knows?" said Gran. "You don't need to have everything figured out all at once. You'll sort one thing and then something else will come along. And then it will get easier. And then harder. It's a constant stream of changes and choices. The shop is just a place, Dakota. Your mother was more than her business."

"Gran, that so doesn't tell me what to do," said Dakota.

"No," agreed Gran. "But you can always lean on your family. Hurry and get dressed now. We've a big day ahead, and I could use some help getting to your great-grandfather. I do so every Christmas Eve."

Dakota changed into jeans and a soft sweater, then slipped

into her thick boots and heavy coat and accompanied Gran to the cemetery.

Dakota glanced around at the stones. "This isn't exactly my idea of Christmas, Gran," she said. "It's a bit morbid."

"Just an old habit, I suppose," said Gran, leaning more heavily on Dakota than she had during the last visit as the twosome made their way through the snow. "The holidays can be difficult. All these reminders of other times. Long ago."

After many minutes, Gran stopped at a square stone with "Walker" etched on its front and the names of family members listed below. Dakota saw her mother's name, Georgia Walker, after her great-grandfather's.

"Gran, Mom's not here!" exclaimed Dakota, worried that her great-grandmother was seriously confused.

"I know that," tsked Gran. "But your great-grandfather's not really here, either, you know. This is just a place for bodies. Not for souls."

"Did you tell anybody?"

"I just liked the idea of Georgia being with all the family and had it engraved so. No one says no to you when you're almost one hundred years old," she continued. "Remember to use that to your advantage someday."

Dakota used a branch of pine she'd brought to sweep some snow off the grave, hoping Gran would hurry with whatever she needed to do.

"So, now what?" she asked after a few moments.

"So, now we think," said Gran. "It's quiet enough here that a person can finally hear her thoughts. Say a prayer, perhaps."

"I don't pray, Gran," explained Dakota. "It's just not my thing."

"Definitely not," agreed Gran. "Let's just stand, then, and pay our respects."

Dakota waited, standing silently as Gran, she imagined, said her prayers. She watched the clouds roll slowly across the sky, and she felt the cold in her toes and wished she'd put on a second pair of socks. But her mind, even as she sought to be as calm and clearheaded as befitting a graveside think, still felt crowded. And her thoughts kept coming back to her mother.

"I'm sorry, Gran, but this is awful," she blurted. "Christmas should be about opening presents and eating buns."

"That's just what I was remembering," said Gran, a faraway glint in her eye.

"What?"

"There's a lot to learn from memories," said Gran. "The fun ones and the hard ones. Simple things, really. Just the idea that this was a real person, with a real life. With a temper, maybe. Or a penchant to be a bit of a grump. Not perfect. But loved."

"Yeah, okay," said Dakota. "But this is still weird."

"Do you not go to your mother's grave, then?"

"Sometimes," said Dakota. "Like after the funeral."

"All those years ago?" Gran was bemused but tried to hide her smile.

"Yup," said Dakota. "It feels weird to just be talking here, you know, chitchatting."

"As good as the kitchen, I'd say," said Gran. "Less interruption, perhaps."

Dakota rolled her eyes.

"Oh, there she is," said Gran. "My cheeky little Dakota hidden inside this grown-up girl."

"Not so grown-up," said Dakota. "I know I am kinda all over the place lately. I just feel so much pressure. As though I'm going to ruin everything. You know, make a mistake, choose the wrong thing."

"Can't have that," agreed Gran. "You might learn something that way. Though it would take quite a power to ruin absolutely everything."

"It's been a tough fall, okay?" Dakota sighed. "It seems as though everyone—Donny, Bess, Catherine, Anita—is just bursting to tell me all these sides of my mom. Like crazy stuff she did when she was a teenager, or that she loved to bake when she was a little girl. Details I never really knew. It's disconcerting. I thought I knew my mom better than anybody."

The wind picked up a bit, and the air began to feel moist, as though warning of snow—or rain.

"Memories add color to the facts," said Gran, sliding her arm through Dakota's for the return walk, moving somewhat more slowly than before. "All the different pieces, all the different relationships, come together to make up a life. You were insulated when you were a child, and now that you're an adult, you are growing to understand your mother in a fresh way. It takes some getting used to, this new perspective. She made mistakes, and so will you, and no one will love you any less for it."

"I remember my mom used to like leftover turkey sandwiches," said Dakota. "We used to eat them while watching the lights of the Christmas tree late at night, at the farmhouse in Pennsylvania."

"And if I recall correctly, Georgia sent me a pair of legwarmers she knitted for me in 1982," said Gran. "And I wore them, too, in the garden to keep warm. That was almost as nice as the Christmas we celebrated in October."

She and Donny spent weeks preparing for their visit to Gran's house, doing up all the chores around the farm and helping Dad finish up with the harvest. But it was worth the effort, thought Georgia, sleeping on the cot in Gran's sewing room, smelling the scent of grass from the back garden on the crisp, white sheets. Mom had been resistant to the entire enterprise, had insisted that missing three weeks of seventh grade would leave Georgia behind her classmates. But she'd done extra homework beforehand and brought worksheets from her teacher as well. She wasn't about to miss Gran. They were able to visit only every few years, anyway. And they hardly ever got to spend the holidays with Gran, posting their gifts weeks and weeks ahead of Christmas so they would arrive before the big day.

"Wake up," she hissed, poking Donny awake on the daybed. "Did you forget our plan?"

"I'm sleepin'," he muttered. "Go away."

"Donny, if you don't wake up this instant, I'm going to spill my glass of water on you," she threatened. "We have to go home tomorrow, and there's no other chances."

Stumbling upright, Donny reached out toward his older sis-

ter, who zipped him into a coat and then put on her outerwear herself.

"Let's go," she whispered, picking up a flashlight and a duffel bag and creeping down the hall to the kitchen door. "No talking," she warned, putting her finger to her lips. Donny nodded.

For days now, the two of them hadn't complained when Gran announced it was bedtime. Instead, they'd run to get their pajamas on, waiting for tucking in and stories, closing their eyes as soon as the light was turned off. Then Georgia would count, under her breath, to two hundred. Around which Gran would do her last check of the evening and turn out the hall light, and thus unknow-ingly give them their cue to begin. Using discarded funnies from the Sunday paper, the two of them cut out a series of snowflakes and then used fabric scraps to make Christmas trees in florals and ging-ham. With enthusiasm, Georgia tried to teach her brother how to knit so they could make round ball ornaments, but he failed to master casting on.

"I can't waste any more time teaching you," she told him. "You just cut, and I'll knit." And even though they were groggy in the mornings, and Gran and Dad would wonder why they were such sleepyheads, neither caught on to their late-night activities. And so Georgia and Donny continued with Operation Gran's Best Christmas until they had only one sleep left until returning to Pennsylvania.

Outside Gran's bedroom window, to the side of the front garden, lay an alder tree that was just the perfect size for Donny to climb. One by one, tongue firmly pressed against lip, he strained to place each homemade ornament that Georgia passed him from below.

"And now these yarn strings," she said. "Put them on like tinsel."

Donny took a handful and threw it at the tree, much to Georgia's consternation.

"No, with precision," she corrected. "Always care about what you do. Don't just go fast."

Finally, at the base of the tree, they placed her presents: a dishrag Georgia had knitted, a handful of cookies, and a photo album that Georgia had made of their visit, taping the snapshots to paper she'd colored and stapled together, and adding bubble captions above the heads of everyone in the photos. "I love Gran," she'd written over a picture of herself and the cat.

Without warning, a lamp came on in Gran's bedroom, and Donny practically fell off the branches in his haste to get down.

"Hurry. Be quiet," said Georgia, shushing Donny as he rubbed at his knee. She half dragged him back to the kitchen door, turning to admire their brilliant tree with its yarn and paper decoration, catching sight of a squirrel already joining in on the party by stealing Gran's cookies.

She dropped Donny's hand and ran over to shoo the fuzzy interloper away, tugging off her shoe and throwing it at him.

"Those are Gran's cookies," she yelled, her hand flying to her mouth just as she heard the door opening.

Georgia turned, one foot barefoot on the cold, dewy grass, framed by the oddly decorated tree.

"Merry Christmas, Gran," she said.

"Aye," said Gran. "What a happy October Christmas indeed."

The holidays were absolutely not the same as having a vacation, Dakota thought as she tried to sneak off for a quiet moment of knitting. She had a lot to think about since her long walk with Gran. But she didn't get past the hallway before another task required full attendance.

Gran was keeping everyone on the go, from hoisting lights onto the roof to assembling wreaths from the cut branches of the too-big-but-getting-smaller Christmas tree, tying the pieces together with leftover red yarn and finishing with a crisp white ribbon from which they could hang. They made a wreath for every window, and still the tall tree Gran had selected would not fit in the door, and she reluctantly agreed that the tree would have to stay outside.

"Do it up like you did that time," she said to Donny, and they put the Scots pine into a pot in the front garden, next to the tall alder tree already growing there. Under her uncle's direction, Dakota used lights and fabric scraps from the sewing room to add dashes of color. And yarn as tinsel, just as her mother had done for the tiny tree they had in their New York City apartment.

Then Donny and Tom had returned to the bog to find a more suitably sized Christmas tree, which the entire group admired as they set it in a bucket to prevent it from tipping, as carols warbled on an old record player that Gran ferreted out from the back of the closet. Dakota sang as the others hummed along, all sipping cups of mulled wine from the top of the kitchen stove and sharing secret laughs when Gran insisted on going up to the attic to point out the boxes of decorations.

"It'll be the ones marked 'Christmas,'" she said repeatedly. "Don't miss a box."

"She's a bit bossy," Donny remarked in a loud voice.

"I heard that," said Gran. "But I want to make sure you get the good ones." She removed the dusty box top to reveal painted paper bells and wreaths made from dyed coconut and ribbon, a few almost-crumbling newsprint snowflakes, and a cardboard angel with a lace-knitted halo.

"That's my angel," exclaimed Dakota, raising it up to show her grandmother Bess. "I made that when I was eight years old."

"Quite the impressive halo," said Bess, touching it quickly with her fingertips.

"Mom made that part," explained Dakota. "I did the cutting-out and coloring parts."

"Indeed you did," said Gran. "And it goes at the top of my tree every year since your mom sent it over. Donny, let's put her there."

She continued to pull out crayoned Santas and fuzzy snow-men made from cotton balls, childish, awkward ornaments going as far back as those made by her now gray-haired son, Tom. At the bottom of it all, coiled upon itself, was a series of thin, inter-locking rings knitted in every color of the rainbow, alternating ribbing and garter. Gran looped her finger through the top ring and slowly pulled out the string of red followed by green followed by yellow followed by white followed by violet. And on and on.

"It's a garland," breathed Dakota. "A gorgeous knitted garland."

"How unique," added Bess, who admired the neatness of the stitches.

"Put this on carefully, now," Gran instructed Tom, scooting over to the love seat in the far corner of the lounge to sit down and soak it all in. "Georgia and I spent years working on that garland, our international project. She'd send me the long knitted rectangle and I'd loop it in and sew up the ends. She and I always said we'd get the whole family together at a Christmas in Scotland, all of everyone. And now we have." Gran beamed at the room, at her family.

"This is just what she wanted," she concluded with satisfaction.

There was a heartbeat, and then another, when no one spoke. And then the timer on the oven beeped and everyone started busying about, setting the table and putting away the empty boxes. Each person took turns wrapping gifts in the sewing room and bringing them to the tree, while the rest of the house drank wine while they waited their turn and greedily devoured the butter tarts that Bess had been baking.

And even Gran said she liked them.

chapter thirteen

The coal-burning stove in the lounge was cooling, prompting Dakota to nestle under two of Gran's afghans and wear a pair of her hand-knit multicolored slippers as well.

"Can't let this Scottish chill into our bones, can we, kitty?" she murmured to Gran's fat orange tabby, who was preoccupied with stalking half of a dropped shortbread cookie. Dakota had decided, after talking to Gran, that not only was she going to finish the sweater her mother began knitting for her father twenty-one years ago, she was going to wrap it up and give it to her dad on Christmas morning tomorrow. She wasn't likely to get much sleep before the presents were opened, she realized, but she was determined.

She reached into her knitting bag for her circular needles, leaving most of the sweater to rest in the bag so the cat wouldn't sit on it, stitching her knots one after the other. She wasn't even certain her father would recognize the sweater, wasn't sure if he ever knew Georgia was making it for him. But as Anita had said, her mother had planned to complete the piece, had planned to give it to James that Christmas if complications from the cancer surgery hadn't gotten in the way. And now Dakota was going to do her work for her.

The cat jumped up to her lap, meowing for attention, batting at her circs with his paws. Dakota kissed the top of his orange head and gently placed him on the floor.

It was soothing, to be alone in the quiet of the tiny, dollhouse-sized cottage. To listen only to the ticking of a clock and to knit in the glow of the indoor Christmas-tree lights. They hadn't left any cookies for Santa, she mused, remembering how she'd slice up carrots for the reindeer with her uncle Donny, leaving a handful outside the farmhouse window in Pennsylvania.

She'd always had fun at Christmas when she was a little girl. Even though she was vaguely aware that Bess and Georgia didn't connect, she never really felt it had anything to do with her. It's not as though there were blowup fights, exactly, just a tense sort of formality when they spoke to each other. Which Dakota mainly ignored, content to wander about with Grandpa Tom and chat to black-and-white cows and observe Grandma Bess roll out pastry for tarts. The smells, the routines, the same old same old of their holiday habits, were what made the day special. And Georgia, although present, typically made herself scarce on Christmas Eve.

Dakota imagined she was behaving tonight just like her mother, no doubt, finishing up some last-minute garment the night before Christmas. Georgia never had much energy for her own projects, Dakota knew, too busy creating for everyone else. And yet she always had something homemade waiting under the tree, even something as simple as a barrette stuck into a knitted flower that Dakota could put in her hair.

She would do the sweater, she decided, and then she would sit her dad down for a discussion about Sandra Stonehouse. And this time, she thought, she would ask questions. And really listen to his answers.

Dakota finished a row and switched hands, starting again. Peri, she thought, would likely be doing a last check of the Walker and Daughter shop before racing down the steep stairs, her rolling carry-on bouncing behind her, to frantically flag a cab and obsessively watch the minutes tick by on her cell phone, hoping against hope not to miss her flight. How would it work if Peri went to Paris? What sacrifices would Dakota have to make?

She could end up more like her mother than she anticipated, she thought.

"There you are." Dakota turned around to see Bess, in a thin cotton housecoat, standing in the doorway of the lounge. "I thought we'd forgotten to turn the tree off," she said, coming over to sit beside her granddaughter.

"I'm making a present," Dakota explained. "For my dad."

"Aren't you tired?"

"I need to do it," she said. "It's from my mom. I mean, she was making it when, you know."

Bess glanced away quickly, then took a breath and returned to the conversation.

"She liked to create, your mom did. It's one of the ways she wasn't like me," said Bess. "But that shop was something. Never really saw it until the memorial service. Never had much cause to go. And yet there was so much to see, all those colors of yarns and on such a busy street. I nearly got hit by a car as I crossed the street."

"You're not a city girl, Grandma," said Dakota. "That's okay."

"Oh, I wasn't always itching to live with cows, that's for certain," said Bess. "I had my own city aspirations once."

"Maybe that's where Mom got it, then," said Dakota, still working up her rows. "You planted the idea when she was little."

"When she still listened to me, you mean?" mused Bess. "Maybe. I used to tell her stories some nights, if I wasn't too tired. Running a farm is hard, hard work. And I had two kids and a husband who required attention as well. I never felt I had the luxury to slow down."

"I feel that way a lot," agreed Dakota.

"Well, let me give you some advice, then," said Bess. "Don't be so afraid of messiness in life. I always was. Worried about having extra work to do. Or not feeling appreciated. But you know what? The mess isn't going anywhere anytime fast. The world doesn't stop if you take a break. And I wish I'd been more of a pest and found a way to ingratiate myself with your mother."

"It wasn't so bad, Grandma," said Dakota, reaching out to reassure her. She couldn't remember ever having a conversation with Bess when they weren't working on a chore together. She wasn't like Anita, ready to listen over a cup of coffee, or like Gran, who always knew just what to say. Bess was more distant, and yet Dakota could see that now she wanted to be a part of things as well. She just didn't know how to go about it.

"It wasn't so good, either, Dakota," said Bess. "I've spent years reconsidering my relationship with my daughter, and I finally think I've figured it out. I'm going to listen first and open my own mouth second."

"Uh, Grandma, isn't that a little . . . challenging to do now?"

"Sometimes it is and sometimes it isn't," said Bess. "It helps me to recollect some of the disagreements your mother and I had, to try and see it now from her point of view. Some days a fresh insight hits me quite clearly and I feel I know her better somehow. Makes me a funny old woman, doesn't it?"

Dakota shrugged.

Bess reached out an arm to stop Dakota from knitting.

"All my life I held back, thinking it was safer that way," said Bess. "But let me tell you, holding people at arm's length doesn't make you love them any less, and it doesn't make it any easier when something happens. It just means you miss out on the chance to get to know them. You remember that, Dakota. It's always easier to keep to yourself, but it's not always for the better."

"Want to learn how to knit, Grandma?"

"I might be too old now," said Bess. "It'll probably be a waste of energy."

"Nah," said Dakota. "It's just a way to spend some time together."

"But it's the middle of the night," reminded Bess, pursing her lips.

Dakota leaned over. "Live a little," she whispered, before reaching into her knitting bag for an extra pair of oversized bamboo needles.

"These are 35s," Dakota said. "They're like training wheels."

Bess wrapped her hands around the needles as Dakota put aside her knitting and, her arms around her grandmother, showed her the motion of picking up stitches. Then she did a slipknot, cast on several short rows, and, hand on hand, demonstrated to her grandmother how to stitch. After a few moments, Dakota picked up her circs and the two women sat together in companionable silence.

Tom ambled into the lounge, his gray hair poking up.

"Bess, it's half past two," he said sternly. "You haven't even come to bed."

"I know," said Bess, feeling more relaxed than she had in ages. "But Dakota is teaching me how to knit."

"That's new," he said, knowing his wife had refused to learn from his mother and then waited, without saying a word, for her own daughter to offer to show her. Which never happened.

"She's not bad," said Dakota. "I cast on for her, and she's doing up her first scarf."

"I am?" said Bess. "I didn't realize. Well, it might have been a gift for you, Tom Walker, if you'd just minded your own business."

"And I'm finishing up a present for my dad," said Dakota, finally lifting the bulk of the sweater out of the knitting bag, almost the full back attached to her circs. The turquoise stripe running down the length looked even more retro than before.

"It's beautifully knit," said Bess. "But the color. It seems a bit out of step."

"My goodness," said Tom, looking at the knitting carefully. "I'm sure I've seen this before. Did you tear out your mother's blanket to make this?"

"Huh?" asked Dakota. "It wasn't a blanket. I just found it among her UFOs."

"That's an unfinished object, Tom," said Bess. "Dakota's been teaching me all about the knitting-isms. Knitters are punners, apparently. Ewe'll love it."

"I see," said Tom, amazed at his wife's behavior. She reminded him a bit of when she was young. He pointed to Dakota's knitting. "That's shaped like a blanket."

"It's part of a sweater, Grandpa. You make the different pieces and put them together. Though it was next to impossible to find this pale turquoise," Dakota explained. "I don't think there's much call for the color. So I really had to search. Because Mom didn't leave much extra yarn with it. That wasn't like her at all—she always saved the right amount of yarn with whatever she was working."

Tom was certain now where he had seen this pattern before.

"My guess is that she used it for something more important," he said. "And I'm pretty sure it's in one of the boxes that James sent up to our place after the funeral."

"I never looked into those," admitted Bess. "But maybe I should."

Georgia stocked her extra change in a glass jar, her homemade savings plan supposed to leave her enough to buy Christmas gifts for Dakota.

"She's a baby," her mother had said over the telephone when Georgia boasted about her hopes. "She won't even know."

Still, Georgia collected her dimes and pennies, dipping into the jar sometimes when she was low on money for diapers. Or when Dakota had that bad cough and she had to pay for that pink syrup that the baby spit up for each dose. She was always meaning to pay back her jar loan but never had quite enough left over to make up the difference. Still, she considered her financial planning a success when she rolled up her coins in the middle of December and exchanged them at the bank for thirty-seven dollars.

Anita offered to take Dakota for the afternoon, and Georgia enjoyed the freedom of an afternoon alone, walking down the street without a heavy diaper bag on her shoulder. She went to three toy stores, comparing prices, squeezing the talking dolls, and admiring the stacks of games that went as high as the ceiling. It seemed there were a lot more toys than there were when she was a kid, and that didn't seem that long ago, thought Georgia. In the end, though, she went home with as much money as when she started, carefully tucking it into her sock drawer and thanking Anita for watching her Dakota.

"I couldn't decide," she said. "I want to get her something just right."

"She really will be happy with a cardboard box," Anita said, tickling Dakota. "She's barely a year and a half. Anything colorful will catch her eye, and then she'll be on to something else."

"I know," said Georgia, who wasn't entirely convinced. "But I only got her a rattle last year. How dinky is that?"

"Well, you certainly brought back an entire toy store with you," said Anita, nodding to the stack in the corner.

"Between you and my dad, Dakota is not going without," said Georgia.

"And your mom," said Anita, as Georgia shook her head. "I'm sure she's pushing that cart down the aisle of the superstore. I don't think your dad knows as much about Barbies as you give him credit for."

Later, when the baby was napping, Georgia whipped out her journal. She'd always kept a notebook—a different color so she could tell them apart—in which she wrote down everything, from her secret thoughts to her favorite pizza toppings. Old filled notebooks were stored in a box in the closet, along with some photos, her high-school yearbooks, and random crap from the James era. That's what she ought to do this Christmas, she thought, purge her old life. She carried in a chair so as not to wake the sleeping baby and clambered up to take down the box from the top of the closet. There were a lot of remnants of her life with her baby's father.

She lifted up a sealed envelope that he'd mailed, holding it up to the light to see if she could read anything through the paper. Nothing legible, certainly. Georgia tucked her little finger under a corner of the flap, daring herself to open the note.

"Nah," she said, tossing it back into the box. "If I had a fireplace, I'd burn it," she declared, remembering how her father, Tom, had taught her and Donny to burn their letters to Santa Claus in the fireplace, just as he had done during the Scottish Christmases in his childhood.

Georgia rummaged through the rest of the contents, coming across a needle raggedly broken in two. The sweater! That's what she had. She could take all the remaining yarn—not like she was ever going to finish now that he'd hightailed it outta here—and make something for the baby. A blanket, she decided. Her baby never needed to know what the yarn was intended for, and she didn't plan to tell her. Instead, she'd have the most unique camel-and-turquoise striped baby afghan, better than anyone else's on the playground. She ducked under the bed, grabbing a garbage bag in which she had a few projects waiting, the sweater shoved down to the bottom. She considered tearing out what she'd made of the sweater already but opted to leave it as is, an unfinished chunk existing as a reminder of the foolishness of believing in a future before it was certain.

She wouldn't make that mistake again. She wouldn't focus on anything but making a life with her daughter.

As for the thirty-seven dollars? Well, thought Georgia, she'd just use that to start Dakota's college fund.

chapter fourteen

 She always felt like a kid on Christmas morning, the overpowering desire to upend her stocking and hunt for chocolate balls causing her to sit straight up in bed.

"Wake up, sleepy," said Gran, attempting to rouse the lump of Dakota next to her, her mouth open and a mostly finished camel-and-turquoise sweater gathered under her arm. "You'll miss the holiday."

Gran hummed to herself as she ran a brush through her soft white hair, then chose a very special green cardigan with white snowflakes.

"I made this one a lifetime ago," she said, though Dakota's breathing indicated she was hardly awake. "It was Tom Senior's favorite. I wear it every Christmas."

The tradition of it all was part of what made Christmas so

magical, even though it had been decades since she was a little girl with a stocking at the end of her bed.

Gran knew, without question, that she'd awaken and put on this very cardigan that she only wore this one day a year, and she knew she'd race to the kitchen to put in the turkey she'd carefully ordered, and she knew she'd pour a last coating of brandy on the Christmas cake she'd been soaking for weeks (and a wee drop in a glass for herself), and she knew that she'd attend eleven a.m. services at the Presbyterian church in Thornhill, and she knew that the cousins from both sides would come over to eat her Christmas lunch in the rose-wallpapered dining room. She knew that she'd get out the good china with the border of leaves and vines, and the sturdy silver she'd been polishing for weeks, the table extended into the hallway with the wooden leaves she kept wrapped in cloth at the back of the coat closet and the extra chairs gathered up from the kitchen and the bedrooms, the stool that sat in front of her sewing machine commandeered for the youngest member of the family. She knew that they'd take turns snapping one another's gold-foiled Christmas crackers, twisting the tube apart so the goodies inside would tumble out and they could eat Christmas lunch properly, with colored paper crowns mashed down onto their heads to keep from sliding off as they read aloud the jokes and sayings from the printed tidbits of paper inside the cracker. And she knew her family would bow their heads to listen to Glenda Walker commence to say a grace for the food before the entire clan dove into the best meal of the next 364 days.

There'd be presents, and chocolates, and fancy nuts still in their shells, the cousins' little ones taking turns operating the heavy wooden jaws of the nutcracker until one of them dropped it on a toe, and there'd be the requisite crying but no parent would get mad and say, "I told you so." No, there would be only hugs, and little shared smiles among the adults, and no prohibitions on desserts. "It's Christmas," someone would say every few minutes, justifying another snack or a catnap or just an excuse to give a peck on the cheek and a bit of a squeeze.

The family would rise up from lunch and leave the dishes on the table as they gathered in the lounge for the Queen's address on the telly, and then clean up in the kitchen before heading out en masse for a quick walk on the banks of the River Nith. As the darkness grew, even though it was afternoon, they'd make their way back to Gran's cottage for a snack of smoked salmon and bread and butter, reveling in one another's company and delighted to have an excuse to see one another and catch up.

They'd comment on who had changed, and who looked the same, and who was working at what job and whether it was suiting them all right. Gran looked forward to being complimented on her hand-knit cardigan by every member of the family—and why not, as being worn only once annually meant it was practically brand-new—and she braved herself for the moment they'd all drink a toast to the loved ones who were gone. Like her husband, Tom Sr. And Georgia.

And this year, with the family all around, she knew they'd spend the morning exchanging gifts, and she'd been preparing for weeks. Had wrapped her gifts tidily and stored them under the bed. Going so far as to tie on ribbon, when everyone knew that just got torn off.

Quite simply, it was going to be a glorious day. The most triumphant Christmas, a perfect capstone to a lifetime of memories.

Gran padded down the hallway to the kitchen in a pair of her soft knitted slippers. After all, she thought, the turkey wasn't going to jump into the oven himself.

Dakota had disappeared behind the mound of crumpled gift wrap piled high on the love seat, where she and James sat opening presents across from Bess and Donny. Tom stood, coffee cup in hand, as Gran watched the entire proceedings from the center of the room, sitting in a hard-backed chair brought in from the dining room. She'd gotten a stocking after all, bursting with oranges and chocolate and a lacy knitted bookmark in candy-cane stripes.

Dakota had been bleary upon waking, coming around to the sound of pans being dropped in the kitchen, but the fatigue passed quickly. She finished the sweater as everyone took turns showering in the one bathroom, hiding out in Gran's bedroom and pretending she was still asleep. Caught up in the frenzy to complete the sweater, Dakota realized that all the gift wrap was still in the sewing room, where Donny was getting dressed. So, she dashed into the kitchen for the tinfoil and wrapped the sweater like a food parcel, tying it with kitchen string. It would have to do, she decided, as Gran rang a bell and announced that it was time for everyone to get their hides into the lounge.

"We're going to open one at a time," she said, settling into her chair with a large film camera in her lap. "And I'll take some snaps. Donny, you play elf." And, without a thought of doing otherwise, Dakota's forty-two-year-old uncle began handing out gifts, one to a person.

Donny reached under the tree to see if everything was handed round.

"This one," said Dakota, waving her tinfoiled package in the air. "Give Dad this one."

"I'm sitting right next to you," said James, the end of a candy cane sticking out of his mouth. "Give it to me yourself."

She handed over the present gently. "Don't just rip it," she joked. "I took a lot of time with that wrapping."

"Obviously." Her dad laughed. "Now, what is it . . . ?" He shook the gift so vigorously that as the tinfoil crinkled and crackled, the entire packet opened up and the camel-and-turquoise sweater flew right out of the package and onto Gran's lap.

"I know that sweater," said James, pointing. "I remember that sweater."

"My goodness," said Gran, picking up the garment and holding it out in front of her. "I'd recognize those stitches anywhere. Each one as perfect as the one before. It's Georgia's knitting."

"Just the front, Gran," said Dakota, worried that she'd miscalculated and that Gran—or her father—would be upset. "I'm

the one who finished the back. Mom was making it for you,
Dad, before I was even born."

"I know, I know," said James, stammering. "It's just . . . I
don't know. I haven't thought about this sweater in decades. It's
the most beautiful thing. From her hands. From yours. I can't
wrap my head around it."

"You like it, you really like it?" asked Dakota.

"I do," said James, rising from the love seat. "It's just that it
brings everything back."

*Georgia had been looking forward to the tree lighting all day. She'd
only ever seen the lighting of the giant tree in Rockefeller Center on
television, and now she and her boyfriend were going to stand—
along with thousands of other people, of course—and see it happen
in person. It was the New Yorkiest thing she'd done since moving
to the city. Best of all, it was free.*

*What could they do without cash? That was essentially the
discussion she and James had every Saturday morning, ready to
savor another weekend in the city but lacking any cash with which
to do anything. Their jobs didn't result in any extra income, and
after pizza and rent, they did a lot of walking around and window-
shopping, sharing soda in the park, and hanging out at home,
enjoying each other.*

*"We practically live together," he mused one crisp morning,
snuggling closer because the heat hadn't kicked in. "Maybe we
should cut out one of our apartments."*

"Maybe," she said, returning his kiss. "Let's decide in the New

Year." They had lots of time, she knew, so no need to rush. Besides, who wants to move apartments in the middle of winter? If New York in December was anything, it was damn cold.

She'd arrived at her desk an hour earlier the day of the tree lighting, so she could say good-bye to her boss and to KC and exit the door at a reasonable hour, burrowing into her cloth coat and fuzzy earmuffs—there was no pride when it came to the New York chill—and lugging along a manuscript or two in her worn backpack.

"Don't be late," James had teased her that morning.

"You, either," she'd replied. The two of them often found it hard to coordinate schedules, always leaving one waiting—at the movies, at the park—for the other.

But tonight was different. James had brought a thermos of hot chocolate, explaining how he'd bought packets of cocoa mix and then boiled water in the kettle at the architectural firm. Then Georgia surprised him by revealing an airline-sized bottle of brandy in her pocket.

"I bought it at the bodega near work," she said. "And it cost way too much for two sips of booze."

They mixed the two beverages together, sipping their toasty drink, surrounded by masses of excited tourists and a few New Yorkers feigning disinterest.

"No doubt they're just here because they have friends visiting," said James.

"And we're here because we love Christmas," shouted Georgia.

"And each other," said James, wrapping his arms around her as the switch was thrown and the multicolored lights on the huge green pine tree glittered. They stayed there, hugging and holding, as the other onlookers slowly began to move away.

One day we'll have a big Christmas tree, imagined Georgia, though she didn't say it. James hadn't even met her parents, nor had she met his. They were both broke, and, besides, everyone would say they were too young. Settling down at their age was fine in the 1950s, but the world wasn't like that anymore. She shouldn't be so foolish. Still. She loved him. She really did.

Georgia kissed James's cheek, rubbing her cold nose into his skin until he laughed.

I'd like to get a fresh tree, thought James, not exactly as big, of course. Something he'd haul in and put up in the living room. The room in the big house he dreamed about, something impressive, something to make his family proud. Sometimes, when they were grocery shopping or doing the laundry, he pretended he lived there already with Georgia. But that would be someday, in the future, he reminded himself when he started to feel nervous. She made him feel that way. Caught off guard because he enjoyed their chats in bed after making love almost as much as the lovemaking itself. That was new. That was different. Sometimes, he felt overwhelmed by it.

But tonight was just right, like the city was lit up only for them. That their little thermos of brandied hot chocolate was the most delicious dessert coffee in a five-star restaurant.

"C'mon," he said, kissing her hair. "Let's go home."

"Let's walk around," said Georgia. "I don't want it to stop. This is our Christmas together." In a few weeks, she'd go to her parents' and James to his, to spend the holidays as expected.

"Yeah, okay," he said. "So, what now?"

"Chocolate!" she said, as she dragged him down the street to the chocolate shop, James's eyes widening when he saw the price per piece.

"We'll just get one caramel," Georgia said to James. "We'll share."

"I'd like a pound," said James. "Actually, I'd like two pounds."

"James, you can't afford that," whispered Georgia, worried and yet excited as the clerk rang up the triple-digit sale.

"I can tonight," he said. "It's Christmas."

The clerk shot them a quizzical look.

"Today is Christmas for us," she explained, grinning. "We just saw our tree. You know, the big one."

"We come from GeorgiaJamesville," said James as Georgia giggled, clutching his arm. "You've probably never heard of the place. But we like it. We love it."

The twosome wandered over to the Avenue of the Americas to eat their supper of chocolates, sitting on the edge of a planter across from Radio City Music Hall as they watched ticket holders rushing in to catch The Rockettes.

"This is freezing," said James, holding Georgia tighter. "Nice, but I'm still turning into an ice cube."

"Oh," said Georgia, trying to wipe her hands free of chocolate. "Let's not go yet. I have a present for you."

"What for?"

"For Christmas," said Georgia. "And now seems perfect. It's not done, but I'm going to show you anyway." She opened her backpack and gathered up a bundle of yarn in her arms.

"You got me yarn?" said James. "You knit? Like an old lady?"

"Yes and no, not like an old lady," said Georgia, dropping the yarn in the backpack and lifting up a small square. "Pay attention. This is going to be your sweater. Meet the beginning."

"Hello, sweater," said James, bending low as though talking to the stitches. "I look forward to wearing you. Someday."

"Oh, I'll finish it," said Georgia, poking him gently with the end of a needle. "I am better than you know."

"That I do not doubt," said James. "And I know I'll always think of you whenever I wear it."

Donny returned to the love seat as they all waited, fidgeting a bit here and there because they knew James. Dakota stood to go find her father but sat down again after a quick shake of Gran's head. Several minutes later, a red-eyed James returned.

"You could've gone on without me," he said. "I'm sorry about that."

"I'm sorry, Dad," said Dakota.

"No, no," he said, putting on the sweater over his oxford shirt. "This is the most perfect gift. It's a memory all its own."

Gran abruptly left the lounge, coming back promptly with five large, flat beige boxes, none of them wrapped. She handed them out—one apiece—to Dakota, James, Donny, Bess, and Tom.

"No more of this hiding our heads," she announced, clasping her hands together. "I meant to give these to you tomorrow. But better now, I think. We're going to stand up straight and not be afraid. We're going to celebrate."

She scooted over to squeeze into the love seat between James and Dakota, removing the lid of the box she'd given Dakota and lifting out a thick mahogany picture frame, turning the frame and holding it high, her arms shaking just slightly from the effort, so everyone could see the picture inside.

"This is the fearsome trio," said Gran, tapping the glass of the frame with her finger and lowering it to her lap. "This is Georgia Walker with her Gran and her not-quite-a-teenager daughter, Dakota, smiling on the high street of Thornhill. We look silly. And relaxed. It was taken, if I recall, by your mother's friend Cat on the day we put those prejudiced old biddies in the tearoom in their place."

"You guys hit a bunch of old ladies?" asked James.

"With words, dear James," explained Gran. "Glenda Walker has never resorted to fisticuffs."

"I beg to differ, Mum," interjected Tom. "I seem to remember a spanking or two when I was a boy."

Dakota chuckled, and then Donny smiled, and then even James nodded.

"Open them, open them," said Gran, bouncing a little in her seat. "I searched through all the pictures I ever took or was ever sent to find the times when Georgia was happiest." She handed the framed photograph back to Dakota and pushed herself up off the love seat, coming around to catch another peek at each of the photos she'd chosen for every member of the family. There was James with Georgia the night he flew to Scotland to tell her he had always loved her. Donny and his older sister going for a drive on the afternoon he passed his driving test, making a big thumbs-up as he sat in the driver's seat, his sister riding shotgun with her arm wrapped around him. And there was Tom as a dark-haired young man, bouncing on his shoulder a little brown-haired girl with pigtails bobbing, her mother's hands visible in the edge of the frame, fluttering about protectively but not actually touching her daughter.

"Put these on your dresser, in the front hall, on the kitchen table," she declared, ready to march about if only she could get past the mountain of gift wrap. "I've lived long enough to tell you that these are the times you must remember. Not just holidays and birthdays. All the everyday moments. We may cry every Christmas, but we will not forget to laugh."

There was nodding and agreement around the room, as Bess, having waited her turn, finally opened the box to look at her photograph. Dakota could tell, by the flush in her grandmother's cheeks, that she was excited.

But instead of smiling in recognition at the picture, as the others had done, Bess dropped the lid of the box onto the carpeted floor of the lounge.

"Oh, Glenda, why?" she cried out, starting to suck in ragged breaths. "And on today of all days. How could you?"

Inside was an image of her daughter Georgia in a nightgown, her curly hair sweat-soaked and matted to her head, as Bess and Tom, dressed in their good navy suits, flanked either side of her hospital bed.

"Oh, Mum," said Tom, stepping over the box tops and gift wrap to comfort his wife. "What were you thinking? This was taken not long before Georgia passed away."

Gran, her back as straight as a ruler, took a few steps toward Bess. "I want you to look at it again, more closely," she said, pointing. She waited, and then, getting no response other than tears, cleared the love seat of the stray pieces of paper and ribbon and settled herself in tightly next to Bess, who stiffened as Gran drew near.

"I don't want to see," said Bess, craning her neck toward Tom, who leaned on the edge of the love seat.

"Then I'll describe," said Gran, caressing the glass of the photo frame lovingly. She beckoned to Dakota to join them.

"Look here," she began, "and notice how Georgia is beaming. I know her skin is pale. She's tired. But her face is absolutely glowing."

"It's hard, seeing Mom like that, Gran," ventured Dakota, feeling caught between her constant loyalty to Gran and still savoring a new sense of connection with Bess from Christmas Eve.

"Aye," said Gran. "But all these hospital doodads can make it so we don't see her beauty here. She's so happy. Joyous, even."

Bess couldn't help herself, turning quickly to steal a glance. Could it be true?

"I know you two had your troubles," Gran said in a quiet voice. "Sometimes, when life happens quickly, the good moments get overshadowed."

"That was one of the worst days of my life," squeaked Bess primly.

"But also one of the best," said Gran. "I don't want you to

forget this moment. We may not be soul sisters or whatever they call it, Bess Walker, but we both loved our Georgia something fierce, and it's about time you forgave yourself. This is my gift to you today. To remind you of what you've forgotten."

"I remember it all," said Bess, her face streaky and flushed. "Too well."

Gran leaned over and lifted Bess's chin with her finger. "Well, then, look through my eyes," she said matter-of-factly. "Because I see a mother and daughter finally fighting together. And you, see that right there? The two of you are holding hands," she said. "Holding hands, Bess!"

"We are?" Bess took the framed photograph in both hands. "Oh, Glenda, we are," she said, gazing up at the roomful of her family to let them know. "Georgia is holding my hand."

"You don't need to feel guilty anymore," whispered Gran so only her daughter-in-law could hear, as Bess nodded and rubbed her eyes with the clean, folded handkerchief Gran produced from her sleeve. "This, dear Bess, is the proof that your Georgia finally believed how much you loved her."

———

The kitchen was a mess of roasting pans and dishes piled next to the sink, as Walkers and cousins alike dug in to Gran's most brilliant Christmas lunch yet. The small wooden table in the kitchen held the final course of Dakota's mince pies, Gran's Christmas pudding with raisins and cherries, a trifle with layers of cake, fruit, and cream, and multiple china and sterling-silver trays bearing shortbread cookies, gingerbread people, butter tarts, and rum balls.

The entire extended family tucked heartily into the meal, enjoying seconds and thirds of gravy and turkey and turnip and potatoes and sage stuffing and thickly buttered homemade buns, all while keeping in mind the goodies that awaited them.

"There's nothing more Christmassy than brussels sprouts," announced Tom, heaping another mound onto his plate.

"Save room," clucked Bess. "You don't want to miss Dakota's pie."

Gran took a final bite, dabbed her mouth with her cloth napkin, and neatly placed her knife and fork on the plate. She cleared her throat, immediately commanding attention even as her purple paper crown slipped sideways off her fluffy white permed hairdo.

"I would like to say something," said Gran, fondly gazing around at all those in the room, her great-nieces and great-nephews, all the cousins, as well as Dakota and the others.

"Andrew, I would like to give you my washing machine," said Gran to her niece Susan's grandson. "You're just starting out and might have use of it."

"I think that's from the 1970s," whispered Dakota, as her father elbowed her under the table.

There was a series of titters around the room. Gran being all together in her mind must have been too good to be true, their bemused looks seemed to say. She's going dotty on us now.

"And that washer's still running, my dear," said Gran proudly.

"I have excellent hearing, or haven't you noticed? Now, where is my list?" She reached into the left sleeve of her green snow-flake cardigan, pulled out a tissue, and then tried the other side.

"There it is," she said, waving a folded sheet of paper. "Susan, I thought you might enjoy my toaster oven. And Felix, the wheelbarrow."

"I work on a cruise ship, Auntie," said a slight gray-haired old gent. "I've no garden."

"Quite right," said Gran. "I just remembered how you and Tom used to play in the garden back when you were schoolboys. No matter, we'll leave it here."

"Don't you need these things, Gran?" asked Dakota, look-ing round the table at relatives she knew well and others she just met, as one by one forks were set down and people leaned in closer.

"Not where I'm going," Gran declared, to a collective gasp around the table.

"Are you sick?"

"Is everything all right?"

"Why haven't you told us?"

Questions flew around the room as everyone spoke all at once.

"Oh, pish!" said Gran, knocking on the table to make a loud noise and recapture her guests' focus. "Today's lunch notwith-standing, I decided a few months ago that I am quite done with dinner."

"What?"

"The making of it, I mean," she said, her eyes twinkling. "I

still intend to eat as much as I can. So you can wipe those horrified looks off your faces. I'm not dying anytime soon."

"Are you getting a cook, Gran?" ventured Dakota.

"Better than that," said Gran. "I'm moving into a small bedsit
in a deluxe residence for active golden-agers. Where they serve
your dinner to you and bring up the tea to the common room
in the evenings. All very fancy."

"You're moving? To an old folks' home?" Dakota's eyes
bulged.

"Not for old folks," said Gran. "Only *active* seniors can move
in here. So you can do the aerobics, you see."

"It'll be nothing but shuffleboard and bridge, Gran," implored
Dakota. "You won't like it. You wouldn't be happy there."

"Now, now," said Gran. "I think I might rather like to join a
shuffleboard league. Maybe they'll make me captain."

Dakota shot a look at her uncle, her eyes begging him to
do something. Donny held up his palm. *Hold on*, he mouthed.
It's okay.

"It's a shock when things change," continued Gran, settling
back into her chair, reveling in holding court over the Christmas table. "But I'm not going far, only to Dumfries. And I'm
leaving on my own terms. I'm not being warehoused. I'm finally
giving in to my inner lazybug. It's my turn to be pampered, don't
you think?"

"Why didn't you say anything?" asked Dakota.

"And have everyone moaning about, bellyaching about our
last Christmas in the old cottage?" said Gran. "No, thank you!"

I, for one, intended to have my best Christmas ever, and so I have done."

"What about the farm?" asked James, considering the practical side of things. "Are you going to sell?"

"Not exactly," admitted Gran. "I've made an arrangement with the new owner that I'm able to keep my room as it is and visit on weekends if I like."

The room was absolutely still. Everyone inched closer to hear.

"It's me," admitted Donny, rising slightly from his seat. "I've agreed to move to Scotland to take over Gran's farm. There are a lot of new things I want to try with the organics, and it's just the right size."

"What about everything in Pennsylvania?" asked Dakota, still feeling off kilter. Although reassured the farm would still be here, that she could hold on to knowing this special place just a bit longer, she knew she'd still have to adapt. To embrace the fact that the circumstances were all changing. That life was constantly in flux. Just when she got all used to one thing, something else would come along. Just like Gran was always saying.

"More corporations are getting into organics," explained Donny. "I leased out my land back in the U.S."

"And, truth be told, we've done the same," said Tom. "We're keeping the house, but the fields are all going to be managed by a company." He caught the gaze of one of his cousins, nodding as he spoke. "We're frankly ready to retire. Bess has done it my way for a long time, and it seemed about right that I should try it hers."

kate jacobs

"So you're moving to Florida or something," said Dakota, incredulous. Why, she wondered, did everyone seem to have a magic "go south" date? "You're not all going to old folks' homes, are you? Dad, you next?"

"We're not old," said Bess. "We're simply moving into a new phase. Maybe going to get a condo somewhere. Or take a photo safari."

"A safari sounds quite smart, my dear," said Gran. "I know I always liked the elephants at the circus."

"A safari? Are you kidding me?" said Dakota.

"It's just an idea," said Bess. "It's never too late. Do you have room for that pie now, Tom?"

"I do," said Dakota's grandfather, as the family shuffled the dirty plates off the table and helped carry in the decadent desserts. Dakota sat glued to her seat as she watched the procession of pie and tart and cake from kitchen to table, dumbfounded that anyone could be thinking of eating after the news they'd just heard.

"One of everything, I presume?" asked Gran, scooping some trifle into a bowl and passing desserts down the length of the table. "After all, it's Christmas, isn't it?"

James rested on the love seat, dozing off the humongous meal, as Gran paid close attention to the Queen on the BBC. The extended family made themselves at home, and Bess slowly stitched up her scarf as Tom looked on in admiration. Donny and Dakota, dish towels over shoulders, strolled into the lounge to pick up the last of the teacups.

"This truly was a wonderful lunch, Mum," said Tom, patting his stomach. "You outdid yourself today."

"Well, I had help," confessed Gran.

"To Dakota," said James, holding up his china teacup.

"And to Bess," added Gran. "Let's toast Georgia's mom as well."

"Hear, hear," said Tom, rising. "To all our family, each one of us here tonight. May the blessings of the holidays keep us safe and happy throughout the coming year. And for my dad, Tom Senior, and my beautiful daughter, Georgia. Here's hoping the turkey is just as delicious in heaven."

chapter fifteen

The crowd was larger than she'd expected, commented Gran, counting heads and nodding appreciatively. Attending was a last-minute decision, debated as they lolled about on the furniture, feeling well fed and content, chatting about everything from the morning sermon to the Queen's outfit on television. But then Gran had clucked her tongue, pulled off her multicolored knitted slippers to reveal the cozy hand-knit white cotton socks underneath, and announced that they ought to all get their boots on. It would be bad form to miss the Christmas concert on the lawn of Trigony House just outside of Thornhill, she declared. Students of all ages, and a few talented parents, had been rehearsing long hours to put on a show.

They'd taken the two rental cars but, due to the earlier arrival of like-minded townspeople, found themselves having to park at the end of the long driveway, joining the procession of con-

certgoers marching up to the seats, kisses and hugs and greetings of "Happy Christmas" being tossed out liberally. Gran was
stopped every few seconds by someone—from the gray-haired
children of old friends to the girl who came out to wash the
windows twice a year—who wanted to wish her well.

"She's like the queen of Thornhill," Dakota murmured to her
uncle. "What if she misses it when she goes to that old folks'
home?"

"Being sad to go isn't always a reason to stay," replied Donny.
"Sometimes going in a new direction—even when it wasn't in
your initial plan—can actually turn out to be the best thing."

"Maybe," said Dakota, considering. She slowed her step to
distance herself from her family, watching how they moved—
Bess with her small steps, James with his brisk pace, Donny
pumping his arms, Tom's hands in his pockets, tiny Gran with
her shockingly good posture. *Here we all are, together, making a memory*, she acknowledged. She knew there would come a moment
when she'd want to call up this image in her mind's eye, this row
of her scarved and hatted loved ones strolling on a most special
Christmas. They'd never been all together in this manner before, and Dakota knew it was highly unlikely that they'd ever be
this way again. Her elderly Gran, still so strong and yet slowing
down. Her own father, possibly, might want to move in new
directions as well.

"Who knows where we'll all be in a year?" she whispered to
herself, aware that she hadn't been able to anticipate the developments of the previous year, from her starting culinary school
to learning Peri had a job offer in Paris.

What will happen to the shop? To my family? To me? Dakota thought anxiously. She hated that she had no idea, had no means of reading into the future. That no one did. Too often, she knew, change simply morphed into loss. And she'd had enough of that in her life already.

She saw her father extend his arm as Gran, not breaking her purposeful stride, accepted the help, her head bobbing slightly as she still glanced down to watch where she was stepping. Careful of the ice and snow. Dakota saw Bess and Tom, more affectionate than she'd ever seen them, Bess tugging on the sleeve of his coat as they intertwined a few gloved fingers, exchanged a private grin. Starting out all over again, she supposed, freed of the strain of the farm in Pennsylvania. And Donny, excited about his new adventure, glancing around to see all the Thornhill folks who would be his neighbors and might well—he hoped— become his friends.

The musicians were tuning their instruments, and girls in tartan dresses were handing out programs, the songs and lyrics listed. Chairs had been set up on the lawn, and, just as in all movie theaters, twosomes and foursomes had positioned themselves to leave a seat here or there between them. There were several empty seats but not enough for the entire family, and so the group split.

"I'll go with Dakota," said Bess, surprising her granddaughter. "I tucked my knitting into my purse. The rest of you can go near the front."

"I'll sit with Dakota," said James. "I'd like to chat. I've hardly seen her since we've arrived."

"No, no," said Bess. "You always get to have her. Let me have one more turn." She pointed at some nearby seats. "We won't be far."

"So, are you looking into Harrisburg proper, Grandma?" Dakota asked Bess, as the two settled in.

"Who said anything about Harrisburg?" said Bess. "No, I want change. Philadelphia, perhaps. Or maybe even Los Angeles."

"You don't strike me as very L.A., Grandma," said Dakota, taking in her gray-haired grandmother in her frilly colored blouse and thick, black winter coat.

"I don't know what I want to be," said Bess. "But it'll come down to costs, of course. We won't be having the penthouse at the Ritz, but we'll do fine. I might get a little job."

"At your age?"

"Your friend Anita is almost a decade older than I am, young lady," said Bess. "And you don't think that's strange."

"Yeah, but she's . . ." Dakota struggled for a word that wouldn't offend.

"Whatever she is, I can be the same," huffed Bess. "You don't want your Gran to move, but you're ready to put me out to pasture."

"Nah," said Dakota, opening up her program. "I actually like hanging around with you, Grandma. It's weird, but sometimes you remind me of my mom. She could be impatient, too."

"I'm very patient when it's called for," said Bess, as the strains of "Silent Night" began to play. "I've spent my life as a country mouse when I wanted to be a city mouse. And now I can do anything I want."

"But what *is* that exactly?" asked Dakota.

Bess leaned in conspiratorially. "Unfortunately, I haven't quite figured that out yet."

Dakota could tell, by the intense way her father was staring, that he wanted to drive back to Gran's cottage with her.

"Hey, Dad," she said. "How about I ride with you?"

"Fantastic," he said, his face breaking into a relieved smile. "I thought we could talk."

"About me?" Dakota slid into the passenger seat on the left-hand side of the car.

"Sure," said her dad. "What's up?"

"Nah," said Dakota, being playful. "You first. How's your new friend? Ms. Stonehouse?"

"Sandra, yeah. She's good, really nice," he said. "I bet you thought so when you interviewed her."

"More scary, really," said Dakota. "But seeing the two of you kissing kind of took away that illusion."

"I'm going to call her tonight, wish her Merry Christmas," continued James. "She's gone to her parents' house."

"Thoughtful, Dad," Dakota said in a slight mocking tone. "Maybe you're getting this relationship thing down. Finally. Don't need to run away for twelve years or anything."

James did not look amused.

"I cannot undo the past," he said. "This is the real deal, Dakota. Your mother was one thing. This is another. They're not the same; they're not to be compared. But it's genuine. I have real feelings for Sandra, and I need you to recognize that."

"Some things are hard, Dad." Dakota looked out the window as the car moved down the road, wishing she was standing out with the sheep in the fields. Or doing more dishes with Gran. Or knitting with Bess. Or playing Scrabble with Tom and Donny. Just anywhere but here.

"We're taking a step," ventured James. "A big step."

"Oh, not the two of you," cried Dakota, as James drove the car right past the driveway to Gran's cottage. This was going to be a long ride. Obviously. "Let me guess. We're going to have a triple wedding, and I get to be the bridesmaid at that extravaganza, too."

"*Noooo,*" said James, drawing out the word. "I thought you were happy for Anita. For Catherine."

"I am," said Dakota. "I'm happy, happy, happy. But it's just like 'splat.' Everything is happening all at once. Weddings and marriages, and Roberto came back, and that was just plain awkward. Old loves are better in the past, Dad."

James raised his eyebrows as his daughter continued to rant. He'd choose to assume he was the exception to the rule.

"Then it's eat up the turkey, happy last Christmas, because Gran is deep-sixing the farm." She twisted in her seat to view her father more clearly. "Gran thinks going to an old-age home is all about captaining shuffleboard and doesn't have any idea how awful it's going to be for her. Donny is a . . . a . . . what do you call it? A reverse immigrant. How crazy is that? Who on earth does that?"

"Your mother wanted to do that," said James. "Had this whole fantasy she'd raise her own sheep for Walker Sweaters."

"But instead she died," shouted Dakota. "Died and left me to figure it all out. So it's still freakin' crazy. Why can't anything stay where it's good?" She took a breath.

"Good for whom?" said James, his voice very quiet.

"Good for me! Me! Me!" yelled Dakota. "There's enough going on in my life. I feel as though all my safety nets are ripping. Like I'm running around with my arms wide, to catch everything that's falling through, but I just can't do it."

James aimed the car toward the side of the road and stopped.

"Shout it out," he said. "Get mad!"

"Shut up, Dad," moaned Dakota. She wanted to cry, but no tears were coming. Instead, she just felt drained. "I'm terrible. Selfish. Me! Me! Me! Who acts like this?"

"Pretty much everybody," said James. "You're just more likely to say it out loud."

"I even hate that Grandma and Grandpa are giving up their farm," said Dakota. "I hardly get a chance to see them. And you want to know something? I like those two. I know Mom had her issues, but the fact is she was just like Grandma Bess, prone to having fits of temper just as often as being nice."

"It's a family trait," James said calmly. "The storm cloud of emotion. It usually passes quickly."

"Ha, ha, ha, Dad," said Dakota, leaning her head on his shoulder. "I feel out of control. That's my problem."

"Get used to it," said James. "It's a common part of being grown up."

"So, now what?" she asked.

James kissed the top of his daughter's head. "We roll with it," he said. "But Sandra and I are going to move in together. In the spring."

"Are you sure?"

"Am I sure we're moving in together," asked James, "or am I sure about Sandra?"

"Both, I guess," said Dakota. She liked sitting here with her cheek on her father's shoulder, with him kissing her head.

"Well, that's my answer, too," said James. "I'm sure."

He told her that Sandra was funny, and intelligent, and made very good French toast. That they'd known each other in Paris but had never dated until she was transferred over a year ago, and hadn't believed—until she saw him—in the rumors that James Foster had abandoned his player ways to become a devoted dad.

"So, you're saying I got you a real girlfriend?" asked Dakota. "Ick."

"I'm more committed and caring that I once was," said James.

"Double ick," said Dakota. "Dad, no offense, I get that you were pretty hot stuff back in the day. But first, you're practically fifty. And second, I so don't want to know. You can't comprehend how little I want to know." She mimed covering her ears.

"I get it," said James. "But just because I'm moving in with Sandra doesn't make me any less your father."

"Yeah, I know," said Dakota. "Big question. What's happening to your apartment?"

James chuckled.

"Good to see you're feeling better. I won't put it on the market for a while, if that's what is worrying you," he said. "You can stay there until at least September, probably longer."

"Dad," said Dakota, getting serious. "If you're going to have any shot at making this romance work, you can't actually hold on to your place with a wait-and-see attitude. Even I know that much. What about renting it out? To me, I mean."

"Well, I know you can't afford the cost," said James. "I pay for your bills, remember? And I was worried how you'd feel."

"I could pay for the apartment if I had roommates," said Dakota. "And I spend the week at the dorm anyway."

"Most twenty-year-olds don't maintain a pied-à-terre, you know," remarked James.

"I hear your point," said Dakota. "So, let's just table this part of the discussion and pick it up again later. Just don't say no yet."

"Okay," agreed James, more to maintain this sense of equilibrium than anything else. "I know this move is a big step. How do you feel?"

Dakota appraised her father. On the one hand, she'd had her outburst. So maybe she could tell him she wanted him to just be happy. This was true. Technically. But on the other hand, maybe she ought to just be honest.

"I'm kinda uncomfortable," she admitted. "I don't want to be. I'm good with the idea of a theoretical serious girlfriend. But in reality . . ."

"So, you'll get to know Sandra. Slowly," said James. "No one is saying you have to be best friends."

"I can't wait to call Catherine," said Dakota. "I wonder what she's going to think about all this."

"Oh, I don't know," said James. "She'll probably understand how complicated it is. After all, Catherine is marrying a man who has his own memories. She's going to become a stepmom."

Dakota narrowed her eyes suspiciously. "You're not leading in to anything parallel here, are you? Because a stepmom is not something I need, in case there was any confusion," she said quickly. "Either way, I don't want Sandra Stonehouse to think she's going to become my new best friend. She's not going to want to hang out, is she? Go shoe shopping?"

"No," said James. "Because I'm her new best friend. Not that we've gone shoe shopping. But I'm pretty sure I still qualify."

"I mean, this moving-in thing," ventured Dakota. "It's not just a precursor, is it? Like you'll invite me over for a barbecue and then a minister will be there and then, whammo, you'll get married and stuff?"

"Hold on there, Dakota," said her father. "I'm just figuring out my way here."

"It's just that I don't want Sandra—or any girlfriend of yours, I'm not singling her out—to not get it," explained Dakota. "I want them to understand I have a mom. Who was my friend. Who still is my friend, you know? So I'm not looking for someone to play parent to get into your good books."

"She's already in my good books," said James. "And last I heard, you'd declared yourself too old to need a parent. Who knows what will happen to your dear old dad because of it."

"I'm still keeping him," said Dakota, poking her finger into

kate jacobs

his shoulder. "Pending the outcome of the apartment rental situation."

"So we're good, then," said James, dodging the topic.

"We're always good, Dad," said Dakota. "But I can't pretend there isn't this part of me that just wishes we could be a real family. You, me, and Mom."

"I don't think that feeling is ever going to go away," admitted James. "But all we have is what is. There's no way for us to resurrect what might have been. And finally, I think I've found a new way to be happy. It's something I never believed would ever happen again for me."

"Then you have to do it, I guess," said Dakota, sighing. "And somehow, we'll figure it out. That's what mom would say when I had a problem."

The scent of pine was soothing, filling her nose and lungs. Dakota lay flat on her back underneath the Christmas tree, the lights still on even though everyone else had gone to bed. It had been a good Christmas. Lots of butter tarts and an iPod from her uncle Donny, a knitted photo album cover that Gran had sent from Scotland, and an expensive jacket from a fancy store, courtesy of James. Mister Mystery Father. It had been a good haul.

Dakota felt her big toe being squeezed.

"Hey, muffingirl, you going to sleep there all night?" asked Georgia, before easing herself down to slide under the tree branches with her daughter. "Looks different from this perspective. Pretty."

"Yeah," said Dakota, reaching up to poke at the tree's needles. "I don't feel like going to bed."

"Seems a shame, doesn't it, for Christmas to end?" said Georgia. She wanted to reach out and hold hands with Dakota but knew her tweenage daughter well enough to resist.

"I waited all year for Christmas," grumbled Dakota. "And then it's just one day. One good day. But just the one."

"The letdown after the big buildup, right?"

"Makes me kinda sad, I guess," admitted Dakota.

"Well, there'll be another Christmas next year," said Georgia, giving in to her urge and snuggling in close to her daughter. Miraculously, Dakota didn't budge. Maybe, even, if Georgia was correct, she was leaning in. Just a tiny bit.

"But it won't be the same," said Dakota. "I'll be older. I'll be a teenager."

"That's okay," insisted Georgia. "You'll still be my muffingirl when you're fifty-two. Even eighty-two."

"Don't tease, Mom," said Dakota.

"Okay," said Georgia, lying side by side with her beautiful daughter, taking in the intoxicating aroma of the tree and the glittering, twinkling lights. "No teasing. We'll find a way to work it all out. We'll just stay here together. All night. That way our perfect Christmas never has to end."

the new year

This is the most powerful of tomorrows: one moment that overflows with renewal, with resolution. The exhilaration of being able to start anew, when there are no mistakes. Not yet, anyway. In a similar way, each knitting project starts fresh—yarn still untouched—and all outcomes are possible. So grab your needles. It's the only way to ever know what the result will be.

chapter sixteen

Although there was mention of a possible blizzard in the weather reports, the city streets remained clear of snow and slush when Dakota and James returned from Scotland. A good thing, really, because Dakota needed to get around quickly: She had to dash up to the kitchens at school in a few hours and mix all manner of batters with her classmates who were assisting on the wedding petit-fours project. The catch was that she had to train back into Manhattan tomorrow night for a New Year's Eve bachelorette party bankrolled by Marty and organized by Peri and KC. The men were scheduled to attend a tasting of regional Scotch at James's apartment. It was all quite a lot, mused Dakota, for a girl who'd never even been a guest at anyone's wedding. Ever.

"Not only that but you get to be maid of honor twice over," shouted Catherine, standing in garters and a tight white bustier in the spacious dressing room as Dakota waited on a bench near the three-way mirror. She'd bought a designer gown off the rack from a famous Madison Avenue designer and paid exorbitantly to have it rush-fitted. Now she stepped into the dress carefully with the aid of the sales clerk. "What a way to celebrate New Year's Day! I'll be a bride!"

Dakota had gotten used to Catherine's exclamations of "I'm getting married!" that popped out of her mouth with alarming frequency, and she'd been with her for only half the day. They'd run through table seatings with Anita and had a long discussion about whether the florist should make the centerpieces even taller, at which point Dakota determined that the safest course of action was to make as many *umm-hmmm* sounds as she could without ever venturing an actual opinion. Her scheme seemed to have worked: After all the chatter, everything stayed exactly as had already been decided.

"Is this all stressing you out?" said Catherine, peeking out of the dressing-room door before stepping back in. "Out in a sec."

"You know," said Dakota, "for once in my life, I feel surprisingly calm. I am drowning in to-do lists—and that internship at the V starts the day after New Year's—but I feel more in control than I have in a long while."

"Good visit with Gran, I bet," said Catherine. "That helped turn my life around back when."

"And look at you now," said Dakota, as Catherine glided out of the dressing room and toward the mirror. "You are stunning."

"Don't tell anyone what I look like," she implored. "I want it to be a surprise. Because I'm getting married!"

"Yes, so I've heard," said Dakota, raising one eyebrow. "Is

getting engaged like taking drugs? You seem unnaturally happy all the time now."

"I know," said Catherine. "It's amazing."

Her first wedding had also been a whirlwind: a miserable countdown to a big day she'd had little role in planning, buffeted between the whims of Adam and the insistence of his mother to have a proper society affair. Even if she'd hated Catherine. Oh, Catherine had been ecstatic, of course. But mainly because she had no idea what she was getting herself into, her brain addled by a fantasy future of living the good life and finding happiness as her due course.

Now she knew that true love was found somewhere between a feverish child and holding a flashlight in gum boots while her lover checked on the vines. Somewhere in the real world. And if she fell a tiny bit into the trap of bridezilla self-indulgence this go-round? Well, at least it was for only a short while.

Catherine wanted to hug everyone she met and encourage them to fall in love. The entire Christmas holiday was beyond compare, she thought, twirling around on the dais in front of the mirror. She'd hosted the Toscanos—er, her soon-to-be family; she had to stop thinking of them as one unit apart from her—as well as Anita, Marty, Sarah, and Enzo. Eight people in all, and Catherine, wanting to give them a feeling of home, had attempted to bake homemade panettone. Well, it was a first effort. She'd be better next year.

The timing meant she went over the wedding details with Anita each and every day (and yes, it was a bit odd to plan someone else's wedding and then become one of the brides herself).

But she also shopped nonstop, buying lip glosses and cute sweaters for Allegra, and a leather bomber jacket for her pilot-in-training almost-stepson Roberto. She shopped so much for the children, and picked up little trinkets for Sarah and Enzo, that it wasn't until Marco presented her with a glimmering cushion-cut diamond ring that Catherine realized she'd forgotten to get him any sort of gift at all.

"A good sign," he'd said later that night, as she apologized once again, and he meant it. Marco felt reassured that she, like him, thought initially of his children.

Only two more days, thought Catherine, and she would see him waiting for her as she walked herself down the aisle.

Dakota checked the clock on her cell phone as she exited the subway steps and hoofed it over to Walker and Daughter. She wanted to go over the holiday sales with Peri, and also just visit. Of course, she had hundreds of teeny-tiny cakes to bake, so she wasn't going to be able to stay long. Peri was putting together goody bags of candles, chocolates, eye masks, and knitted slippers when she arrived.

"Favors for our bachelorette party," she explained.

"This I like," said Dakota, peeking into the bag. "But something tells me I should worry that KC has invited oodles of naked guys to shake their junk around."

Peri laughed. "Because that's what Anita and Sarah really want to see," she said. "Nah, even Silverman knows there's a line not to cross. Of course, if it were just Catherine getting married, we'd all be at a strip club in Vegas right now."

Dakota waved at a few regular customers knitting at the table as she sauntered past the register to scoot up onto the counter. It was the ideal vantage point to look at the shop in its entirety, the rainbow rows of yarn, the light streaming in the tall windows, the shelves of reds and greens and blues and whites a wee bit low after a swift holiday sales cycle. She smiled at the black-and-white photo of herself with her mother taken years before that held a spot of honor on the wall.

"So, Peri," she asked. "Think you're going to miss this place?"

"I, uh, uh," Peri stammered. "How did you know I decided to take the job?"

"It's the best choice," said Dakota. "And it's Paris. And soon it'll be Peri Pocketbook all over the world. You must go give it a try. You'll always wonder if you don't."

"I'm nervous," said Peri. "I'm handing over my baby. Sure, I'll be president of Peri Pocketbook but a subsidiary of the major corporation. Plus I've been asked to oversee all the knitwear lines."

"That's a lot," said Dakota. "But you've got management experience. We have part-timers. Your new gig's just going to be on a bigger scale. So I couldn't think of anyone more suited."

"I haven't spoken French since college," continued Peri.

"Get those little tapes," said Dakota. "All you need to do is learn how to look mysterious and glamorous, and no one will guess you're not French."

"You mean I don't look glamorous now?"

"Okay, even more glamorous, then!" Dakota threw up her hands. "So, what about the boyfriend? Is he still the one?"

"I ditched him as soon as I returned from seeing my parents for Christmas," said Peri. "It wasn't just Thanksgiving, though his behavior was irritating beyond belief. But then I found out from a girlfriend that he'd updated his profile to 'single' on the online dating site where we met."

"Youch," said Dakota.

"Not youch," said Peri. "Because he called me the same day to say that he loved me. And no, he wasn't asking to come on over. But that's when I knew."

"Huh?"

"That he couldn't resolve the conflict between what he wanted and what his mother was pushing for," said Peri. "Then I called up Lydia Jackson and accepted the job. I wanted Paris more than I wanted Roger, and that sums it up."

"Wise moves all around," said Dakota. "So, admit it, aren't you a little thrilled?"

"I'm ecstatic," said Peri. "But I'm worried about the shop. I'm worried about Georgia. What would she think?"

"She'd be packing your bags for you," said Dakota. "And I know that, because I was going to march upstairs and do the same thing myself if you'd chickened out."

"What about you?" Peri frowned. "That's what worries me most of all."

"I am fine. More than fine, in fact," said Dakota. "I'm going to buy out your share of the shop."

"You are? How?" asked Peri.

"Not sure yet," Dakota admitted. "But I'm working on a plan."

"You know, I might refuse to sell."

"Of course you will," said Dakota. "All to spare me the expense, I have no doubt. But I'm going to make you a good offer someday soon. In the meantime, we'll just work things out, won't we?"

"You know it," said Peri, spontaneously hugging Dakota. "I'll miss you, you know. You're like my little-sister-business-partner-best-buddy."

"Hey, I'm not going anywhere," said Dakota, returning the embrace. "I'm already home. With the shop. My café and recipes. My mother's pattern book and her designs. This is what I'm meant to do. And so I'll always be right here."

———————

The dress code on the bachelorette party invitations was clear: Pajamas only. Slippers optional. The Friday Night Knitting Club was having a New Year's Eve slumber party.

"Well, I've never heard of such a thing," said Sarah, as Anita bundled her sister, in a pair of navy striped pajamas under her heavy winter coat, into the waiting car.

"You never can know with the club," said Anita, who wore an old pair of Marty's sweats and a T-shirt. No one needed to know what she really slept in. "I only hope someone thought to get some cushions for the floor of the shop."

But the car didn't take them to Walker and Daughter. Instead, all the cars that had picked up the guests arrived at a secret party location almost simultaneously. At a lovely hotel overlooking the very heart of the city on the last day of the year.

"We're in Times Square, everyone!" shouted KC in the lobby as she handed out the goody bags Peri had made. She was delighted that all was coming together, as generous patronage from Marty was able to make happen. KC winked at Anita and her sister. "Strippers come after midnight. Big, naked men!"

"Really?" gasped Sarah, clutching her coat tighter.

"No," said Anita, shaking her head. "Not really."

She entered the door to the hotel suite that had been arranged, a room filled with her dearest friends clad in sleepwear and nibbling on smoked salmon points and chocolate-dipped strawberries.

"Champagne punch," said Darwin, wearing a red nightgown covered in images of multicolored snow people, as she offered glasses of bubbly liquid to Anita and Sarah from a tray. "This is the first alcohol I've had since weaning Cady and Stanton. I'm on my third glass."

"Take it easy, young mom," said Anita. "I expect the whole family to make it to the wedding tomorrow."

"We will," said Darwin, beginning to rush her words with excitement. "It's the twins' first wedding, and I have the most perfect outfits all picked out, and they'll look so cute on camera—"

"What did I tell you when you called?" chided Anita.

"That I have to enjoy moments," said Darwin. "Not try to

capture them to lock away." It was difficult advice to follow. But after returning back to Jersey from the holiday with her parents (and Dan's always difficult mother), she'd spent hours upon hours downloading photos of the twins' second Christmas. So much so that Dan couldn't pry her off the computer.

"I have to record it all so we don't miss it!" she'd pleaded, secretly relieved when he abandoned his efforts. She didn't even join him when he'd bathed the kids that night, mousing and clicking as she captioned the pictures of Cady ripping open her gifts and Stanton climbing inside an empty cardboard box. Darwin had just been fantasizing about a Christmas some day in the future when she and Dan would laugh about these images with the twins, all grown, maybe with kids of their own, when she heard Dan screaming for her.

She knew immediately that the twins were drowning.

Ripping the mouse from the computer, she unconsciously kept it in her hand as she ran to the bathroom, flying through the open door and slipping every which way on the wet floor, much to the amusement of her twenty-month-old twins, who giggled and splashed.

"Nobody's drowning?" she cried, dropping the mouse and practically climbing into the tub with her babies.

"Nope," said Dan, still kneeling at the side of the tub where he'd been washing the kids. "But you missed their first full sentences 'cause you were too busy categorizing last week's photos. What'd you just say?"

"Wash me up, Daddy," shouted Stanton, trying to stand

but being gently encouraged to sit down on his bottom by his father.

"Wash me toe," said Cady, pushing her foot closer to Darwin. "Wash me toe."

And Darwin sat on the wet floor next to her husband.

"I may have broken the computer," she said to Dan.

"Good enough," he said. "Because I was thinking of doing so myself."

Now, at the party, Darwin held up one finger to Anita. "I'll take it as it comes," she said. "I'm getting better. I'm trying."

Catherine joined them, her face a mask of white cream, with Lucie at her side.

"Try this, then! I'm taking years off my age, ladies," she insisted. "It's crushed oyster shell from the French Riviera." She went over to talk to Peri, who, with Dakota's blessing, had just announced her new job. Already Catherine was insisting the club needed to take another field trip.

"It's actually not oyster shell," Lucie explained to Darwin and Anita. "I just told her that because I knew she'd love it. It's really Pond's cold cream with a drop of vanilla extract mixed in."

She took a sip of her punch and pointed to a plump woman getting her toes painted bright red.

"I put the same mask on my mother, Rosie, over there," she said to Anita. "She's doing great. The doc says the meds have her mind holding steady."

"She's not going to get back the memory she's lost," continued Darwin. "But the progress of the dementia is slowing down."

"And the rest of her body is A-okay," added Lucie. "So I'm trying to obsess maybe not so much."

"Not tonight, anyway," said Anita. "We have life and love to celebrate tonight!"

All around the suite, the members of the Friday Night Knitting Club and their friends were chatting and giggling, painting nails, playing at spa treatments, and sipping fruity drinks with tiny paper umbrellas floating inside.

"Hey," said Dakota, opening and closing hers. "I used to beg my mom to get me these for my pretty Anita Barbie." She picked up a clean spoon resting next to a display of fruit and cheese and tapped her glass until the room quieted down somewhat.

"As maid of honor times two," said Dakota, "I'd like to propose a toast to my dear friends, Anita and Catherine. It's not every day that a twenty-year-old such as myself is very best friends with two . . . twenty-nine-year-olds . . ."

"She read my birth certificate," said Anita, in mock horror.

". . . but you've both been mainstays in my life for many years now, and I couldn't be happier you finally have someone else to pester!" Dakota joined in the laughter, then waved the group quiet again.

"In all seriousness, it's also beautiful to remember how my late mother played a role in both of your romances," said Dakota. "Anita, you're the kind of woman who stops when you see a girl crying on a park bench. Kind. Openhearted. And fate, God, somebody must have noticed. Because this girl ends up living in a walk up two floors above Marty's deli, and you somehow stop in for your coffee every morning on your walk to the coziest yarn shop on Broadway and Seventy-seventh, and, after a long think, you and this Marty guy finally go out after ten years of chitchat about one sugar or two, and then finally decide to make it legal after seven years of living together . . . I'm just saying. This is more than coincidence. It's magical. This is meant to be."

"Yes, it is," shouted Catherine.

"And Catherine," said Dakota, "you're an adventurer, a dreamer, and in spite of a blip or two, a loyal friend. You met Marco because you wanted to open a wine bar next to your antiques shop. And you opened an antiques shop because my mother gave you the big, fat kick in the pants just when you needed it."

"Also true," agreed Anita, wagging a finger at Catherine.

"So, on behalf of my mother, and myself, I say, 'Here's to both of you and your respective grooms, wherever they may be. I wish you every happiness.' You deserve it, and if I may say so, it's totally about time, ladies!"

Dakota lifted her glass, as did all the guests, congratulating the brides.

Together, the group savored the final night in another momentous year as they watched the crowds gather in Times Square below.

"Get over here, girls," shouted KC, flagging everyone to the huge picture window. "The moment is now."

Even though they were many floors up, they could hear the million or so individuals chanting on the street, counting down

to the dropping of the ball on the Square and the official beginning to a new year.

"Nine, eight, seven, six . . ."

The women in their pajamas joined in the shouting, some
with arms around each other's waists and dancing along to the
counting. "Five, four, three, two, Happy New Year!"

Dakota watched the women kissing cheeks and hugging and
toasting with champagne. She raised her glass but stayed back,
watching. She'd planned to do so many things over the course
of the past year but, after 365 days, had to admit she hadn't quite
managed to get it all done. Such as the pattern book, for example. Or starting the reno. She sighed.

"Just move whatever's still relevant onto this year's wish list,"
whispered Anita as she came up behind her beloved Dakota and
slipped an arm around her waist. "You'd be a miracle worker if
you accomplished everything you wanted to."

"Still a mind reader," said Dakota.

"Or maybe every woman feels the same way," said Anita,
looking at the white flakes highlighted against the window.
"Look, the snow is finally here. Just in time to wash away the
old and bring us into the new."

chapter seventeen

The snow had continued throughout the night, painting the city and its New Year's revelers in a cloud of white. Anita and Sarah had snoozed in the bedroom of the hotel suite as the pajama party continued until the early hours, ensuring they were well rested for the wedding and reception later that day. Catherine, who insisted every woman try a little of Lucie's oyster-shell mask, eventually nodded out on the sofa.

"I can't believe we're finally at the wedding," said Dakota, as she sat up with Lucie and KC and Peri. Darwin had flaked out long ago, barely able to keep awake past midnight. ("It's the kids," explained Lucie. "There's no sleeping until they're about six.") She knew her classmates were—just like real wedding-cake caterers—renting a vehicle to bring down the petit-fours they'd spent most of yesterday decorating in buttercream and fondant. All she had to do today was keep the brides under control. Plus remember to carry an emergency kit of nail polish for torn stockings, breath mints, combs, hair spray, Band-Aids, tissues.

"Don't forget tampons for Catherine," said KC. "You just never know when there could be a little surprise."

"Good point," said Dakota, adding to her mental checklist. "Were your weddings like this, KC?"

"More like Anita's October wedding-that-wasn't, I'd say," said KC. "A lot of fuss about not much at all."

"So, what's the dealio with Nathan," said Lucie, as Darwin snored loudly to her left. "I want you to know I was always blaming Dan when I heard this through the walls. But no, it's our professor who has the deviated septum, apparently."

"Nathan's going to cause trouble," said Dakota. "He's done so every other attempt."

"I thought her sons were going to walk her down the aisle?" said Peri.

"That's Benjamin and David," explained Dakota. "Nathan isn't talking to them anymore. That's what Anita says."

"She's going to back out again," said KC. "Let's just call it. We're all afraid."

"Marty's only caveat to the bachelorette party was that I make sure we have no men—especially ones named Nathan—and our location be kept a secret," said Peri. "Last wedding he worked her over but good the night before."

"This isn't a wedding anymore," said Dakota. "It's a top-secret mission."

"So, what happens now?" asked Lucie. "Anita's always there for us. We gotta be there for her."

"We could sneak into his room and change his clocks so he'll miss the ceremony," said Peri.

"Do you know where he's staying?" asked KC eagerly. "Because I could pick a lock."

"No," said Peri. "I was just brainstorming."

"We should move the wedding and not tell him," said Dakota.

"Right," said Lucie. "Not like that's difficult. We'd lose half our guests to the change in address and the rest to the blizzard."

"Wait," said KC. "Let's not change the location. Let's change the location his car service is going to . . ."

"There's car services arranged for all the family," confirmed Dakota. "As maid of honor, I'm privy to these things. But I wouldn't know the name of the company."

"But I do," said KC. "Because Marty had me arrange cars for all of you tonight. Bet they used the same folks."

"This is wrong, guys," said Peri. "You know that? Anita wants him there."

"Oh, we'll get him there," assured KC. "We'll just get him there *late*. And Nathan Lowenstein may pull all sorts of shenanigans when it's just him and Mommy in private, but I'm not so sure he wants to make a fool of himself in front of his entire family."

"He's gone pretty over the top," said Lucie. "Remember the fake heart attack?" She mimed a fainting spell.

"You really think Nathan is going to stand up during the service—in front of a rabbi, no less—and whine about his mother getting married? In a room filled with people ready to take him on? I don't think so, girls," said KC. "This time around, the Friday Night Knitting Club is going to have its wedding. I am going to wear that damn fancy dress Peri talked me into buying, and then I'm going to eat more than my fair share of petit-fours."

"I made extra dark chocolate just for you," said Dakota.

"That's my kiddo," said KC. "Now grab my purse. I need to find the name of this car company."

———————

A string quartet played in the spacious and beautiful rented space in the Morgan Library and Museum as guests filed in to take their seats, which had been arranged in a semicircle, leaving an aisle in between. At the end of the room stood a white gazebo, in which white organic cotton had been stretched inside to form the huppah, the traditional open-sided canopy under which Jewish couples, such as Anita and Marty, were married. Catherine and Marco would also be married, by a justice of the peace, under the same gazebo.

"This is quite the show," murmured KC as she loitered around the entrance. "Two marriages, two faiths, two brides, two grooms. Two of everything."

"Only one maid of honor," said Dakota, sneaking up on KC in her strapless silver gown. She wore a very light, lacy knitted wrap around her arms. "Anita's asking about Nathan. What should I tell her?"

"He's on his way," said KC. "Then tell her he's seated."

"This is deceptive," hissed Dakota. "That's not good."

"This is manipulative," said KC. "Not the same at all."

"She wants to see him beforehand!" Dakota felt very uncomfortable.

"Kiddo, you are not very good at this game," said KC. "Tell her he was talking to the rabbi and you didn't want to interrupt. Then go see Catherine and stay occupied."

Dakota lifted the skirt of her gown to do just that when she saw her father in her peripheral vision. On his arm, as she had been told to expect, was his date. Sandra Stonehouse. She turned, just in time to see her father, in his tuxedo, and his friend, in a cap-sleeved red gown and sheer black wrap, smiling in her direction. Dakota moved closer.

"Hi, Sandra," she said, extending her hand. "It's nice to meet you. Properly."

Relief washed over Sandra's face. "Your father is very proud of you," she said. "He brags about you always."

"Well, he's said nice stuff about you also," said Dakota, beginning to sense that squeezed-up feeling whenever she thought of her father with someone other than her mother. "Excuse me."

She fought her way through the crowd of eager, excited well-wishers, an even mix commenting on how they remembered her when and a range of so-called gentlemen (even the oldies!) appraising her figure.

"That's how you know you're grown up," said Peri, catching up alongside and carrying a good-sized white box under her arm. "When they look at you as date material instead of like a daughter."

"Kinda creepy," said Dakota.

"Well, you look pretty smashing in that dress," said Peri. "And I helped Anita with your stole."

"A designer original," said Dakota. "I'm going to sell it on eBay when you're famous."

"Naturally," said Peri, letting Dakota go first as they entered the space where Catherine was surrounded by a team of hair and makeup artists.

"Oh, thank God you're here," said Catherine. "My stomach is in knots." She stood in her ivory-with-a-hint-of-sage halter dress, shimmering sequins outlining the generous V neckline and the hem of the trumpet skirt. Her blond bob was styled in a loose updo with dozens of tiny white flowers and crystals dotting her hair.

"You look like a movie star," said Peri. "Very chic."

"It could be too flashy," said Catherine. "Dakota, what were you thinking? Why didn't you pay any attention when I had them deepen this neckline? I like skin, guys, but what if I'm showing a bit too much?"

"You can have my wrap," offered Dakota, removing it from her shoulders.

"Holy Nelly," said Catherine, appraising Dakota in her strapless gown. "You look like you're at least . . . older than I want you to be. Now, listen to me. Go home with your father at the end of the evening. You're going to be getting a lot of attention to-

night. So put that wrap back on and pin it or something. If somebody is going to be revealing their assets, better it be me."

"You actually look very pretty, Catherine," said Dakota, re-
adjusting her knitted wrap. "Dare I say even tasteful?"

"It's nerves," determined Peri, presenting a substantial box
to Catherine. "I brought you a gift from Anita and Sarah. Maybe
it will make you feel better."

She removed the top to reveal an open-front sheer hooded
ivory cape with a thin silk knitted edging, similar to the finish
around the shawl collar of Anita's wedding coat.

Catherine gingerly lifted the cloak and placed it around her
shoulders, the hood puddling gently around her neckline.

"Here," said Peri. "There's a buttonhole on the one side and
we can connect it with this tiny, almost sheer, chain. It doesn't
cover up the front of your dress but you seem more . . . covered,
somehow."

"I'll take it," said Catherine. "After the ceremony, then I'll
va-va-voom."

Dakota dipped into her Peri Pocketbook clutch, in which
she kept her emergency supplies, and brought out her gift for
Catherine.

"Ta-dah!" she said, dropping something into her hand. "Put
it on the ribbon wrap of your bouquet."

"What is it?" asked Peri, peeking into Catherine's palm.

"It's a loaner," said Catherine. "Georgia's butterfly pin."

"Took it to a jeweler for polishing," said Dakota. "So it's very
spiffy."

"She would have loved to be here, wouldn't she?" said Catherine. "Only she would have freaked out about you in that dress. Are you sure Anita picked it out?"

"No," said Dakota. "I chose it myself."

Catherine looked down at her wrist to check the time and then realized she would have no watch all day.

"Time check," she said. "Is that part of your duties? Aren't we getting close to starting?"

"Yup," said Dakota.

"How's Anita?"

"Good." Dakota hesitated.

"Don't tell me she's backing out again," said Catherine. "I can barely breathe in this gown as it is."

"Uh, she's waiting for Nathan," said Dakota. "Only he's not here."

"Where is he, that dirtbag?" said Catherine.

"He's in a car that's gotten itself lost," said Dakota. "It's KC's plan. I only did nothing to prevent it."

Catherine broke out into a broad grin. "This is a gorgeous day," she said. "Listen to me: Do whatever KC said. Let's help Anita stand up for herself."

"How?"

"Let's start this wedding now," said Catherine. "Nathan is crafty—don't ask me how I know—but we're better off not taking chances."

"Plus, you're losing oxygen," added Peri.

"And my feet hurt," said Catherine. "There's that, too."

Marty waited, as did Marco, under the gazebo, for the first sight of his beautiful bride. He stood, smiling, waving to the occasional guest. Minute after minute.

"I should just text Nathan," Anita was saying to Dakota as Sarah kissed her cheek and left her sister to be ushered to her seat. "Just let him know I love him."

"There's a blizzard," said Dakota. "All the towers are scrambled. The message won't get through."

"Really?"

"No, Anita," said Dakota. "Look, I've got to level with you. Nathan *is* late. There was a mix-up. But he'll be here soon. And outside this door are your sons Benjamin and David, and they're ready to go. And there's Catherine, her feet swelling in her too-high heels as she waits to walk down the aisle to meet her happiness. Or Marty, who has been pouring coffee for years while dreaming of you. You've got to decide if you really need Nathan's blessing or if you're ready to just accept that sometimes people get mad at your decisions."

"Since when do you give advice to me?" asked Anita mildly.

"Since I learned from some of the best," said Dakota. "You, Gran, and Mom."

Dakota giggled, waiting for the music that was her cue, as she practiced how she was going to take mincing steps down the aisle.

"You are magnificent," whispered Roberto, and Dakota was

surprised at how much she enjoyed the compliment. "Don't forget we're supposed to dance."

"Don't forget you're supposed to be up there with your father," reminded Catherine, as Roberto blew kisses to his almost stepmother and winked at his onetime girlfriend. Maybe, thought Dakota, not everything had to change.

Both their hearts stopped as the music picked up. Dakota waited a beat and then moved forward, incapable of removing the goofy grin that was plastered to her face. Catherine, practically born in stilettos, prayed she didn't trip over their high heels as she strode up the aisle, discreetly waving to her siblings and their families, to finally take her place under the gazebo next to Marco, uncharacteristically shy and slightly embarrassed to be the focus of so much love and attention. Then they, like all the guests, paused. Waiting for the next bride.

They heard the sound first, before they could see her. A collective gasp from the entire room—of relief, of sheer joy, of being near her absolute radiance—as Anita Lowenstein, hanging on to the arms of two of her sons, followed her heart to her husband-to-be.

She wore a simple, square-necked white sheath covered with a smattering of tiny glittering crystals, topped by the exquisite shawl-collared knitted wedding coat that she'd designed and redesigned with her sister, Sarah. Dropping lower than the skirt of her dress, the wide hem of her coat glided along the floor of the library, creating the effect that Anita was merely floating down the aisle. In her shiny silver hair she wore one single lily pinned behind her ear, showcasing the sparkling sapphire earrings that her beloved Marty had given her the day before. Her blue eyes, as bright as the sapphires, shone with excitement as she approached the huppah.

"Yes," she murmured in Marty's ear before the rabbi had even said a word. "I *will* marry you. Over and over."

She gazed lovingly as Marco and Catherine exchanged vows with the justice of the peace, and then, when it was her turn, she twisted to get a better look at the roomful of guests. There, pacing at the end of the aisle, were Nathan and Rhea and their three children. He looked so much like his father, she thought, it was almost as though Stan was in the room with all of them. Gently, she rubbed Marty's hand, wondering if Nathan was going to attempt a power play, and then decided enough truly was enough. Ready to turn around, she waved. Nathan, nodding slowly, stopped pacing and raised his hand. And then, finally, he waved back.

Dakota stood, transfixed, watching guest after guest bite into their petit-fours. Were they smiling? Going back for seconds? She'd already watched Roberto eat three of each flavor, pressing him for his culinary reviews. Dakota thought back to when she once kept a notebook of the reactions of the club to her scratch muffins, grilling her mother about her friends' opinions of her baking. Some things change, she mused, but some things never do.

She watched Ginger stream on by with a tiny cake in each hand, icing smeared on her chin.

"Dance with me," said James, tapping his daughter's shoulder. Dakota turned, feeling secretly happy to see Sandra trapped in a corner with Catherine and Anita, who were very eager to know all about this new friend of James Foster's. "C'mon, Dakota! I'll show you the Robot."

"Uh, please, no," said Dakota, holding her dad's hand as she followed him. "Let's just dance like normal people."

Of course, there was hardly anybody with the chops to be invited on a reality dance show at this shindig, thought Dakota. They joined Darwin and Dan, wiggling out of step to the music, and Marty and Sarah, keeping it old style, cheek to cheek, as they grooved around the dance floor. Ginger, having consumed her cake as rapidly as possible, joined hands with the little twins to run around in dizzymaking circles. Marco, abandoned by his bride in her quest to suss out the secrets of James's new lady friend, enticed KC to join him for a twist, as Peri and Roberto tried to rustle up the crowd to start a conga line.

"I love weddings," screamed Dakota at her father, trying to be heard over the music.

"Oh, yeah?" he asked, moving his arms in slow motion.

"Try not to get any ideas, mister," she said. "This Walker has had more than enough to handle this holiday. Let's just take it easy for once."

The music shifted and the 1980s anthem "Walking on Sunshine" started to blast as Catherine came running, grabbing Allegra's hand as she sped over to join her new family for a group dance.

"Your mother loved this song," said James, bouncing on his toes.

"Let me guess," said Dakota. "Just like the rest of you, she couldn't really dance, either."

She spun around and around on the dance floor, singing the words—"I feel alive, I feel the love"—along with everyone else as she absorbed the joyous energy of her father and all her dearest friends.

chapter eighteen

The February club meeting was the first full session of the year. Also the last day for Peri to manage the shop. Finally ready to go, having flown to Paris for a week to find an apartment and returned to sort through her belongings, she checked the various cupboards and drawers in her apartment as she waited for Dakota to arrive.

"Nearly lost my soufflé with all the rush to see you," said Dakota as she knocked on the open apartment door and strolled inside. She knew Peri had to leave at eight thirty to catch her overseas flight and the shop was closed early so the club could meet. "I wanted to say my good-byes before everyone else."

"Good. Now I'm officially off the clock," said Peri. "I'm just a friend with a new job."

"And an owner until I buy you out, remember?" said Dakota.

Peri dug into her oversized, candy-apple-red Peri Pocketbook hobo bag and pulled out a leather business card holder. She handed a card to Dakota.

"Hello, Madam President," said Dakota, offering a salute.

"Hello, Ms. Walker," said Peri. She displayed a sheaf of papers in a manila envelope and passed it along. "I'd like to make you an offer *you* can't refuse."

Dakota giggled nervously. "You don't want to take over the shop, do you?"

"No," said Peri. "But, in my new capacity of head of knitwear for Lydia Jackson, I'd like to license the original designs made by your mother. That Italian *Vogue* cover did not go unnoticed. And when I mentioned the design for the Blossom dress was not a one-off . . . well, let's just say there is enthusiasm for your mom's work."

Dakota took the envelope and peered inside. Yup, there really were lots of pages with small print. "Are you serious?"

"Completely," said Peri. "Trust me; I've been working on my bags for years. You saw me—manufacturing is difficult. This way, you don't sell them outright, just allow us to use them. I'm hoping to start an entire line of clothes made from undiscovered designers called Tricoter."

"Wow," said Dakota, taking a deep breath and letting it out very, very slowly. "But what about the pattern book?"

"You can still do that," said Peri. "We'll just work together to pick and choose what you license exclusively and what you want to put in the book."

"So, what now?"

"You get a lawyer," said Peri. "You read over the papers, and we come up with a good deal all around." She reached over and tapped Dakota's nose. "This is going to be lucrative, Walker. I'm talking marble counters for the kitchen of the café if you want."

"I never thought about my mom's designs as being anything but a way to honor her talent," said Dakota.

"That's what this will be," said Peri. "And, in the meantime, you get a big fat paycheck to finance the remodel and reinvent the shop. For you. For your daughter, maybe. And that's far off in the future, you hear me?"

Dakota affected a dramatic sigh. "I don't even have a boyfriend right now. Will there come a day when everyone isn't over-involved in the details of my life?" she asked.

"Never," said Peri. "Now, what about this mysterious new manager you've hired? I guess I'll have to meet her when I come back for a visit."

"Nope," said Dakota. "I invited her to come to the shop tonight."

"To a club meeting? Whoo, boy, KC is going to have a field day," said Peri. "No more changes! That's her motto. She's already had several tantrums about my move. Told me I had to go, mind you. And then told me she was never going to visit me because I'd probably move on and forget about her."

"So, when is she coming?"

"In April," said Peri. "When the weather starts improving and we can ride bikes in the countryside. Drink wine and charm handsome French men."

"With your inability to speak the language," commented Dakota drily.

"Oh," said Peri. "That wasn't how I was planning to charm them."

Anita's honeymoon to Australia had returned her tanned and rested, and Catherine's ski holiday (including a week with the kids, as previously scheduled) left her happy but frazzled.

"I always just hung out with Dakota," said Catherine. "But much more is expected of me regarding Allegra. I can't just read her teen magazines and do facials."

"Uh, didn't you just ship her off to boarding school again?" asked KC.

"Yes," said Catherine sheepishly. "But it's the middle of the school year. No one wants to upset her routine just yet. It's enough we got married."

"Are you staying in New York?"

Catherine shrugged. "Yes, no, maybe?" she ventured. "We're here for the moment, while Marco figures out the new vineyard. But there's the property in Italy, and even though it's managed, he still needs to be there often. So, I think we'll be binational for a while. See what works best for us."

"What about the antiques shop?" asked Dakota.

"My manager is quite used to my jet-setting ways," she admitted. "So, we'll keep on as we've been doing. But I'm going to do more writing."

"You finished the novel?"

"Not quite," said Catherine. "Marco hired me to write an online newsletter about Cara Mia. Who knows where I'll go from here."

KC made a face. "That's two," she said with finality. "Peri and Catherine. Moving."

"Very dramatic," said Anita. "KC, you will be fine. We will all be quite fine. Most friends don't have the luxury of living so near one another. We should celebrate our luck instead of bemoaning our new directions."

"Speaking of living near one another," began Dakota. "My father has agreed to let me sublet his place with some new roommates."

"Really?" said Darwin, who'd arrived a few moments earlier with Lucie and Ginger. "I thought he was concerned you'd throw wild parties with all the other chef kids."

"He was," said Dakota. "But we all had a sit-down, laid out some ground rules, and I think this situation is going to work itself out. I even invited one of them to join the club."

"You're replacing Peri?" KC was horrified.

"I am not replacing her," insisted Dakota. "I'm simply expanding the group."

"We've never laid out a charter," pointed out Darwin. "We've never really considered the impact of strangers."

"We were all mostly a bunch of strangers not so long ago," said Lucie. "It's easy to forget that sometimes."

"I look forward to meeting your new girl," agreed Anita. "Is it your NYU friend, Olivia?"

"Nope," said Dakota, jogging lightly to the closed shop door. "It's a lady I've known my whole life but only recently got to know well. I even hired her to work part-time at the shop."

She stepped back to introduce a gray-haired woman who bore a strong resemblance to an old friend of theirs.

"My goodness," exclaimed Anita, reflexively smoothing her hair. She wanted to make a good impression.

"Everyone, this is Bess Walker," said Dakota. "My mother's mother."

"Hello," said Bess, remembering to smile even though she was intimidated by her late daughter's friends.

A chorus of "Hello" and "How are you?" rang out automatically, as Anita made her way to Bess and hugged her in a long, teary embrace.

"Thank you, thank you, thank you," said Anita. "I've always meant to express my gratitude to you. For raising your wonderful daughter. She was such a dear friend to me. Literally saved me, being able to come to this shop, after my first husband died."

"There's nothing to thank me for," said Bess, so quietly that Anita had to strain to hear her. "I'm the monster mother, you know. Georgia couldn't wait to get as far away from me as possible for most of her life."

"That's what some children do, though, isn't it?" asked Anita, her voice low to keep the conversation just between the two women. "Make a big fuss when really they've just been testing their ability to be independent all along? You and I both know

Georgia didn't raise herself. There's a lot of you in her. I can see that."

"There's a physical resemblance, that's all," said Bess. She felt anxious, all the women in the club staring at her. She hoped this wasn't a mistake.

"It's much more than that," said Anita, nodding. "Bess, I have one of my own who took issue with me once he hit his fifties. He could get a senior discount in some places! So, it's a challenge no matter how grown-up they may look on the outside. They're always our babies within, aren't they?"

Bess nodded vigorously, certainly not about to blubber in front of everyone. She'd often worried about this moment, having spent many evenings of her life practicing in her mind all that she might say to this Anita Lowenstein for her belief that this wealthy New York matron was usurping her role as mother, grandmother, dear friend. Needing to believe that if Anita hadn't been around—the type of exuberant woman, eagerly doling out hugs, that Georgia seemed to want in a parent—she might have been more willing to accept Bess, with her reserved manner and preferring things to be just so.

Of course, Bess's regrets and frustrations hardly disappeared in an instant. There was a lot of history to sort through. But she was contending with a new emotion she didn't anticipate: gratitude. Because as much as she wanted her daughter, Georgia, to reach out to her and to Tom, it was a relief to know that Georgia felt she was able to turn to this elegant, silver-haired woman with the crinkly blue eyes to help her when she needed it. In spite of everything, Bess had never wanted her daughter to feel alone. And Anita had made sure that was the case.

"Thank you," said Bess now. "For all that you did for my daughter. You were a true friend, and her father and I appreciate your support."

These were words she'd simply been unable to express—to even imagine saying!—when she last had a conversation of more than pleasantries with Anita, back when Georgia was ill.

"That's very kind," said Anita, who then raised her volume. "I can't think of a better decision, Dakota. You've proven that you really are in charge now."

To herself, Anita decided it was a good month to take another trip with her new husband. Just keep a low profile for the next while as grandmother and granddaughter figured out a rhythm on their own. Then she'd be back in her beloved Walker and Daughter, as usual.

"We'll have some part-time help, of course," explained Dakota, as she slid out a chair so her Grandma Bess could join the others at the table in the center of the shop. "But we'll manage. And then the reno will get under way."

"It might take a while though," Bess said quickly, blushing a little as she spoke. She wasn't used to this kind of togetherness, just chatting and knitting and eating between stitches. "James just won a new contract today. He got the news while we were unpacking our suitcases."

"And you are going to live with your grandparents, kid?" asked KC.

"On the weekends," said Dakota. "I still have school, you know."

"This is something else," said KC. "Well, I'm still coming here every Friday. I hope you know that, Dakota. I expect muffins."

"She's not been taking things well," said Darwin, quite loud enough for all to hear. "So, maybe we shouldn't tell her we got a little nibble, Lucie, about Chicklet."

"That's our positive television programming for young girls," Lucie told Bess. "We kind of function as part knitting club, part support group, part career coaching, around here."

"And we've been invited to make a pitch to some new investor-producers," said Darwin.

"Where? Out in L.A. or something?" said KC, catching Catherine's eye. "Remember that night at the movies? I said it: Everyone is just going to move apart. The Friday Night Knitting Club blown to smithereens."

"Oh, no, KC," said Anita.

"Not moving apart, I don't think," Dakota said thoughtfully. She finally brought forth a box of chocolate chocolate-chip muffins from her backpack and presented the largest one to KC. "There's a tremendous difference between moving away and moving apart. Just because we're not together in a physical way doesn't mean we're any less together. That's something I learned because of my mom. And I believe it."

"So, then we'll have club meetings over the Internet?" asked KC, taking a nibble at her muffin and then immediately taking a second, larger bite.

"If we have to," said Dakota.

"We'll still see each other," said Peri. "You know you're fly-ing over in just a few months. And of course we'll talk."

"And one meeting does not equal a move to L.A.," said Lucie.

"Or packing up everything for wine country in Italy," said Catherine. "Did I just say that?"

"Why are you so damn nonchalant?" KC said suspiciously. "You're changing, kiddo."

"I am," agreed Dakota. "I have. Maybe it was hearing the memories of my mother. But I've finally figured out this place has a story and we're all a part of it. It doesn't matter what changes. All that simply adds to our history."

She leaned into the stiff door to get it to open, struggling to make her way in without jostling the baby's calm sleep.

Inside remained a stack of old boxes lying in a corner of the back office and a faded yellow sofa, although Marty had mostly swept the room. Still. A good cleaning—and polishing the deep wooden floors on her hands and knees—would certainly bring this room alive, thought Georgia, striding across the room to catch a sunny view of Broadway. She opened the window, ever so slightly, to fully appreciate the honking, vibrating city one floor below.

This was it: her own shop in Manhattan.

Georgia studied the space, as she'd done for weeks, visualizing just where she would place the shelving, the register, the table. She imagined a future in which her yarn shop would be crowded with customers and her daughter sat on a stool while she rang up sales.

Dakota, all soft cheeks and dimpled knees, yawned and stretched, secure in her mother's arms, opening her eyes wide and staring as Georgia slowly turned in a circle to show her absolutely everything.

"This will be our shop, baby girl," she whispered. "This place will always be Walker and Daughter."

acknowledgments

True confessions: I came very close to skipping a family reunion as I was writing this story.

You see, husband, dog, and I drove up from our cozy home in California to soak in the natural beauty of Hope, British Columbia, Canada, where the extended family get-together was to be held, and I immediately squirreled myself away to write. But somewhere between hearing the hum of happy voices and the squealing of young cousins meeting one another for the first time I realized, like Dakota, that perhaps I needed to reassess my priorities. So I stepped away from the computer, and I'm tremendously glad that I did. What fun to catch up with everyone! That weekend also refreshed my perspective and provided some clear thinking amid the chaos. Ultimately, I rewrote large parts of this book and ended up with quite a different story altogether. Living the themes and not just typing about them.

It takes a team to publish a book, and I so appreciate the cheerleading and sage advice from my dream agent, Dorian Karchmar of William Morris Endeavor Entertainment, and the invaluable support from her assistant, Adam Schear. Heartfelt thanks to everyone at Putnam and at Berkley, including Ivan Held, Leslie Gelbman, Shannon Jamieson Vazquez, Kate Stark, Stephanie Sorensen, Melissa Broder, and my insightful and talented editor, Rachel Kahan. I remain ever grateful to everyone in sales, marketing, publicity, editorial, production, and design for all of their efforts.

I'm lucky to have a dear group willing to read (and reread) early chapters. This list of names hardly changes from book to book, which says something about the amazing support and commitment of these

acknowledgments

women and why I'm lucky to call them my dear friends: Rhonda Hilario-Caguiat, Kim Jacobs, Shawneen Jacobs, Tina Kaiser, Rachel King, Sara-Lynne Levine, Alissa MacMillan, Robin Moore, and Christine Tyson. And thanks to Dani McVeigh for all her efforts designing my Web sites and helping to test recipes in my kitchen.

This story is special to me for many reasons, not least because I worked on the story mere steps from where my family typically gathers for our holiday meals. Although my dog, Baxter, who typically keeps my feet warm as I type, all but abandoned me for chasing tennis balls with his dog cousins and the chance to take daily swims in the Coquihalla River, I was hardly alone. My mom, Mary Lou Jacobs; my husband, Jonathan Bieley; and my sister-in-law, Shawneen Jacobs, eagerly discussed the pros and cons of rice flour in the shortbread and how many cranberries are just a bit too many in the muffins. I cobbled together leftover yarn, almost the same age as I am, from the top shelf in my mother's sewing room to stitch some easy patterns. Even my nephews, Kevin and Craig Jacobs, willingly made room for my laptop and my notes amid the LEGOs, going so far as to create my very own "Auntie Kate's Office: Do Not Disturb" and "Please Knock" signs to keep interrupters away. (Thanks, fellas!) As always, I worked on this book at odd hours and in all sorts of places, from my kitchen table in California to my mother's desk in Hope to accompanying the boys on the Whistler Mountaineer train, scarcely able to keep my eyes on the page because of the gorgeous scenery distracting my attention.

Above all, I want to let you know how sincerely I appreciate *your* support. Go on and send me an e-mail at katejacobs.com, pop in to book signings, and invite me to telephone your book groups. I'm grateful to hear from everyone who reads my stories. Because together we're all just members of the club.

knitting patterns

ginger's easy bookmark

The idea is to use up the odds and ends in your stash and experiment. Bookmarks are a good way to try out new stitches and make lovely small gifts, perfect for Hanukkah or for stocking stuffers. Below is an easy pattern, with a seed-stitch border around reverse stockinette.

needles: Smaller is better. You want a thinner bookmark to fit between the pages. Opt for number 3 or 4.

yarn: Opt for lightweight. If you want to be more playful, use self-striping or sparkly novelty yarns.

the pattern: An easy seed-stitch border around a reverse stockinette center. You're just using the knit and purl techniques in varying combinations. Go to www.katejacobs.com for detailed directions about knitting basics.

Cast on 12 stitches

For border:
Row 1 and 3 : k1, p1, k1, p1, k1, p1, k1, p1, k1, p1, k1, p1
Row 2 and 4: p1, k1, p1, k1, p1, k1, p1, k1, p1, k1, p1, k1

Row 5 (and all odd rows after row 3): k1, p1, k1, p6, p1, k1, p1

Row 6 (and all even rows after row 4): p1, k1, p1, k6, k1, p1, k1

Once the desired length is reached, finish off with four rows of border (following the stitch pattern for rows 1 to 4) and cast off.

Now you can hold your place in the story while you try out some of the recipes!

georgia's holiday garland

The beauty of this project is that everyone—especially kids—can play a part! Remember the fun of making garlands from colored construction paper? This pattern applies the same approach to knitting. Simply create similar-sized long rectangles that you can interlock by folding around one another and sewing up the ends, thereby making a knitted garland you can either put on a Christmas tree or use as a wall decoration. Switch up the colors to fit in with your holiday decor.

needles: Opt for number 13 for a chunkier ring, or use number 4 for a more delicate circle.

yarn: Mix and match colors and textures for a varied look, or simply alternate two colors for a more coordinated appearance. The options are endless!

the pattern: Aim to make the rings similar in size—rectangles 8 inches by 2 inches work well. You can either use all the same stitching or vary the stitches used for the rings.

Cast on an even number of stitches (such as 12)

Garter-stitch rings:

All rows: Knit the stitches.

Cast off, but leave a long enough tail of string to sew up the ends together, forming the rings.

Rib-stitch rings:

Row 1 (and all odd rows): k2, p2, repeat to end.

Row 2 (and all even rows): k2, p2, repeat to end. (Think of it as knitting the knits and purling the purls.)

Again, leave a long tail when you finish casting off.

Take the first rectangle, twist it around to bring the ends to touch, forming a ring, and—using a crochet hook—use the long tail of yarn to sew the ends together. Then take a second rectangle, loop it through the first sewn-together ring, and connect the ends of the second rectangle, again sewing it together. Continue until your garland is as long as you like, and voilà! You have created a truly unique decoration that your family can enjoy for years to come.

recipes

dakota's thanksgiving pumpkin spice muffins

Easy holiday snacking while you wait for the turkey!

Makes 18–24 muffins

Ingredients

2 cups all-purpose flour

1 tsp. baking powder

1 tsp. baking soda

½ tsp. cinnamon

½ tsp. nutmeg

¼ tsp. ground ginger

⅛ tsp. cloves

⅛ tsp. allspice

½ tsp. salt

4 eggs

4 tsp. unsalted butter, softened

¾ cup brown sugar

½ cup sugar

1 cup canned pumpkin puree

½ cup molasses

1 tsp. vanilla

1 cup chopped cranberries (chop while frozen)

Optional:

- Streusel topping (recipe follows)
- ½ cup pecans, chopped; you can also add a whole candied pecan to the top of each muffin
- Replace individual spices with 1¾ tsp. pumpkin-pie spice

Directions

Preheat oven to 350 degrees (and make sure the rack is positioned in the middle). Line muffin pans with paper liners.

In a large bowl, sift or whisk together flour, baking powder, baking soda, spices, and salt.

Beat eggs and set aside.

In a separate bowl, cream butter and sugars until fluffy, then mix in pumpkin, molasses, and vanilla. Add beaten eggs.

Make a well in the center of the dry ingredients and add the wet mixture, stirring until just barely combined.

Fold in chopped cranberries.

Fill muffin cups ⅔ full. Top muffins with streusel, if desired (see the following recipe for the topping).

Bake 25 to 30 minutes. Muffins are done when a toothpick inserted in the center comes out clean.

streusel topping
Makes enough topping for muffin recipe above

Ingredients
    2 Tbsp. all-purpose flour
    ½ cup sugar
    ¼ Tbsp. cinnamon
    4 Tbsp. cold butter

Directions
Combine dry ingredients.

Cut in cold butter, using a pastry cutter or two knives held in one hand, until just crumbly. (Butter in the mixture should become similar in size and shape to peas.)

Sprinkle on tops of muffins before baking.

gluten-free pumpkin muffins

Just as tasty but without the flour!
Makes 6 muffins

Ingredients
    1 egg
    1 tsp. vanilla extract
    ¼ cup brown sugar
    ½ cup canned pumpkin puree (note: NOT pumpkin pie
        filling!)
    1¼ cup gluten-free baking mix (for example, Pamela's
        Baking and Pancake Mix)
    ¼ tsp. cinnamon
    ¼ tsp. nutmeg
    ⅛ tsp. allspice
    ⅛ tsp. mace
    ¼ cup water
    ¼ cup chopped frozen cranberries or chocolate chips

Directions
Preheat oven to 350 degrees. Grease muffin pan with butter.

In a medium bowl, beat egg and vanilla together with a fork.

Mix in brown sugar and pumpkin puree.

Mix together the baking mix and spices, and add it to the wet mixture. Stir in water and add berries or chocolate chips.

Spoon into muffin pan.

Bake for 18–20 minutes. Muffins are done when a toothpick inserted in the center comes out clean.

anita's hanukkah latkes

The traditional potato pancake favorite!
Makes 18–22 latkes depending on size

Ingredients

- 1 large white onion
- 2 eggs
- 1 tsp. kosher salt
- ½ tsp. black pepper
- 2 Tbsp. all-purpose flour
- 1½ tsp. baking powder
- 2 lbs. potatoes (the starchier the better; try Russets)*
- ¼ cup vegetable oil

Optional:
Add 1 cup grated apples for a sweet touch.

Directions

Using either a hand grater or a food processor, grate the onion into a bowl.

Separate the eggs, and lightly beat the yolks in one bowl; beat the egg whites until stiff in another bowl.

Mix onions, egg yolks, salt, pepper, flour, and baking powder.

Grate the potatoes quickly: Grate 1 potato, place gratings into a cheesecloth, and squeeze as much liquid out as possible, discarding the liquid. Place the gratings in with the onion mixture and stir. Repeat for all potatoes. Add more flour if excess liquid forms.

Fold in egg whites.

Heat ¼ cup oil in a 12-inch nonstick skillet (the oil should be ¼ to ½ inch deep) to very hot (about 350 degrees).

Spoon the mixture (about 2 tablespoons for each pancake) into the oil and spread into flat, round pancakes with a fork. Place about 3 to 4 pancakes into the oil at a time. Fry until the underside is browned, about 5 minutes. Flip once. Place on paper towels to drain. Add more oil if necessary, letting the oil return to temperature between each batch of pancakes.

Place a cooling rack on top of a cookie sheet, and keep latkes warm in a 200-degree oven. Serve warm with traditional toppings, such as sour cream and applesauce, or offer smoked salmon and caviar as accompaniments. You can also experiment with using grated sweet potatoes or half a zucchini for different flavors.

Alternately, make the pancakes the day before and keep them wrapped in the fridge. Reheat in a 350-degree oven, on a rack over a cookie sheet, for about 5 minutes.

*note: Keeping the potato skins on can add a more intense flavor. If you do choose to remove the skins, keep the peeled potatoes in cold water to prevent them from browning before cooking, and dry them thoroughly before grating.

gran's scrumptious shortbread

Melt-in-your-mouth delicious!
Makes approximately 24 small cookies

Ingredients
- 1 cup butter, softened
- 1 egg
- ¼ tsp. vanilla
- 1 cup icing or confectioners' sugar
- ½ tsp. salt
- ⅛ tsp. nutmeg
- 1½ cup white flour
- ¼ cup rice flour

Directions
Preheat oven to 350 degrees.

Place butter in a large bowl. Using a wooden spoon, combine egg, vanilla, sugar, salt, and nutmeg with the butter.

Mix flours together and then add flour mixture to the egg mixture, ¼ cup at a time, until the mixture is stiff—too stiff to work with a wooden spoon.

Place half the mixture on a floured board and knead lightly. For best results, place hands in cold water before kneading (as long as you can stand it). Slowly add remaining dough while kneading until dough just begins to crack.

Wrap in wax paper and refrigerate for 20 minutes.

Roll out dough until ¼ inch thick and cut into shapes if desired.

Place cookies approximately 2 inches apart on an ungreased cookie sheet and into oven for 20 minutes or until lightly golden.

bess's butter tarts

Sweet and yummy—nicely complements a cup of tea!
Makes 1 dozen tarts

Ingredients
   6 Tbsp. butter, melted
   2 eggs
   1 cup brown sugar
   ¼ tsp. salt
   1 tsp. vanilla
   2 tsp. vinegar
   ½ cup maple syrup
   ⅔ cup chopped pecans
   ⅔ cup raisins
   1 package (12-count) frozen pastry shells (or make your
      own pastry from scratch!) Pastry shells should be about
      3 inches in diameter and at least ¾ inch deep.

Directions
Preheat oven to 450 degrees.

Melt the butter and set aside.

Whisk eggs until well blended. Add brown sugar, salt, vanilla, vinegar, and maple syrup.

Add melted butter, nuts, and raisins, and mix well.

Place unbaked pastry shells on a cookie sheet. Fill shells with mixture, to about ⅓ of the way from the top.

Bake at 450 degrees for 10 minutes, then reduce to 350 degrees for 20–25 minutes or until filling is firm. Do not let filling bubble.

Cool and serve!

knit the season

by kate jacobs

You can also visit www.katejacobs.com to sign up for Kate's newsletter and to learn more about her upcoming events.

And you can even ask Kate to call in to your very own book club!

DISCUSSION QUESTIONS

1. During her lifetime, Georgia was a strong role model for everyone in *The Friday Night Knitting Club*, most of all for her daughter, Dakota. How do Georgia's values of sacrifice and dedication to hard work influence Dakota's choices?

2. Change is a major theme in *Knit the Season*: new romantic partners taking the place of the dearly departed, the shop changing hands, homes being recreated and reimagined. Which characters fear change, and why?

3. How does Dakota bear the burden of responsibility that is Walker and Daughter? What resources are available to her, both tangible and intangible?

4. When KC laments to Catherine about the romantic relationships that are altering the club, KC explains the root of her anxiety this way: ". . . there's a lot of programming about what it means to be women, and not everyone is going to have *that* life. The absence of what you're taught to want can make it hard. Even when you're the one doing the choosing" (page 86). What do you think she means by this?

5. For Darwin, mother of twins and compulsive family documentarist, living in the moment is challenging, and as parents

she and her husband, Dan, "savor an experience only in the retelling" (page 90). Is it possible to make and preserve memories simultaneously? How does she resolve this conflict?

6. Why is Catherine so willing to commit to Marco, yet so resistant to the concept of marriage?

7. As Catherine is preparing for her wedding to Marco, she reflects that she's in control this time, unlike when she married her first husband, Adam. What do you think she means when she describes her true love for Marco as being found "somewhere in the real world" (page 231)?

8. Do you find Anita's son, Nathan, to be a sympathetic character?

9. Gran's home in Scotland is what you might call the birthplace and bastion of Walker family traditions. She wears the same hand-knit cardigan every year, and there's a definite order of activities on Christmas Day: beginning with the turkey in the oven and ending with smiles and satisfied stomachs all around. She predicts this will be the "most triumphant Christmas" ever (page 197). Does this proclamation seem optimistic in hindsight? What gives her such confidence?

10. Is the photo of Georgia in her hospital bed an appropriate gift for Bess Walker?

11. Do you agree with KC's decision to deliberately delay Nathan's arrival at the wedding ceremony?

12. The relationships between Bess Walker and the members of the Friday Night Knitting Club undergo significant change.

Discuss the circumstances that allow Bess's acceptance into the group.

13. While sharing fond memories of Georgia's role in the club, Lucie remarks, ". . . Georgia was not a saint. . . . She was so genuine. That's what drew us all to her. . . . Nobody's completely got it together in the Friday Night Knitting Club. It's a condition of membership" (page 63). By the end of *Knit the Season*, does everyone still fulfill this condition?

14. Will the Friday Night Knitting Club live on? Who will be the chief guardian(s) of the tradition?

FEBRUARY 2006

Gus Simpson adored birthday cake.

Chocolate, coconut, lemon, strawberry, vanilla—she had a particular fondness for the classics. Even though she experimented with new flavors and frostings, drizzling with syrups and artfully arranging hibiscus petals, Gus more often took the retro route with piped-on flowers or a flash of candy sprinkles across the iced top. Because birthday cake was really about nostalgia, she knew, about reaching in and using the senses to remember one perfect childhood moment.

After twelve years as a host on the CookingChannel—and with three successful shows to her credit—Gus had made many desserts in her kitchen studios, from her creamy white chocolate mousse to her luscious peach torte, her gooey caramel apple cobbler and her decadent bourbon pecan pie. A "home cook" without culinary school training, she aimed to be warmly elegant without veering into the homespun: she strived to make her dishes feel complete without being complicated.

Still, birthday cake was something altogether different: one sweet slice fed the spirit as much as the stomach. And Gus relished that perfect triumph.

She loved celebrating so much that she threw birthday parties for her grown daughters, Aimee and Sabrina, for her neighbor and good friend Hannah, for her executive producer (and CookingChannel veep) Porter, and for her longtime culinary assistant who'd recently retired and moved to California.

But Gus didn't stop there. She always made a big ta-da for the nation's anniversary, which wasn't so out of the ordinary for an American, and for December 25, which, again, wasn't all that unusual for someone who'd been raised Catholic. Then she also made a fuss for saints Valentine and Patrick, for Lincoln, for Julia Child (culinary genius; August 15), Henry Fowle Durant (founder of her alma mater, Wellesley; February 22), and Isabella Mary Beeton (author of the famous Mrs. *Beeton's Book of Household Management*; March 12). No matter that those guests of honor were quite unavailable to attend, being dead and all.

Some hostesses love parties because they relish being the center of attention. Gus, on the other hand, found her greatest pleasure in creating a party world with a place for everyone and where she believed everyone would be made to feel special.

"Let me fix a little something," Gus said to her daughters, their friends, her colleagues, her viewers. She truly loved the idea of taking care, of nurturing and nourishing. Especially those guests who found it hard to make their way in the crowd: Gus always looked out for those ones the most.

There was only one birthday that Gus was getting tired of organizing. Tired, really, of celebrating at all. Her own. Because in short order—March 25—Augusta Adelaide Simpson was turning fifty.

The problem, of course, was that she didn't feel as old as all that. No, she felt more like a twenty-five-year-old (ignoring, as she often did, the logistical problem that her older daughter, Aimee, was twenty-seven and her younger, Sabrina, was twenty-five). And, as such, she found herself completely caught off guard—genuinely surprised to add up the years—to find that she'd arrived at the half century mark.

A half century of Gus.

"You'll want to use the best sherry you can afford when making a vinaigrette," she had said on a recent show, before realizing the sherry was almost as old as she was.

"I could be bottled up and put on the shelf," she'd said, laughing.

But a nagging dread had snuck up on her, and she resented it. Forty-six, forty-seven, forty-eight, even forty-nine—all those parties had been smashing. When she blew out her candles on last year's cake—a carrot ginger with cinnamon cream cheese icing—and her producer, Porter, had shouted out, "Next year's the big one!" she had laughed along with the crowd. And she felt fine about it. She really, really did. No, really. She did. She hadn't scheduled a session of Botox, hadn't begun wearing scarves to hide her neck. Fifty, she told herself, was no big deal. Until she woke up one morning and realized she hadn't done a thing to plan. She, who never missed a chance to have a party. And that's when she realized that she didn't want to do anything about celebrating, either.

The problem, she reflected one morning while washing her tawny brown hair with color-enhancing shampoo, developed somewhere between working on the show schedule for the up-coming year and learning that the CookingChannel was slash-ing the budget and ordering fewer episodes than usual.

"All the cable channels are losing market share," Porter had explained. "We just have to ride it out." He'd been in the TV business a long time, longer than Gus, and was enviably suc-cessful, a black man in the very white world of food TV. There were rumblings he was even going to be named head of pro-gramming. Gus's trust in Porter was absolute.

Then the CookingChannel had hired a style consultant who informed Gus that "after a certain age" some ladies do well to add a few pounds to smooth out the face. ("You're wonderfully slender but it wouldn't hurt to fill in the lines, you know," the stylist had said, not unkindly. "Good lighting can only work for so long.") Finally, she'd met Sabrina for dinner one night and admired the couple at the table across from them, a gorgeous black-haired young woman in a bubble-gum-pink dress accompanied by a frowning older woman clad in an oatmeal linen pantsuit, her hair in a medium-length swingy bob. She was startled to realize the wall across from her was mirrored and the grumpy-faced diner was herself. "Are you okay, Mom?" Sabrina had said, signaling the waiter for more water. "You look as though you're a little ill."

Gus wasn't young anymore.

At first she'd tucked this awareness away with her white shoes after Labor Day. But the truth refused to stay hidden, revealing itself when she spotted a wrinkle she'd never noticed or heard a crackle in her knees when she bent over to pull out a saucepan. Or when her longtime sous chef announced, in what seemed like out-of-the-blue fashion, that she was retiring. Which meant she'd reached retirement age. Alarming when you considered that it meant twelve long years had gone by since Gus had had her first CookingChannel show, *The Lunch Bunch*, in 1994. That the young mom who'd twisted her shimmering butterscotch locks into a loose updo, tendrils escaping, had eschewed aprons and whipped up easy, delicious dishes was now a parent of girls with jobs and lives and kitchens of their own. Girls who had, sort of, become women.

They weren't really grown-up. Not in the real sense. After all, she'd had two children by the time she was Sabrina's age—and that was in addition to a husband, and a year of adventure in the Peace Corps. Aimee and Sabrina, on the other hand, were far from self-sufficient. Aimee seemed never to have anyone serious in her life, and Sabrina changed boyfriends with the seasons. It was funny, really, how today's twelve-year-olds were far more sophisticated than any middle schoolers Gus remembered, and yet the twenty-five-year-olds existed in a state of suspended adolescence. She spent more time worrying about them now than she probably ever had.

So it was easy enough to pop along with the day-to-day of life and not really think about aging in a personal way. But then small things—a word from a stranger, a glance in the mirror—startled her fantasy image. Suddenly, reluctantly, one fact became clear.

Gus Simpson *was* going to be fifty.

Not, in and of itself, a remarkable event. It happened to other people every day. Surely. But Gus had blithely assumed getting older wouldn't quite happen to her. After all, she was slim (if not exactly a devotee of exercise), had a thriving career, a chunk of money in the bank (well managed by David Fazio, a top financial adviser Alan Holt had recommended years ago), a closet bursting with pricey clothes—Gus's signature look was a comfortably elegant collarless silk duster, layered over a smooth shell, with wide-legged silk georgette trousers—and a convertible in her garage, dammit. She listened to Top 40. She used a digital camera. She had an incredibly tiny cell phone. She knew how to send text messages. She still dressed up at Halloween to give out candy. Wasn't all that enough to keep maturity at bay?

Turning forty-nine had had a jaunty ring to it; fifty felt like she ought to buy a pair of orthopedic shoes.

"It's quite impossible to figure out how to act these days," she told her producer, Porter, who had several years on her. "My mother had settled into being a grandmother at this age. But today some women are still having babies at fifty—babies, Porter!"

"Do you want a baby, Gus?" he'd asked, joking.

"No! What I want is to figure out this disconnect between a number on a piece of paper and how I feel inside," said Gus. "Do you know that the women from *Thirtysomething* are now fifty-something? And they're still young. What about Michelle Pfeiffer? Meryl Streep? Jane Seymour? Oprah? They say fifty is the new thirty."

"So it should be no problem then," reasoned Porter. "You look great."

"And yet it is an issue," admitted Gus. "I have wrinkles. Real wrinkles, not those little crinkles I used to moan about when I turned forty. Porter, I think fondly about turning forty! I mean, I just can't stop wondering, How did I get here?"

"Where did the time go?"

"Yes, really. Where *did* the time go?" asked Gus. "And when do I get to hit 'pause'?"

And so, she reasoned to herself, it had been natural to fall behind on planning her birthday party. It had been easy to just put it off. Any other year she'd have begun organizing her birthday party immediately after Thanksgiving, deciding first on her cake flavor, arranging the food, sending formal invitations in the mail. (No, Gus Simpson simply did not appreciate the informality of Evite, thank you very much. The little details were what made guests feel most welcome, she knew.) She could have picked one item or concept—a pomegranate, an orchid, the color puce—and built the entire festivities around it as a theme. Her ability to decorate and entertain was so innate that she simply assumed anyone could throw parsley on a dish and make it look better than a haphazard explosion of green.

But not this time; not this year. Suddenly it felt like too much effort: Gus Simpson, one of the most popular entertaining gurus on television, didn't want to throw a party. In fact, she'd have preferred canceling her birthday altogether.

She poured a stream of rich hazelnut-scented coffee from her large French press into an oversized blue-and-white-striped pottery mug. With care she carried her drink to the speckled gray-and-black granite breakfast bar, perching herself on the counter-height navy chair. Gus took a sip, just a little almost slurp (since no one else was around) so as not to burn her tongue, and flipped through the *New York Times*, trying to jolly herself out of her gloomy mood. But her natural habit—it was Monday, which meant the weekly Media section, and she loved to follow her industry—led her to a large article above the fold of the paper.

"The New Faces of Food TV," Gus read to herself, feeling a whoosh of anxiety in her chest. "Food is the new fashion and the latest crop of program hosts look as delicious as their culinary creations."

Gus tapped her teeth against each other as she always did when she was tense and scanned the large photo with all the up-and-coming hotshots in cooking television: there was that *young* surfer chef who always wore shorts and looked barely old enough to be in college, the *young* Midwestern housewife who only made dishes that took up to six ingredients, and the *young* Miss Spain who had turned a gig promoting her country's olives into an Internet cult following on YouTube. From there, Gus read how Miss Spain had created her own ten-minute Web show, *FlavorBoom*, which was also downloadable to TiVo, and had edited a small cookbook that had just come out at the holidays a few weeks before. It had already been a top seller online. The story continued on page two of the section, where there was a glamour shot of the gorgeous, black-haired Miss Spain in her crown and far too much mascara, with a large caption underneath: "Carmen Vega: From Beauty Queen to Foodie Queen."

"I bet she can't even cook," Gus announced to her coffee mug, quite ready to close the paper in disgust. But then a familiar line caught her attention, and she found herself scanning the words carefully.

"Imagine there are only a certain set of ingredients and that's all there is to use," says Gus Simpson, the CookingChannel's ubiquitous program host and star of the well-known Cooking with Gusto! *in a recent interview in* Every Day with Rachael Ray. *"But we don't all create the same thing. So it's not really about what you put in a dish—it's about how you make that meal taste. It's not about how you make it but about how eating it makes you feel. Cooking, like life, stays interesting when you keep the experience fresh."*

And fresh new hosts seem to be how cable is hoping to hold on to viewers, as ratings continue to decline on all channels . . .

Blah, blah, blah went the article. On and on about these exciting new voices in the world of food television, all seemingly sanctioned, via the clever use of already reported quotes, by none other than Gus Simpson. Oh, how she hated that! Being interviewed for one article—which had been published over a year ago—and then finding those same words popping up in every other journalist's food story.

The lesson she'd learned: don't ever say anything, cutesy or cutting, that you don't want to hear parroted back to you for the rest of your life.

Gus thought about crumpling up the paper and tossing it in the bin, but there was no one around to see her dramatics and she always felt that grand behavior wasn't really worth the energy when there was no one to witness it. Television had trained her well. Instead, she sighed and left her spot at the breakfast bar for more comfortable surroundings. She shooed her white cat, Salt, out of an overstuffed wing chair in the bay window and watched her pad her way over to lie in a ray of sun with Pepper, who was black and had a somewhat pungent attitude.

Then, coffee in hand, she settled herself down on the sturdy white twill (for Gus had strong faith in her guests' ability to not spill and in the power of Scotchgard if they did). The large kitchen was a space in which Gus keenly felt a sense of home and was where she did all her important thinking, be it coming up with new recipes or sorting out the endlessly complicated lives of her daughters. The wing chair closest to the French doors, long ago dubbed her "thinking spot" by Aimee, was perfectly positioned to lend a view of the flagstone patio. She could enjoy the color of her divine garden come spring—currently a bit of leftover snow and slushiness from a Westchester winter—as well as have full range of her gleaming kitchen. Sitting in this chair provided what she always called the "viewer's-eye view" because it was how her home appeared on television.

Hers was a dream kitchen, with a deep blue Aga stove, a marble-topped baking area, those granite counters, a deep and divided white farmer's sink, the artfully mismatched cabinets designed to look as though they were pieces of furniture added over time (assuming every flea market and antique shop would miraculously contain wood pieces with precisely the same bun feet and crown molding), and a bank of Sub-Zero freezers and refrigerators along one wall. The pièce de résistance? The substantial rectangular island, with eight-burner cooktop and raised backsplash, ample counter space, and breakfast bar to one side (though not immediately in front of the cooktop, of course, where it might ruin the camera shot). The island was the part of her kitchen most familiar to her viewers.

What a great idea it had been to suggest filming at her home when she began her third CookingChannel program, *Cooking with Gusto!*, in 1999. It certainly cut down commute time and, much more important, had turned the reno into something she could write off. And Gus, for all her professional success, was a devotee of socking away money. For a rainy day. For her retirement. Which had always seemed way, way off, on account of the fact that she was so tremendously, eternally, divinely young. A some-day worth planning for but nothing that seemed as though it was about to arrive soon. She was too busy.

In the early years when she first started on television, long before the plump paychecks and the merchandising deals, Gus hosted a half-hour program called *The Lunch Bunch* based on her menu at her gourmet spot The Luncheonette. It filmed in a studio in Manhattan and she took the train home to the small two-bedroom house she shared with Aimee and Sabrina. It was the same compact Westchester bungalow that she had initially moved into with Christopher, after they'd returned from their overseas Peace Corps stint and had given up living in Manhattan, back when they were barely married. When he'd raved about every dinner she burned and she made him brown-bag lunches, with sexy little notes tucked inside. When they were too new at life and marriage to comprehend the bad that could come. Would come.

The tiny place had been home with their two little girls, and Gus had tried out a variety of careers—taking photographs for the local paper, doing part-time camera work for the local cable station, and making a line of homemade candles—while baking cupcakes for Sabrina and Aimee's school and carpooling the neighborhood kids. Still enjoying the luxury of figuring out what she wanted to do.

Christopher's accident had changed things, of course, spurred her to open The Luncheonette, which attracted the attention of Alan Holt and his cable network. Gus's little restaurant, in Westchester County, just north of New York City, specialized in quick bites and tea parties and the like. She was close enough to the station that commuters popped in for beverages and snacks before catching a train. The decor—bright and light with distressed off-white tables and comfy Parsons chairs upholstered in a wide red-and-cream stripe—had been spruced up to lure in the soccer moms with time between errands and school's end. The small but thoughtful selection of gourmet groceries was selected to entice the adventurous home cooks, both the commuter and soccer mom variety.

It had been a gamble when she opened, a chunk of her late husband's life insurance money dwindling in a bank account and her two young daughters. It seemed as though running her own business would provide her the type of flexibility she needed with two young girls, and she'd always loved to cook. Loved to experiment with flavors and cuisines and making things look pretty. Her friends, though well meaning, disapproved, encouraging her instead to invest and live off the interest. But there wasn't really enough to quite do that, and besides, Gus had wanted the risk. She needed the jolt.

However, taking chances did not translate into being sloppy. No, indeed. And meeting with Alan Holt was a tremendous opportunity she couldn't afford to screw up. She had, in fact, served him several pastries and more than a few sandwiches, never knowing him as more than a regular customer. Until the day he handed her his card and suggested he wouldn't be averse to a home-cooked meal over which they could discuss a business proposal. Gus's fervent hope had been that he was interested in showcasing The Luncheonette in an episode or two.

She remembered vividly when Alan came for dinner in the spring of 1994, when Aimee and Sabrina were both young teens and she was a harried single mom, still keenly missing Christopher though he'd been gone six years by then. It was as though she'd hit the "hold" button on her life when he died, waiting for something she couldn't quite place her finger on that might make it somewhat better, and had instead filled up her days with working and organizing her girls. She hadn't much energy left over, which had been her intention. Just enough to wish for the ability to provide her daughters with the life their father would have wanted for them.

All Gus had asked the day Alan Holt came for dinner was to be left alone in the kitchen and for her girls to go out and cut some flowers. Something bright and cheery they could bring to her so she could do up a vase. Her oldest daughter, Aimee, had promptly walked outside to the back patio and flopped into a wicker chair, arms crossed, while Sabrina slowly wandered off through the front door, with a look Gus couldn't discern between sulking and concentration.

In fact, Gus had been quite prepared for the girls to come back empty-handed from the garden and had put together her own centerpiece hours earlier, working efficiently while her just-turned-into-teenagers slept away a gorgeous sunny Saturday morning. She'd tucked her arrangement onto a shelf above the washing machine, knowing her girls were hardly about to go near anything that seemed like a chore. Her request about gathering flowers had really been a mother's trick to get the kids out of her way while she seasoned and sampled in the kitchen.

And then she saw it: seven stones and one feather.

That's what Sabrina had placed on the center of the polished rosewood table.

"What do you think, Mom?" asked the thirteen-year-old,

brushing her glossy black bangs out of her eyes as she gestured to a lineup of polished river rocks arranged by size and a random piece of gray fluff that looked, at a distance, more similar to dryer lint than to something that once winged through the sky.

Gus Simpson had chewed her lip as she pondered her younger daughter's contribution that day and cast her eyes down the length of her table, covered with her good ivory linen place mats, clean and crisp, her collection of quality china—the artistically mismatched pieces of creamware she'd collected at estate sales and flea markets and the occasional full-price purchase at a department store—and the genuine crystal goblets and glasses she'd brought back from Ireland years ago. Red, white, water. They'd cost more than three months' worth of mortgage when she'd made the splurge and Gus felt both guilty and exhilarated every time she saw them. Every mouthful—even plain old tap water—tasted better, too.

The Ireland trip had been her last vacation with Christopher, a romantic trip without the girls and filled with night after night in which they turned in early, eager to be alone. They'd laughed as they steered awkwardly around the jaw-droppingly beautiful coast, neither of them quite comfortable driving a stick shift on the other side of the road. But they'd managed it just fine, thank you very much. This made the accident all the more incomprehensible: Christopher had driven the Hutchinson River Parkway every day. Every single day. And then he made a mistake. That's what happened when you let your guard down.

Gus Simpson kept a vigilant watch: she knew that every moment, every detail mattered. Even the table setting.

The just-polished silver had gleamed as it lay on the linen place mats; the sixteen settings had been her great-grandmother's. Every clan has its own version of mythmaking—the hard winter everyone barely survived, the long and impossible transatlantic voyage from the Old World—and Gus's family had their own, of course. It was The Quest for Fine Things. And so the silver service (much more ornate than current fashion) had been purchased, at great sacrifice, as a setting a year from Tiffany & Co. and used only for the big three—Christmas, Easter, and Thanksgiving—in later generations. Sometimes, the story went, a spoon was all that could be afforded, the knives and forks left waiting for a fatter year. And so the set had made its way—though not without causing tension within the family—from mother to oldest daughter to daughter's daughter and finally to Gus, where the flatware had been put to more cutting and eating than ever before. No doubt her grandmothers would have thought it frivolous the way Gus delighted in her good plates and knives, and frowned upon their frequent use. Save, save, save it for later. That had been their motto. Tuck away the good to use only when you really need it. The thing was, Gus always felt as if she really needed it.

Though the night Alan Holt came to dinner, surely, even her grandmothers would have approved Gus setting such a grand table, all ready for the gorgeous meal simmering and roasting away in the kitchen. Cream of asparagus soup. Rack of lamb with herb jus. Gently roasted baby potatoes. Fresh, crusty bread she'd made from scratch, using a wet brick in her oven to generate steam (thanks to the advice of Julia Child in a well-worn copy of *Mastering the Art of French Cooking, Vol.* 2). All followed by a rich, buttery financière with homemade raspberry sorbet.

She'd wanted the meal to be delicious. Homey. Welcoming. After all, it wasn't every day that the president of the Cooking-Channel came over for Sunday dinner and the prospect of a different future hovered.

"Mom? The table?" her daughter had said.

Ah, yes, the table. Sabrina's display had been the one element of discord in a perfectly arranged tableau: it was clearly unacceptable.

Gus had opened her mouth to tell Sabrina to clean up the mess she'd created. To go upstairs, change out of the clothes she was wearing and put on something decent. To go find her sister and tell her to get ready.

The words had been all ready to tumble out. Even without seeing herself she could feel the frown, her furrowed brow. How many times had Gus criticized Sabrina and Aimee? Change your clothes, turn down that music, tidy up your room, don't leave wet towels on the floor. She, like all mothers of teenagers, had keenly felt her transformation into a walking cliché, as so many of the little issues that had seemed trivial and fuddy-duddy when she was young had stretched to matters of tremendous importance. A widow with two daughters, no less. Turning lights out when she left a room. Wearing a sweater instead of turning up the heat. Using a coaster on the coffee table. Eating leftovers. It was paying the bills that did it. Changed her perspective. Suddenly everything had mattered.

Every *thing* mattered. Even the table setting. She knew it had to be fixed.

But then she had caught the look of anticipation on her youngest daughter's face. The wide eyes, the mouth slightly open, just enough to catch the glimmer of her metal braces. Her heart caught in her throat: Gus had assumed the sad little decoration on her table was a way for Sabrina to make clear how little she cared about Gus's career. But could her daughter have been trying to help? she'd wondered.

At precisely that moment, Aimee had slouched into the room, alerted, no doubt, by the radar all kids have when they sense— hope—their sibling is about to get in trouble. What is it about family that makes them close ranks to outsiders but attack one another with impunity in private? Thinner and two inches taller than Sabrina, her light brown bangs dyed pink from Kool-Aid, fifteen-year-old Aimee grinned slyly as she saw her mother frowning at the table.

"Nice!" Aimee said, catching her sister's eye, gesturing toward the stone-feather combo. "Mom's totally going to throw that away. It's not perfect. And Gus Simpson doesn't do anything that's not perfect. Right, Mom?" Then Aimee shifted all her weight to one hip, as though standing up straight would take too much effort. She waited.

Sabrina waited.

Gus hesitated as her mom side duked it out with her career side.

"I think Sabrina's arrangement is lovely," Gus declared. "It's very modern, very sleek. It stays on the table."

Aimee rolled her eyes.

"Shut up, Aimee, it's a very karma design," shouted Sabrina.

"I think you mean Zen, dear." Gus smiled, recalling Sabrina's huge ear-to-ear smile, the silver braces gleaming on her teeth, her sweet blue eyes wide and shining. It was the right choice, even though she'd felt a twist in her stomach when Mr. Holt, the CookingChannel president, had looked questioningly at the table as he sat down. But Gus had made no apologies, aware of Sabrina hanging on her every word, and in fact praised her daughter's creativity.

"Part of being a good host is to let everyone feel they've played a part," she'd told him with confidence that spring day long ago.

Mr. Holt, a divorced father, had nodded thoughtfully. "You're just the type of person I'm looking for," he announced. And by the end of cake, Gus Simpson—an unknown gourmet-shop owner without a cookbook to her name—had been asked to host a few episodes on the fledgling cable channel.

Sabrina's display, it turned out, had been karma after all.

And voilà! A few years on TV's CookingChannel and she became an overnight sensation. That was the thing with all that "overnight" business: it typically took a lot of work beforehand.

And now here she was in 2006, the very heart of food television, The Luncheonette long since sold away. She lived in a stunning manor house in Rye, New York, precisely the style of house that Christopher would have loved: a three-story structure, white with black shutters, with a large formal dining room to the left of the foyer, a conservatory, a small parlor that Gus had converted to her private den, a wood-paneled library, a glassed-in breakfast room, and a cozy sitting room off the kitchen. Plus all the requisite space for her camera crews. There was a spacious patio immediately through the French doors from the kitchen, and a lush back lawn, edged in flowers, that was crowned with a decorative pond and waterfall that gurgled soothingly when she was out among the rosebushes.

There were far too many bedrooms in the manor house for a single woman—her children had been practically packing for college when she signed the deed but she forged ahead anyway—and there were definitely not enough bathrooms for a modern home. It was her plan to update the upper floors, though she'd been too busy over the years to do that just yet.

The house was the proof of her professional success. It appealed to her not only because of its magnificence but also because of its imperfections. It had a history that left it a little worn in places.

And so Gus had purchased the home when she was developing her most popular program, Cooking with Gusto! It was her third program for the network and the most well reviewed. Every week she hosted a brilliant chef in the manor house's amazing kitchen (renovated twice since the program had started), and she and her guest drank good wine and chatted as together they prepared an incredible meal, discussing amusing stories from the world of professional restaurant kitchens and doing their sincere best to convince the viewer at home that she, too, could make the scrumptious dishes they were preparing.

Gus Simpson had always been a good home cook. But she was no chef and she knew it: she'd been a photography major at Wellesley and possessed a great eye for visuals, and she'd had an idea ripe for its moment with The Luncheonette. Still, her gift—and it was a gift—had always been about creating an amazing experience. She was a true entertainer: Gus made her guests feel alive—even when her guests were on the other side of a TV screen—and her joie de vivre made every mouthful look and taste refreshing. Gus's main product was Gus, and she sold herself well: she was mother, daughter, best friend, life of the party. And she was good-looking to boot. Not so gorgeous that a viewer simply couldn't stand her, but undeniably attractive with her big brown eyes and her wide, toothy smile.

Gus Simpson was eminently watchable. Her viewers—and therefore her producers—loved her.

Her friends, her daughters, her colleagues: everyone wanted to be around Gus. And Gus, in turn, had been enchanted by the idea of looking after all of them.

Yet now it felt as though the spell was lifting.

So, okay, she didn't want to plan her own party. Who said she had to have one? Gus began pacing about the kitchen, ticking off a list on her fingers of all the people who would be disappointed if she didn't put something together, her frustration rising with every step. She was always doing, doing, doing.

Maybe turning fifty simply meant it was time to shake things up.

"Knock knock?" Shuffling open the white French door from her garden patio was Hannah Levine, her dear friend and neighbor. The two of them had shared an easy intimacy over the seven years they'd been friends. It hadn't been quite that way when they first met, on the very Sunday Gus moved into the manor house during the summer of '99. Gus had walked over to each of her neighbors' homes and presented a freshly baked raspberry pie, expressing how thrilled she was to be in the neighborhood. It was a brilliant touch, of course—pure Gus—and reciprocated by several dinner invitations and the beginning of many warm acquaintanceships. And then there had been Hannah, who lived immediately adjacent in a crisply painted white cottage, converted from what had once been the carriage house to Gus's stately home. Hannah had come to the door in faded gray pajamas, her medium-length red hair pulled back into a low ponytail. Her skin was pale and free of makeup, and she eyed Gus suspiciously through thick black glasses.

"What kind is it?" Hannah had asked, gesturing toward the pie, her body partially hidden by her wide mahogany door. She was even thinner back then, all sharp clavicle and bony wrist. And nervous, tremendously nervous. Of course, Gus was immediately smitten: she simply had to add Hannah to her collection of darlings. To the ones she wanted to nurture and nourish. Her girls, their pals, her coworkers: everyone was clay that Gus was eager to mold. She made a pest of herself that summer, dropping over next door with all manner of muffins and cookie bars, her resolve to befriend her neighbor only heightened by the fact that no one else seemed to visit the gentle, wary woman in pajamas. Certainly Hannah, already in her thirties then, was far too old to be a surrogate daughter; Gus imagined she would become like a little sister. But what happened instead was far more welcome: the two women found they had much in common—a shared love of gardening, an unconventional work schedule, a devotion to finding the perfect chocolate chip cookie, and a love of rising early—from which a true friendship sprang.

When the body wakes up before dawn, as Gus's typically did, there can be several hours when it seems as though there is no one else in the world. A peaceful time for some. Not Gus: she found these early moments, the house dark, the girls' rooms empty, the cats snoozing in far corners, to be tremendously lonely.

Fortunately, Hannah was quite likely to be on her way over by 7 AM, crossing the unfenced property line between their two homes. Because once it became clear that Gus was going to be persistent, Hannah accepted her friendship as the most natural thing. From early on, she had the peculiar habit of never tapping on the door when she came by, always calling out and making her way inside. With anyone else Gus would have found such a gesture intrusive; with Hannah it seemed perfectly normal. The two of them spent many an early morning sitting in Gus's bay window, on those overstuffed chairs, dipping biscotti into their cappuccino and having the very same conversation they'd had the day before. That was the thing about their friendship: it was all about the being together, never about doing anything. As such it made few demands. Theirs was an easy intimacy.

kate jacobs

It was also precious: Hannah was the first real friend Gus had made after becoming well known. There was no handbook for becoming semi-famous. (Or at least nothing that had been handed to Gus by the CookingChannel.) In a society thirsting for celebrity, it didn't take much for people to elevate a widowed mother with a knack for entertaining into a culinary guru. And so even by the late nineties, Gus had developed quite a following, with the requisite cookbooks and calendars, too. It was great; it put Sabrina and Aimee through some good schools. But her sort-of-but-not-quite fame also made it a hurdle to connect—people already "knew" her from TV and therefore it could be a tremendous disappointment to them if Gus turned out, for example, to be even slightly different than they envisioned. To be plain, it had been difficult to make friends. Oh, easy enough to meet people who wanted to say they were chummy with the host of *Cooking with Gusto!* More challenging to get to know individuals who wanted to know Gus.

Hannah Levine had been entirely different.

For one thing, she didn't watch television. Well, not exactly. Hannah watched multiple channels nonstop: CNN, MSNBC, and CourtTV. But dramas, comedies, home decor or cooking shows? Hannah didn't watch any of it. Instead, she holed up in her home office—with its built-in bookcases and large television—and wrote article after article for women's magazines. Sometimes in jeans but most typically in pajamas, with fuzzy slippers on her feet, and a bowl of M&M's nearby. Hannah was a busy freelance journalist, and her area of expertise was health, which pushed her slightly in the direction of obsessing over whatever she'd written about most recently. But she obsessed in a rather benign, almost kindly variety, as concerned for a stranger's odd throat clearing— could it be whooping cough?—as for her own potential ailments. Having the Internet as her main companion all day merely encouraged her cyberchondria.

That was one reason Hannah had been wary of the pie that first summer, having just written an article about an epidemic of *E. coli* on fresh berries, but seemed rather unfazed to learn about Gus's career. And frankly, in all the time since, she seemed yet to have watched one of her programs. Gus absolutely adored her for that.

Now she waved Hannah inside, though of course her friend was already halfway to the coffee. Gus had already left a mug on the counter, spoon on a napkin, and a few slices of fresh banana loaf arranged on a plate.

"I just finished a piece on the dangers of ignoring sore feet last night," Hannah told Gus after swallowing her first mouthful of hot coffee. "Do you stand for the entire time you're on TV, Gus? Because I've got a few ideas to make it a little easier—"

"Don't worry—from now on I think I'll be doing my show from a wheelchair," Gus said, shaking her head at Hannah's worried expression and reaching to show her the section of the *New York Times*. "Apparently I'm over the hill."

Hannah scanned the article. "Look, at least you're in it. You know you're still important when a journalist declares it so." She pulled a face at Gus to show she was joking.

"I'm just feeling a bit of I-don't-know, you know?"

"Is that why I haven't received my invitation to your birthday party?" said Hannah. "If it was anyone else I'd assume I was off the list. With you, I've been worried something's wrong. Your birthday is a few weeks away and I still have to plan my outfit."

Now it was Gus's turn to smile. "Why don't you wear your gray coat dress?" she suggested. That was the same outfit Hannah wore every year, purchased on a rare shopping trip with Gus. Hannah hated to leave her comfort zone of home. Hated to wear anything other than casual, loungy clothes.

"I think I'll just do that," Hannah said, nodding. She didn't mind being teased by Gus.

The two of them settled into a kind of cozy silence, munching on banana loaf and sipping coffee and intently dawdling to avoid the day's work. It was what they did every morning and they loved it.

The phone rang. It was only 7:08 AM.

"Who could that be?" Gus knew she wasn't needed in the studio for a meeting, and the TV crew filmed at her house on Wednesdays. Maybe something was up with Sabrina? Aimee was certainly still asleep at this early hour.

She picked up the cordless and said hello.

"Of course, of course, yes, definitely," she said, jumping up and almost spilling coffee on her white chair. She hung up the phone.

"Well, thank goodness," Gus said, drawing out every syllable for Hannah's benefit. "That was my exec producer. The bad news is that I have to be in the city and ready to be on air in less than two hours. The good news is that Gus Simpson isn't quite yesterday's leftovers."